XpressYourself

Publishing, LLC
www.xpressyourselfpublishing.org

Literature for the Grown & Sexy

Xpress Yourself Publishing™

In
My
Sisters'
Corner

ALSO BY JESSICA TILLES

Anything Goes
Apple Tree
Sweet Revenge

Published by Xpress Yourself Publishing™
P.O. Box 1615
Upper Marlboro, Maryland 20773

PUBLISHER'S NOTE
This is a work of fiction. Names, characters, places, and incidents either are the product of the author's imagination or are used fictitiously, and any resemblance to actual persons, living or dead, events, or locales is entirely coincidental.

ISBN: 0-9722990-1-7

First printing in the United States of America

For Leslie

Acknowledgements

I am grateful to everyone who gave me the time, space, confidence and love to pen my second novel: my parents, Jesse and Wallace Wright, are my biggest motivators and supporters; my editors Carla Dean and Jo Hawley Chubbs for putting up with my many revisions and doing a great job; my sister, Leslie Martin, whose love sustains me—I'm glad you are my best friend; Victor Tilles, for the challenge—you knew I had it in me and for that, I am forever grateful; my brother, Herb Lipscomb, for believing in me; Darlene Rowe-Stukes, for her continued motivation; the Jackson Mississippi Readers Club for their continued support—I am where I am partly because of them; Tahira Chloe Mahdi, author of *God Laughs Too* and *Queen of the Universe*, for being a wonderful author friend; and James Lilly for keeping me sane and focused.

Author's Note

This is a work of fiction. Any references to actual events, real people, living or dead, or to real locales are intended only to give the novel a sense of reality and authenticity. Other names, characters, places and incidents are either the product of the author's imagination or are used fictiously and their resemblances, if any, to real-life couterparts, is entirely coincidental.

Jessica Tilles

In
My
Sisters'
Corner

Maya

All hell is about to break loose.

Jonah uses his key to blow through the apartment like the Tasmanian Devil, throwing shit everywhere and overturning furniture. We meet eye-to-eye. The coldness in his eyes sends chills up and down my spine. "What happened to you last night, girl?" he spews in a southern drawl, enunciating every word. He lowers his head while his eyeballs roll up toward his brow. A satanic smile spreads across his full lips. This bastard looks like the one who flew over the cuckoo's nest. Like a vulture, he starts encircling me, sizing up his prey.

"I was unavailable," I stutter, biting down on my bottom lip, causing a tear. I lick my lips nervously, tasting the fresh, salty blood.

His expression holds a note of mockery. "Yeah, I gathered that much."

"I'm sorry. It won't happen again," I plea, backing myself against the wall, fear and anger knotting my insides.

His tall figure stiffens. "You damn right it won't happen again," he snarls, temper flaring.

Jonah's temper, when crossed, could be almost uncontrollable. Fear of my fate weakens my body. Like a rag doll, he grabs me by the throat and slams my head against the wall. A sharp pain shoots from the back of my head to the front, bringing on a serious migraine.

"The next time you miss an appointment, girl, I will put my foot up that pretty lil' ass of yours," he bellows, leaning in close. His liquor-drenched breath blows like the Sahara across my cheek. "You hear me?" he barks, ready to attack my jugular. The stench coming from the bowels of his stomach is foul and making my stomach gurgle.

"Yeah, I got it." I gulp hard as the hot tears flow down my cheeks.

Jonah releases his grip, takes a step backward and lightly fingers a loose tendril of hair away from my brow. Dried saliva holds the toothpick dangling from his bottom lip in place. He looks me up and down as though I am on an auctioning block and he's making a bid. "You know you gotta be punished for makin' Jonah look like a fool in front of his client." He turns his back on me and walks toward the black marble and brass dining room set that I found at one of those posh Beverly Hills secondhand shops. Jonah carries himself with a conceding air of self-confidence. With his back to me, he clears his throat. "Now you know we can't have that." He looks over his shoulder at me while making sucking noises with the toothpick between his teeth. "You know what I mean, Maya?"

"Jonah, please don't hurt me," I cry. "Please, not in the face. I have an audition tomorrow."

He cocks his head to one side. "Naw, I won't touch that pretty face 'cause that, along with that tight ass of yours, is what makes me my money." He takes off his camel colored, wool cardigan jacket and tosses it across the dining room chair. "I got something better you can do."

I feel like I am eight years old again, taken back to the time when Daddy sent me out to pull a switch off a tree because I bit the babysitter on her inner thigh. I sunk my fangs deep into her inner thigh until the white meat showed. Who told her she had the right to spank me? So what if I was running around acting like a spoiled brat when I should've been in bed? She called Mama and Daddy at the Jones', where they were having dinner, and told them what I had done. Later that night, Daddy came storming in the house yelling, "Maya, go get a switch!" Reluctantly, I pulled the smallest switch I could find from the oak tree that leaned in the front yard and took it inside to Daddy. That only added fuel to the fire. "Oh, you're trying to be a little smart ass," he said. Daddy yanked my pants down, turned me over his knee and tore my ass up with the palm of his strong, rough hand. The babysitter stood nearby watching and laughing. Free, China, and Jade were upstairs peeping over the banister. Daddy whipped me so bad I peed on him, which made him whip me even harder. Daddy was a massive presence. He had an air of authority and demanded obedience from his daughters. Today, an ass whipping like that is a form of child abuse that could land your ass in jail.

Don't think that babysitter got away with that shit, though, because she didn't. Free was furious that, because of her, I had received the whipping of my life and she was determined to get her back, and get her back good. The next time the babysitter came to sit for us, Free poured the soda from her Sprite bottle down the toilet and filled it with Citrate of Magnesium and Epsom salt. The last we saw of her was her back. She shitted all the way home and never sat for us again. Word got around about the instant laxative, and Mama and Daddy caught hell trying to get another babysitter. Eventually, they gave up and decided that Free was old enough to take care of us. It got a little too good to Free, though—she planted switches to our tails every chance she got, especially mine. "This gone hurt me just as much as it's gone hurt you," she would say, all the while laughing.

"Jonah, I didn't mean to stand up your client," I quickly say, attempting to smooth over a hostile situation. "I got delayed at my audition and I might get the part. It's not the lead, but if I get this gig, it will lead to bigger and better things. . ." I gasp at the look of scorn in his eyes. "But, I promise you, it won't happen again, baby," I whimper, my voice fragile and shaking.

"Bitch, will you please shut the fuck up?" he snaps. His voice, which was generally deep with a rough edge, was now crisp and clear, causing me to jump and tumble backward onto the sofa. "You 'bout to make my goddamn head hurt."

I jump to my feet and rush to the kitchen, getting the hell out of his way. "Would you like a cocktail or something, baby?" I ask, hoping to calm him down so that he would change his mind about my punishment, whatever that is. "Let's have a drink and relax. Okay, baby?"

"Nope, don't want no drink," he smirks, his tongue heavy with sarcasm. He unzips his camel twill slacks, allowing them to drop to his ankles. Jonah has always been a snazzy dresser. Even his boxers have creases. "And, you not getting out of your punishment that easy," he growls. "So you can cut out all that goddamn game playing, girl."

"Baby, I'm not playing any games with you. I wouldn't do that."

"Smart move," he says, clenching his jaw. Jonah takes a seat on the sofa and kicks off his shoes. "Maya, it's time." Jonah shoves his right hand inside his cream-colored boxer shorts, letting the tip of his penis peep through. "Get to suckin'."

I take a deep sigh of relief and cast my eyes downward. Thank goodness, all he wants is a blowjob. I just knew he was going to put a real hurtin' on me for standing up that client. Hell, I can't stand that client. He grunts like a pig and starts to sweat as soon as the tip of his head touches my snatch. And he stinks, too—smells like something you find on the side of the road dead. So, if all I have to do is suck Jonah's dick as punishment for missing that appointment, let's just say, it's well worth it. Then again, maybe not. Jonah is a good twelve inches rock hard and likes to be deep-throated. I just can't take that entire dick down my throat, not without throwing up.

I kneel before him, lower my head and try not to bring up this morning's pancakes and link sausages. "Yeah bitch, you a pro at this shit," he moans, tilting his head back and palming the top of my head. "Take it all." He casually stretches his long legs before him and encircles me.

"I can't," I hum, with a twelve-inch sword about to pierce my tonsils. "You are too big."

"Do it!" he demands.

I raise my head and look into his eyes. "Baby, I can't deep throat you. You're too big."

Smoke seems to exude from Jonah's ears as he slaps me silly. "What did I tell you 'bout tellin' me what you can and can't do, trick?"

Blood trickles from my nose and drips onto the commercial beige carpeting. I use my sleeve as a handkerchief to wipe away the blood. I force a smile. "You promised you wouldn't hit me in my face, Jonah," I whine. "You can't honestly think that I can swallow you. I am not that deep, baby." I lick my finger, tilt my head back—more so to keep my nose from bleeding—and stroke myself from my throat down to my kitty cat. "But, I can take you down here."

Jonah pokes out his bottom lip, nods his head and grunts. Before I could blink, Jonah jumps to his feet, grabs me by my shoulder length hair, snatches me to my feet and yanks my head back as far as it will go. I struggle to maintain my balance. "Whatchu say, bitch?"

"Jonah, please!"

Jonah leans in close to me, his eyes dark and cold. "Answer me, motherfucker, before I have to break your fucking neck!" he spit, showering me with his funkiness.

"I. . .I said. . .I can't swallow. . ."

"That's what I thought you said." He raises his arm in the air and forms a fist. "A hard head makes for a soft ass." Jonah plows his fist into my face, knocking me to the floor. He kneels before me. "You do what I tell you to do!" Bringing me to my knees, Jonah strikes a powerful blow to the side of my face, sending me crashing into the glass-topped coffee table. Shattered glass pricks me like cactus thorns. I hear a snap that causes me extreme pain in my lower back. "Bitch, rise to ya feet!" he groans. I can't move. "Did you hear me, cunt? I said rise. . ."

"I heard you, Jonah," I whimper.

"Oh, so that ass ain't soft enough?"

"I can't move, Jonah. I'm hurting."

"Well, you ain't finished with your punishment." Jonah steps out of his trousers and boxers and walks toward me. He stalls, for what seems like forever. Then, using his foot as a broom, he sweeps the broken glass from around me. He straddles me and squats down, his crotch aiming at my face. "Open your mouth," he says. His voice is stern with no signs of sympathy.

Blood trickles from my mouth, down my neck and drips onto my chest. "Jonah, please. Don't do this. I've learned my lesson."

Grabbing me by the throat and lifting my neck off the floor, he leans in, studying me intently. "Don't make me repeat myself." His grip tightens around my neck. Hesitantly, I gradually open my mouth and Jonah inserts his girth. I lie there, peering into his eyes, trying not to regurgitate, wondering how or what could make someone so mean. With his knees planted flat against the floor, Jonah tosses his head back and releases a deep-throated moan. My jaw muscles weaken and my teeth graze him with every thrust. His veins pulsate against my lips. "Fuck!" He pulls from deep within, while releasing his fluids in my mouth. I swallow to keep from choking. Jonah looks down at me with bloodshot eyes. "The next time I tell you to do something, you better do it." After wiping himself off on my face, he rises to his feet and starts to walk backward, his calf muscle grazing the edge of the sofa. He looks down at his knees. "Damnit, look at what you made me do!" Splotches of blood dance around his knees as chips of glass fall to the floor.

I boldly meet his glare. "I hope it was worth it."

"You still talkin' shit?"

"No, I'm not. . ."

He raises his hand in an 'I-don't-want-to-hear-it' fashion. "It's cool. One day you will learn to keep your fucking mouth shut." Jonah slips on his pants, his fake alligator Stacy Adams and grabs his jacket. "You know, Mama, you give good head."

"I'm not your fucking mama, you bastard!"

With the swiftness of a cheetah, Jonah leaps toward me and kicks me in the hip. "That was for my Mama, you ho!" I close my eyes and try like hell to wish him away for good. "Good luck on your audition," he chuckles as the door closes behind him.

Free

From far away, it looks like a burgundy bird's nest, but up close, I see that it's a bad weave. I don't know why people come out of the house looking like someone took a pair of hedge clippers to their heads. And what's with the burgundy? Black folks weren't born with burgundy hair. It's either black or brown. And don't get me started on blonde-haired, blue-eyed black women. Folks just don't care anymore.

When I was a child, I remember my mama never leaving the house unless she was sharp as a tack. She could've been going to the laundry mat, didn't matter. She never left the house without her wig neatly combed and her lips brushed with ruby red lipstick. I've learned many lessons from Mama. Keeping up my appearance was one of them. But the main lesson that I learned was how to start up, run and maintain my own business establishment. At an early age, Mama would tell me, "Baby, keep your ass out of the red. Always stay in the black." Mama wasn't an entrepreneur, but she surely wasn't a dumb woman. She ran a tight ship when it came to the house, the bills and her girls. Mama and Daddy always used cash. They knew that getting merchandise on credit was voodoo. Mama's words stuck with me and by age twenty-four, I had started my own business and twenty years later, I am still the successful owner of Free's Floral Design Boutique located in Atlanta. Just like my mama told me to do, I've stayed in the black, although it hasn't been easy. It's hard being a woman entrepreneur. The opportunities for women aren't the same as they are for men. But, oh well, you will never succeed if you rely on folks to throw opportunities your way, that's for sure. You have to do as I do and not look for opportunities, but instead, make your own.

I am the eldest of four girls and sometimes, I feel like the mother. Every time I turn around, it's always something. Maya, the youngest, decided that she wanted to embark upon an acting career, so she moved to California. I am still waiting to see her face on TV. Jade, the middle sister, is confused. One minute, she's running a marathon to screw every man that crosses her path, and the next minute, she's chosen an alternative lifestyle. Out of my three sisters, however, Jade is the only one who has her head on straight. I don't agree with the lifestyle that she has chosen, but I am very proud of her. Jade is going places, which is more than I can say for China. China has a degree, a husband and two children. Her husband has a drinking problem and acts like a heavyweight who uses his wife for his punching bag. As for my niece and nephew, they are a joy; grown as hell, but still a joy.

"Hey, Free," says Ms. Ethel, chuckling and full of life. "What's kickin', chicken?"

"Not a thing, chicken wing. How are you doing today?" I close the drawer of the cash register.

I count my money at least five times a day. Don't know why though, nobody touches the register but me. That's another lesson I learned from Mama—count your own money. When you let others count your money, they will count you right out of business.

"Just the gout in my knees."

I bring the wooden stool from behind the counter. "Gout? Ms. Ethel, you know you are too young for gout." Ms. Ethel hops on the stool and spreads like pancake batter.

Seven years ago, Ms. Ethel's son moved her into Shady Village, an assisted living community two blocks from the boutique. She has been coming in here on a regular basis. I can set my clock by Ms. Ethel. At the same time, everyday, here comes Ms. Ethel. I guess she's lonely and I don't mind the company. I get tired of just talking to the plants anyway.

"Aw sugah, you are so sweet. You know I'm as old as dirt."

"Ms. Ethel, not true. You are as spry as a youngster."

"Whew, who told you that lie? I can't even give it away," she chuckles.

"Say what?"

"You heard me. Humph, been so long, I'm just like a sand castle. . ."

"All right now, Ms. Ethel." I interject because I know that she is about to give me entirely too much information, which is normal practice with her.

"My kitty crumbles if you glance at it," she finishes, slapping her thigh with laughter.

"Ms. Ethel, now you know. What about Mr. Perry that stays in your building? He does have a crush on you."

"Honey, I want a man who doesn't have to swallow that little blue pill every single day," she says, cracking herself up, and me too. "What about you, baby?" she asks with quiet emphasis.

"What about me?"

"Don't you have a man in your life?"

I'm not sure I like this line of questioning, but I appease her just the same. "Ms. Ethel, you know I do not have a boyfriend."

"I don't know why not. You're beautiful, successful. . .what more can a man ask for?"

"A lighter skin tone, maybe?"

"Shucks, you're talking foolish. What's wrong with your color? White folks trying their best to be your color."

"Ms. Ethel, not that I really care but, men do not care for women with my complexion and. . ."

"And who told you that lie?" she asks, her eyebrow rising in confusion.

"No one had to tell me. I'm not blind."

"No, not blind, but you are ignorant."

"Excuse me?"

"No excusing needed. Has it ever occurred to you that maybe it's your attitude about yourself that run off the men?"

"My attitude is just fine," I snap, getting mighty irritated with this old woman.

"Your attitude is very negative, Free. You should put it in check."

"I beg your pardon."

"No begging needs to be done. Just put yourself in check."

I gasp in astonishment. "Ms. Ethel, I respect you and. . ."

"Listen, baby, I'm just telling you like it is. Stop blocking your blessings. All Ms. Ethel wants you to do is enjoy life to the fullest. Besides," she says in a low voice, with a hint of curiosity, "don't you get the urge every now and then?" The warmth of her smile echoes in her voice.

I lean in and whisper, "The urge to do what?"

"Sex. You know, doin' the nasty. . .doin' the wild thing. . ."

"I get the point. I'm just fine in that department, thank you."

"How so if you don't have a man?"

"I don't need a man, Ms. Ethel. I have accepted the fact that I will be single, and I am okay with that. It is obviously in God's plans that I am to remain single."

"Hogwash!" she replies sharply. "God has made someone for everyone."

"Well, he forgot all about me then," I frown, beginning to feel sorry for myself.

Ms. Ethel peers at me with disgust in her eyes. "God does not forget about his children. He's waiting on you."

"Waiting on me to do what?"

"To help yourself."

"Huh?"

"Yes, Ma'am. God only helps those who help themselves," she said, dismounting the wooden stool. "Well, let me run. I don't want to miss my stories."

"Well, all right. Will I see you tomorrow?"

"Yes, Ma'am," she smiles, turning her back and walking toward the front door. Opening the door, she glances at me over her shoulder. "Free, remember what I said. God helps those who help themselves."

"See you tomorrow, Ms. Ethel."

China

"Ashley! André! Time to get up!" I yell from the bottom of the winding staircase. "Come on, get up! You're going to be late for school," I holler, returning to the kitchen. "Don't let me have to come up there," I threaten over my shoulder.

"Dang Mama, we comin'!" André yells from the top of the stairs, trying to make it to the bathroom before Ashley, his only sibling.

"I don't feel good, Mama!" Ashley whines, running as she tries to beat André to the bathroom. "I won!" she bellows like a banshee, slamming the bathroom door in André's face.

"Ma! Ashley put her hands on me!"

Ashley flung open the bathroom door. "No, I didn't! I ain't touch you!"

"Yes, you did! You pushed me out the way and then slammed the door in my face!"

"Stop lying, you pussy!"

"Ma, did you hear what she called me?"

"Damnit! Is it so bad to want to have a cup of coffee without a lot of daily bullshit from those two?" I mumble. It's the same shit every morning. Seeing who hits the bathroom first has been a daily ritual from the time André took his first steps. Ashley always has a jump-start on him because her bedroom is diagonal from the bathroom. "All right now, I want you two to stop it. You hear me?"

"But Mama…"

"But Mama nothing. Go in my bathroom, André," I demand. "Ashley, you wash your mouth out with soap!"

"Mama, I ain't do nuffin," Ashley shrieks. "You always yellin' at me."

"Hurry up and get dressed. Your breakfast is getting cold. It's getting late, so I will have to drive you to school."

"She gets away with everything!" André pouts and stomps off to my bathroom.

Walking past André, Ron playfully smacks his son upside the head. "Boy, do what your mother says." Jogging down the staircase, Ron makes his way to the kitchen and stands in the doorway looking at me with my hair in rollers, covered with a flower print scarf and wearing his sweatpants and tee shirt. "What the hell is going on?" he snaps. "Can't we have one morning when there's no damn yelling and screaming?"

"Did we wake you, honey?"

"Did we wake you, honey?" he mimics. "What do you think?" He looks at me intently, then strides to the kitchen table and plops his ass in the wooden chair, causing it to inch backward. He and his funky attitude are going to scratch up my damn floor.

I ignore Ron's sarcasm because I do not feel like arguing this morning. "How about some eggs?" I give my husband a cup of black coffee and a kiss on the cheek. No cream, no sugar, black and bitter just like his ass. "Scrambled or fried?"

"China, you ask me the same damn dumb ass question every single morning," he barks. "How long have we been married?"

"Ron, you don't always want them cooked the same way every..."

"Twenty years. And for twenty years, you ask me the same damn dumb ass question every single morning!" Ron snatches a piece of dry toast from the flower-embossed china dish. He takes a bite and frowns up his face. "This toast is always dry too," he mocks.

"Honey, the butter is sitting in your face," I retort. "Okay, how did you end up on the wrong side of the bed this morning, sweetie?"

"Don't start with me, China. I ain't in the mood," he snaps, his body becoming erect.

I pick a lint ball off his shirt. "Baby, I'm not starting anything. You are the one in a foul mood."

"Ma, I can't find my pink sweater and I want to wear my pink sweater today." Ashley shifts irately from foot to foot.

"Ash, why are you going to wear a wool sweater in this ninety-degree Florida heat?"

"It's not hot in the classroom," she whines.

"Your pink wool sweater has been packed away with the other sweaters, and you will not walk out of this house with a wool sweater. . ."

"I want my sweater! André can have whatever he wants and all I want is my sweater!" she hollers, stomping her feet.

"Girl, I know you are not stomping your feet up in here!" I snap, vigorously shaking my finger toward her. "You better get out of my face with that mess." Leaving Ashley to her whining, I direct my attention back toward my forty-year-old child. "Ron, I'm not trying to argue. I just want to know if everything is all right. What's bothering you, honey?"

"You want to know what's bothering me."

"Yes, I do."

"China, you obviously don't pay attention to. . ."

"Ma, I can't find my pink sweater and I want to wear my pink sweater today!" Ashley cries again, tears glistening her sable cheeks.

God, give me strength not to smack the snot out of this child. She is getting on my last nerve. "Ash, I heard you the first time. Find something else to wear," I reply through stiff lips.

"I don't want to wear anything else, I want to wear my sweater!" she yells, twisting her neck and rolling her eyes. "Why can't I wear my sweater if I wanna? André gets to do whatever he wants to do and I can't do a damn thing!"

My body stiffens. "Come here," I say sternly. Ashley plants her feet, as if in dried concrete. "You hear me talking to you, Ashley?"

"Ut oh. . .you're about to get a beat down." André raises his hand to his mouth to stifle his giggling.

"Shut up!" Ashley screams.

I fold my arms across my chest. "When I count to three, I better be able to smell your breath."

Looking down, Ashley scuffs her shoe on the kitchen floor. Licking her lips nervously, she slowly moves toward me. I snatch her little ass by her arm and yank her toward me. "Ash, what did I tell you about your mouth? You aren't grown, so cut out that damn cursing," I snap. "Now, get your fast ass upstairs and find something else to wear. You are not wearing that damn sweater. Do I make myself clear?"

Ashley steps back, takes a deep sigh, props her hands on her 'missing in action' hips and sticks out her right leg. "Yeah, whatever. I swear!"

"Excuse me?" I am seconds away from slapping the shit out of this pissy tail child.

"You saw right, Ma. She rolled her eyes and did that ghetto head snap too," André instigates.

"Shut up, you pussy!" Ashley barks at André.

"All right, enough!" Ron shouts in an authoritative tone, making us all jump out of our skin. "Ashley, do what your mother says," Ron scolds. "You aren't wearing nobody's sweater today. It's going to be too hot and you will look like a fool."

"But Daddy, it's cold in the classroom," she pouts, trying to play on her father's emotions.

"Well, take your windbreaker because you are not wearing that sweater out of this house, and that's that, Ashley!" I snap.

At twelve years old, Ashley is five–feet-five inches tall. She and I stand eye level.

"Ashley, don't start tripping in here. I suggest you do what I tell you before I set fire to that ass and then you won't need a sweater!" I bark.

She stomps out of the kitchen and up the stairs. "Fine!"

"Na, na, na, na, na!" André teases, with his face in his plate.

"André, you hush up, finish your breakfast and finish getting ready for school. We are leaving here in fifteen minutes." I take a sip of lukewarm Hazelnut coffee, but really, I need a sip of whiskey. These kids get on my damn nerves. Ashley thinks she's grown. Too grown for her own good. She has one more time to stand up to me and I'm going to knock her on her ass. She is just like her father, stubborn as a damn cotton field mule.

Ron picks up his packed brown paper bag lunch and grabs a Granny Smith apple from the fruit bowl that sits in the middle of the kitchen island. "I'm out of here," he growls.

"You haven't had your breakfast. You aren't hungry?"

"I'll pick up something at the office."

"Ron, we need to talk. Call me later?" Ron looks at me, mumbles and then leaves through the kitchen door that leads to the garage, without so much as a kiss on my cheek. Damn, what did I do to him? "Okay y'all, let's go!"

André grabs his books from the family room. "Ma, you going out the house looking like that?"

"Looking like what?"

"Looking like you belong in a flower garden."

"Hush up! I'm not getting out of the car, so I won't embarrass you."

"Well, you will embarrass me looking like that." Ashley looks me up and down. "Suppose the car breaks down, then what?"

"Girl, you have worked my nerves enough this morning. Get in the car and let's go!"

"Well, can you at least take that scarf off? You look like Aunt Jemima."

I pop Ashley upside the head and shove her out of the kitchen through the garage door. "Get in the car! I've heard enough from you today."

Jade

I was a real hot ass.

Todd was my first love and my first sexual encounter. After twenty years, I am still trying to find him. I'm curious to see what he's been up to and if he is still looking good. The last I'd heard, he had left the area and had relocated to the West Coast. From time to time, I reflect back on those days—filled with laughter, fun and tears. We were only fifteen and had experienced a lot for kids our age. After Todd, my life changed and I started experimenting with many different men. Some were good, but most of them were awful. There I was, inexperienced, still smelling like breast milk, and screwing every brother in sight, which is probably why I am the way that I am today.

With Todd, I didn't know the first thing about being intimate, let alone anything else. Hell, for that matter, neither did Todd. Nevertheless, just like all teenagers, we thought we knew it all. Our first encounter was awful. I laid there motionless while he tried to figure out where to insert his dick. After watching a few of his parent's homemade porn tapes, you couldn't tell us we weren't getting our groove on. I must admit, it was strange seeing his parents naked. Afterwards, I found it difficult to look them in the eye.

I learned how to do all kinds of sexual things with Todd, which I believe is why I am so good at pleasing my partner. One day, Todd and I decided to ditch school and hangout at his house. His parents were at work and we had the house to ourselves. One thing led to another, which led to us doing the nasty all over the house, which in turn led to us ditching school at least once a week to have an eight-hour screw-a-thon, trying to see if I was orgasmic. He never found the G-spot. Of course, we didn't know anything about any 'spot' back then. Our condom-free screw festivals eventually led to me having a baby on the way. Mama said she was too young to be a grandma, not to mention the fact that I was too young to be someone's mother, so I had an abortion.

I remember as if it were yesterday. That was an awful time in my life. I was terrified. I thought that I could make my period come by inserting a Q-tip into my cervix or douching. I confided in my best friend. She consoled as much as she could. She convinced me that I needed to tell my parents and Todd. After all, it was his child too and he needed to be included. It took me weeks before I told Mama that I had missed my period. When Mama told Daddy, his response caused me to lock myself in the bathroom. He was hurt that his baby was about to have a baby. He did not speak to me for weeks. When Mama took me to see a doctor, I was over three months and needed to go out of town for an abortion. What a horrible experience for a child to go through—a hospital ward with five other girls, having my bellybutton injected with saline solution, cramping half the day and most of the night, being awakened by my water breaking and giving birth to a dried up fetus. If I had known what I was in for, I would have kept my fucking legs closed.

Through all of the turmoil, Todd stood by my side. His mother raised him right, that's for sure. He called me every day I spent in the hospital. It made me feel good to know that I was the only girl in the ward whose boyfriend was calling. After I had the abortion, Daddy acted as though nothing had happened. It hurt me that he stopped speaking to me and although I did not understand what he was feeling at that time, I did not stop being Daddy's little girl.

"Jade, I'm sorry to disturb you, but Mr. McAfee would like to see you in his office," Sherrell announces, peeking her head inside my office, her voice laced with a hint of apology.

Sherrell is a tall, amazon woman with broad shoulders and a Chia Pet hairstyle that glistens from the curl juice. Can you say Soul Glo? She favors a linebacker for the Chicago Bears too. I don't care for her and I guess it shows.

"Thank you, Sherrell," I force a smile. "Let him know that I am on my way, please."

Chester McAfee is my boss and the CEO of McAfee & Associates. He will lick and lap my tail if I bend over for him. He has been trying to smell my underwear for as long as I've been working here, which has been eight years. If he's not careful, his wife is going to find out about his little romps. That man plays tiddly winks in the supply closet after hours with the majority of the females in this office. I don't want nor need my job that bad. If I am going to give my stuff away, I will give it away on my terms and no one else's, especially when it comes to giving it to a man.

Pushing myself to a standing position, I reach for a pad and pencil in case I need to take notes. After reaching in my top desk drawer for a breath mint, Sherrell buzzes the intercom. "Jade, Joy is on line three. Shall I tell her that you will call her back?"

"Do you know why Mr. McAfee wants to see me?"

"Nope, not at all. But I don't think you would want to keep him waiting. You know how he can be," she advises.

"I don't recall asking for your fucking advice," I think to myself. "Yep, I know. I'll take the call, thank you," I sigh.

I fall into the chair and lay my head on the desk. "Damn, what is it now? Joy calls me fifty times a day." This is Joy's fifth time calling me today. It seems as though she's monitoring me. It drives me up the wall. I snatch the phone from the cradle and swivel quickly, facing the breathtaking view of New York City's skyscrapers. "Hey girl, you're going to have to make it quick. Mr. McAfee wants to see me."

"Damn Jade, what did you do now?"

"Beats the hell out of me. I thought I had been a good girl," I chuckle. "What's up?"

"We still hookin' up this evening at the Red Dog?"

"Yep, what time?"

"I will be there around six o'clock."

"I can't get there before seven."

"That's fine. I'll be there waiting."

"Are you sure?"

"Yep, I'm sure."

"Great, see you then." I pull myself up and head toward Mr. McAfee's office on the tenth floor.

"Looking good, Jade. How are you doing?" Shawn Maxwell, an associate with the firm, is always complimenting me. He is such the man. Hell, if I swung that way, I would give him some. But then again, he would end up falling in love and I would have to quit my job. Besides, I just don't feel like being bothered with a nagging ass man.

"I can't complain, Shawn," I smile, walking slowly by him, my hips intentionally sway enough for him to salivate.

I stop at the elevator, tug at my collar, adjust my skirt and take a peep at my stockings. There is nothing worse than wearing shear, off black stockings with a run from the toe to the thigh. I glance over my shoulder at Shawn, flash a smile, strut onto the elevator, turn to face him and as the doors begin to close, I pucker my magenta-stained lips. He drops his papers and I lean against the wall in laughter.

As I approach Mr. McAfee's office, I take a deep breath to calm my nerves. Standing in front of his office door, I take another deep breath and then knock. I feel like I am about to hyperventilate. "Mr. McAfee?"

"Yes, Jade. Please, come in and have a seat."

I walk into his office and take a seat on the sofa. Oops, wrong spot. I can smell the pussy. I quickly jump to my feet and dart for the chair that's positioned in front of his desk. Trying to maintain my cool, I put a warm smile on my face. "How are you, Mr. McAfee?"

I feel moist between my legs and I'm sure it's these flannel draws. There ain't shit about this man that turns me on. Unless, of course, you like the short, stout men with a comb-over to make it appear as if he has more hair than he does. I need to do laundry. Shit, I should've left these damn things at home. My pussy can't breathe and I do not do yeast infections.

Standing behind me, he rests his hands on my shoulders, in a possessive manner. "Please, enough with the formalities. You've been with me long enough to call me Chester," he smiles. "Care for a drink?" he offers, walking over to his glass-encased bar.

Mr. McAfee's. . .I mean, Chester's office is immaculate. You could eat off the floor, and from what they tell me, he does a lot of eating off his floor and his grand oak desk too. Rumor has him being a nasty old man who chases behind his female employees because his wife is a valium junkie and is always too mellow to rock his world.

"No thank you, Chester."

I don't feel comfortable calling this man Chester. I might end up having dreams about him or something. I shiver at the vision of Chester naked with a roll of quarters protruding from his M&M-sized testicles. I picture myself stretched across the desk with my panties dangling by the heel of my pump, Chester's potbelly rubbing against my abdomen, and his piss stick trying to find its way to my garden. "Oh God," I mumble.

"Excuse me?"

"Oh, um. . .I just realized that I forgot to unplug my iron."

Yes, I lied. What was I supposed to have said? 'Chester, I just imagined us trying to have sex, but you couldn't find the hole because your dick is too small and your stomach got in the damn way?' He would've fired me on the spot.

"Are you sure you won't have a drink?"

"Yes. It's too early in the day for me." I ease back into the chair, wanting him to hurry up and get to his reason for summonsing me into his den of raunchiness. I can still smell the stench of pussy in the air. At least keep a can of Lysol nearby for goodness sakes.

"Jade, I suppose you want to know why I've asked to see you."

"Well, yes. The thought had crossed my mind. Is everything all right?"

"Everything couldn't be better," he smiles and takes a seat behind his desk. "I wanted to tell you before you found out through the McAfee & Associates grapevine. . ."

"Yes," I nervously interrupt. Lord, I wish this man would stop beating around the bush and just get it over with, fire me and let me walk out of this place with a little dignity. "On second thought, Chester, I would like to have a drink." Enough of this Chester shit. I don't want him to get the wrong idea. Besides, just the mere thought of him naked scares the hell out of me.

"Sure." He walks over to the bar. "What will you have?"

Now sitting on the edge of the chair, stroking my stocking-covered thighs with the palms of my hands, I am nervous as hell. "Whatever you're having will be fine."

"Martini, shaken, not stirred," he smiles, extending the drink toward me.

"Thank you." I take the Martini and quickly take a sip to calm my nerves because I just know I'm about to be fired, and this is not a good time. I owe everybody and their mamas. On top of that, I am a month behind with my rent. I already have to hide my car at a friend's house in Jersey so the snatchman doesn't snatch my shit.

"Jade, as I was saying, I would like to tell you before you hear it through the grapevine. I am sure that you have heard that Jeffrey Christianson has left McAfee & Associates. . ."

"Yes, I believe I've heard something about that." I take another sip.

"Yes, well, now that he is gone, we will need someone to run the Human Resources Department. I don't feel that we should recruit outside of the firm when we have qualified people who can fill Christianson's shoes."

"Yes, there are many qualified people here." I take down the rest of the Martini. "May I have another?" I pray this man would stop killing me a slow death.

"Sure," he smiles, probably thinking I have a drinking problem because of the way I took that Martini to the head. "Jade, I called you here today because. . ." he extends me the drink, "I need you to pack up your office. . ."

I become hysterical and knock the drink out of his hand and onto the floor. "Oh no, Mr. McAfee!" I exclaim. "I will work harder. Please don't fire me. I can't afford to be out of work. I have bills out the ass and a layaway in every store up and down West 34th Street. Please, I've been loyal to this firm for eight long years. . ." I gasp for air.

Mr. McAfee looks at me and falls out with laughter. "Jade, it must be the Martini."

"What? But, I don't. . ."

"No, Jade, I am not firing you. I am promoting you to Director of Human Resources," he announces with his hands jammed inside his pants pockets and a smile so wide I can see the cavity on his wisdom tooth.

"Oh, Mr. McAfee, thank you! Thank you so much!" I leap to my feet, run around behind his desk and wrap my arms around his neck. I quickly catch myself when I feel his stubby hand tap me on my ass. I jump back from behind the desk. "Oh, I am so sorry, Mr. McAfee. I don't know what came over me." I hold my head down in shame. "I will clean up this mess also."

"Nonsense! I love to see enthusiasm from my employees, and you will do no such thing. We have a cleaning staff," he chuckles.

"Yes, sir, and I will do one hell of a job too!"

"I know that you will, Jade. That's why you got the job."

"Thank you. . ." I begin walking backward toward the door. "Thank you, thank you!" I back into the hallway, smiling and closing the door behind me. "Yes!" I exclaim. "Hot damn, wait until Joy hears about this!"

Free

What a day! I need to hire an assistant. Since my floral business has become so popular, I am overwhelmed with orders. Today, I filled six orders for funeral sprays. Can you believe that? People are dropping off like flies, especially our young people who live on and by the streets. When will they ever learn that the only place the streets will get you is in a wooden box, spending eternity next to someone you don't even know? On the bright side, Spelman and Morehouse are having their homecoming festivities in a few weeks, so they are ordering every flower imaginable.

My feet hurt, I'm hungry and I'm too tired to cook. I am going to order in a large meat and cheese pizza, eat myself into oblivion and watch my two favorite shows, My Wife and Kids and The Bernie Mac Show. But right now, I have a craving for a nice cup of Hazelnut coffee with a hint of Amaretto cream and a chat room. It's been days since I've checked my email.

Porn, porn and more porn. I've never been to a porn site before, so why am I receiving all of this junk? Is somebody trying to tell me something? I know it's been a while since I've even thought about doing some of the mess they do on those sites, but this is ridiculous. This reminds me of a person I used to date who, every time I turned around, was stroking his you-know-what while looking at one of those porn sites. This person and I dated for about three years and I had a key to his place. One day, I stopped by unannounced. I didn't think I needed to call if I had a key. I caught him stroking his penis and looking at some hoochie (I got that from China) on the computer screen sucking on a penis that barely hung past the man's testicles. I'd never seen anything so small before in my life. Well, needless to say, my relationship with that pervert ended. He said it was my fault that he was looking at that mess. I wouldn't give him head, so I forced his hand. Whatever. I don't do that kind of stuff. If God wanted us to do that nasty thing, he would've had Eve doing it to Adam on a regular basis. Besides, I believe it was the little penis he was getting a thrill out of, rather than the hoochie.

Sorting through the tons of junk email, I come across an email from Jade. It's been quite a while since I've received any form of communication from her. She hasn't had two words to say to me since her last visit, which was my first time meeting her significant other, Joy. It was the strangest relationship. First, I couldn't understand why Jade would be interested in a woman. Secondly, Joy was so possessive and demanding, it was sickening. Every move Jade made, Joy had to know why she was making it. She was so far up Jade's behind she had a personal relationship with her hemorrhoids. The moaning and groaning at night drove me so far up the walls that I had to let Jade know that I didn't like that kind of stuff going on under my roof. I don't believe in same sex relations and never will.

To: ForeverFree34, LadyActor275, ChinaCloset24
From: NeverJaded69
Subject: Good News!
Hello Sisters,
Guess what? You are now reading mail from the new Director of Human Resources for McAfee & Associates! Hot

damn, can you believe that shit? Mr. McAfee called me into his office and I just knew he was going to fire my ass, but instead, he promoted me! I am so happy I could just spit! Ladies, we MUST celebrate! I wanted you all to be the first to know!

Free, how's the business going and do you have a man in your life yet? Maya, are you still trying to get into the movies? China, how are things with you? Give André and Ashley a big kiss from their Auntie Jade. Gotta run, Jade.

Well, doesn't that beat all? I am so proud of Jade. She finally got her head out of the clouds and doing something with her life. But I knew she would come to her senses. It's about time, she put that degree, that Mama worked so hard cleaning white folk's houses to put her through Columbia University, to good use. I just wish her choice in partners were the same as most women. Jade is the prettiest of us all, yet she refuses to date men. It's not as if she has to deal with having a deep complexion that resembles a puff of smoke, as I do. Men make passes at her all the time. I just don't get it and I guess I never will. Well, it really doesn't matter, as long as she is happy. I know Mama would be so proud of her girls. Well, except for Maya.

Maya was a handful when Mama was carrying her around in her belly. And when she popped out, she was raising pure hell and still is. Maya is the youngest and spoiled rotten. She was always talking about, "I'm going to be a movie star," while flipping a white towel around her head, pretending she had long blonde hair. The poor child was confused. Maya left for Hollywood five years ago and every time I turn on the television, I don't see her, not even on a Tampax commercial. The last time I spoke with her, she was going from audition to audition and couldn't seem to land a role. She wants to be an actor so bad. I do believe she would sell herself to make the ends meet, if she had to.

To: NeverJaded69, LadyActor275, ChinaCloset24
From: ForeverFree34
Subject: Re: Good News!

Jade, I think I speak for us all when I say that we are so proud of you! You go, Ms. Director of Human Resources! I know you're going to take us all out to Sizzler now that you are making big bank. LOL

I am doing fine and NO, I don't have a man in my life. I don't need a man. The last time I checked, it wasn't a sin to live without a man! You seem to do it without any problems. I wish you would stop riding me about having a man.

With sisterly love, Free.

Jade gets on my nerves with that mess. She's asking me if I have a man and here she is carpet munching (got that one from China too) with another woman. "Mind ya damn business, Jade!" I yell, logging off. Time for my pizza.

China

Twelve years ago, Ron told me that he wanted me to take a leave of absence from my job because he wanted me to stay home and raise Ashley. At least until she was old enough to become a latch key kid. Well, two years later, André was born and I got the same story from Ron. "China, baby, I don't want our kids growing up in a daycare center," he said. "At least wait until André is old enough for Ashley to watch him while we are away at work," he said. Well, Ron, it's been twelve fuckin' years and my degree and knowledge is going right down the toilet, thanks to your ass. I really can't blame it on Ron though, because I am the master of my destiny, or so I think. "Oh well, I love taking care of my family," my thoughts echo as I walk through a desolate house and up the winding staircase with the empty wicker clothes basket balancing between my forearm and my hip. Tonight, I will talk to Ron about me going back to work, and that's all there is to it.

Thursday is laundry day and there is nothing I dislike more than washing someone's dirty underwear, especially the underwear with track stains. I know I taught that boy how to wipe his ass properly. I love my family, but goodness, I swear that damn André is just nasty. I have to step over Nintendo, Game Boy and all kinds of shit just to get to André's clothes hamper. I told that child to clean this damn room. He half does his damn homework, so the least he can do is clean this funky ass room. As I bend down to pick up dirty clothes that have tumbled out of the clothesbasket, I notice something sticking out of André's bottom dresser drawer. Being the mother that I am, and since his ass is living under my roof and not paying for food or mortgage, I slide open the drawer.

"China, what's wrong? You look like you've just seen a ghost," Ron snickers, peeking his head inside André's bedroom.

I am speechless and unable to move. I can't believe my eyes. My baby, my sweet innocent little boy has a strip of Trojan Magnum XL condoms in his dresser drawer. I stand upright to face Ron, straightening my shoulders and clearing my throat. I extend the condoms in his direction. "Look," I whisper.

"What's that?" he asks, walking toward me.

"It's, it's. . ."

"A damn condom!" he exclaims and shakes his head in utter disbelief. "What the hell is a ten-year-old doing with a damn condom?"

"I don't know. I can't believe this. Our baby is having sex?"

"And an extra large condom at that!" Ron laughs. "That's my boy!"

"Ron! I can't believe you are taking this so lightly. Our ten-year-old son is obviously having sex."

"Calm down, China. You don't know that for sure. He could be using them to make water balloons or something," he chuckles, shaking his head and mumbling to himself, "Extra large condoms. . ."

"Ron, this is not funny. Can he even get a hard on at ten years old?"

"China, you are overreacting. Let's wait until the boy gets home and we will ask him, okay?"

"I'm sure it's all very innocent." I turn my back to Ron and walk out of the bedroom.

"Um, baby?"

"Yeah."

"Where are you going with the condoms?"

I stare at the pack of condoms, my hand trembling. "I don't know. I guess I will throw them away," I solemnly say.

"No, don't do that. Here, let me have them." Ron lunges at me in one fluid motion and snatches the condoms from my hand. "I will have a man-to-man talk with André this evening, all right?"

"Yes, that would be best. My head is killing me. I'm going to lie down."

"Yeah, you do that, babe," Ron says as I turn to walk away, while at the same time massaging the knots from my neck. "How in the hell did he get his hands on my condoms?" Ron mumbles to himself.

"Did you say something, sweetie?"

"Uh-huh."

"Okay. I am going to lie down for a bit."

"Uh, yeah, you do that. I've got to run out."

"Where are you going?" I yell from our bedroom.

"Just out. Be back in time for dinner." Ron jogs down the stairs and out the front door.

Maya

"Somebody please help me." The phone rings for the fifth time. "Please, somebody help me," I cry, hoping that whoever is calling could hear me and come to my rescue.

It's been two days since Jonah bashed in my face and I have not been able to move from this spot. "Help!" I cry out, but my cry is a soft whisper. I can taste the saltiness of my tears rolling down my face. My legs feel numb and because I haven't been able to get up, I've defecated all over myself. I smell awful.

There's a knock at the door. A thought of Jonah slamming his fist into my face has me shuttering with fear. I don't say a word. It might be Jonah, coming back to finish the job. I cry silently instead. The mail passes through the mail slot and an ounce of hope gives me energy to mouth, "I need help." Sound refuses to escape me. "I missed my audition." I fall into a deep sleep.

Jade

It is cold as a witch's tit in a brass bra out this bitch. This weather is the only reason why I hate living in New York City. It's cold and dark as hell, even when the sun is shining across the bridge in Jersey. I button my coat up to my neck, slightly choking myself, and partially cover my face with my scarf, wrapping it around my head. I am not in the mood to take the subway, so I'm standing in the middle of the damn street, attempting to hail down a cab. Just as one approaches, a dark figure of a tall and slender woman comes out of nowhere, hops her ass in my cab and the driver takes off. "What the fuck?" I exclaim. "You bitch!" I yell, flipping the bird, and not a soul is paying me any attention. Standing here, pissed off and cold as shit, I raise my hand to hail down another cab—just like a black man—empty cabs are passing me by. "The fuckin' assholes!"

From nowhere, this fine specimen approaches me. "Excuse me, Miss," he says, standing as if he prided himself in his good looks.

"Yes," I smile, my demeanor taking a turn, facing a mouth watering, breathtaking view.

"I notice you are having some issues. . ."

"And how did you notice that?" I snap, because I do not want him to think that I jump at the first dick that approaches me. Hell, I don't jump at dick at all.

"My apologies, I didn't mean to offend you. I saw from my car how that woman stole your cab. I would love to give you a ride to your destination."

"Oh, well. . ."

"I know you don't know me. However, I will be glad to tell you all about myself if we could step in from the cold."

Normally, I wouldn't accept rides from people I don't know, but for the first time, before me stood a man that actually made me feel kind of giggly inside. Besides, it's cold as shit standing in the middle of the damn street.

"Yes, I would appreciate that," I smile. After all, I am the new Director of Human Resources. Fuck a damn cab! I can never understand what those foreigners are saying no damn way. How in the hell are they allowed to stay in this country, take all of our jobs and they can't even speak English? The limo driver appears, takes my satchel and leads me to the opened limo door. Once inside, I immediately warm up. It's so toasty in here. This is definitely better than a cab, plus, I prefer the view.

"So, where are you headed?" he asks, pulling of his black, lambskin leather gloves, one finger at a time.

"To the Red Dog, on West 125th Street," I smile.

"Yes, I am familiar with the Red Dog."

"You are?" I wonder what side of the fence this cutie stands. The only folks who hang out at the Red Dog are folks who prefer same sex relations.

"Yes, I am."

"Oh? I am always there and I don't ever recall seeing you."

"I only said that I was familiar — never ventured inside." He flashes a smile and strokes his top lip with this index finger. "My name is Jonathan Meadows, and you are?"

"It's nice to meet you, Jonathan. I'm Jade Howard and thank you so much for the ride."

"It's not a problem, I am glad to have been able to offer," he smiles. "Robert, let's drop this lovely lady off at the Red Dog." Robert, the driver, nods his head in agreement and pulls the limo away from the curb and into New York's infamous traffic.

"I don't know how I could ever repay you."

"Why would you want to do that?"

"Well, I do like to repay my debts."

I can't help but look out the window at all of the folks walking in the cold, freezing their asses off and looking like icicles, while I am riding in style. I mentally stick out my tongue at all of them, especially that rude bitch who took my damn cab.

"This is not a debt. This is simply a nice gesture. You don't owe me anything. Okay?"

I shrug my shoulders and look around the limo, taking inventory of the Bose speakers, black leather seats, wet bar housing wine glasses that hang upside down and the rack of mini liquor bottles against a mirrored background. The melodic voice of Eddie Levert swoon me with Forever Mine, while The O'Jays back up his plea. I love me some O'Jays. "I only offer a pay back once. So, what do you do, Jonathan?" Here I go, getting all up in this man's business.

"Please, call me Jon and to answer your question, I own my own consulting firm. You may've heard of it, Meadows & Meadows Architectural Design."

I don't realize that my bottom lip is now sitting in my lap. Jon leans over toward me, extends his hand and uses his index finger to motion for me to close my mouth. "I've heard of your firm." I had no idea that Meadows was a black man. I wonder about the other half of Meadows & Meadows.

"You look as if you've just seen a ghost or something," he smirks.

"No, not at all. . ."

"I know, can't believe a black man is the owner of the largest architectural design firm in New York City, right?"

I give him a bashful look. My face warms from embarrassment. "Yes, well, you've just called me out."

"Don't worry about it. Besides, I think you are cute with your mouth wide open. It's a good thing I didn't tell you out there," he points out the window. "The flies would've had a warm place to nest," he chuckles at my expense. I feel like such the idiot. "It looks like we are going to be sitting in traffic for a minute. Would you care for a drink?"

"Sure. After all, I am celebrating. I got a promotion today."

"Congratulations, Jade! Well, this calls for the good stuff." Jon opens the mini refrigerator and pulls out an unfamiliar bottle. "You do like Dom, don't you?"

"Of course, who doesn't?" I ask with excitement.

Truth is the closest I've ever gotten to a bottle of Dom Perignon was staring at it through the glass-encased, refrigerated display inside the corner liquor store. I couldn't afford that shit then and I can't afford it now, even with the promotion.

"Oh snap, that's my song!" I exclaim, bobbing my head and snapping my fingers to Mystikal's Shake It Fast. Damn, how can you go from The O'Jays to Mystikal?

John seems to be getting a kick out of my bobbing head and gyrating shoulders. I'm damn near close to breaking out with the snake. "Show me whatcha workin' with," I sing, exhibiting Jade to the fullest. Take me or leave me, is what I always say.

Jon pours us both a glass. "Here's to your continued success," he toasts.

We tap our glasses together, making that shrieking clinking noise. Okay, is this real crystal or what? That clink sound was too damn crisp to be glass. I close my eyes and feel my lips caress the rim of real crystal.

"Hmm. Thank you. So, who is the other half of Meadows & Meadows?"

"That would be my brother, Paul. He handles the financial end, while I handle everything else." Jon has the most beautiful smile. He has all of his teeth and they are white as snow too. I think he did a Denzel move and had a cap or two placed because his teeth are too perfect. Shoot, I am not mad at him or Denzel. Nothing worse than a brotha with fucked up teeth, which leads to hot, funky breath. And who, in their right mind, would want that anywhere near their puss? "So, what's your new position and where do you work?"

The driver hits a pothole, causing my drink to splatter. "Oh shit!" I exclaim, wiping the spillage from my chin with my finger. "McAfee & Associates and you are now looking at the new Director of Human Resources," I smile, resembling Ms. Celie in The Color Purple.

"Well, that's awesome."

Oh no, did he say awesome? "Yes, it is . . . awesome."

"Chester McAfee, huh?"

"Yes, you know him?"

"Yes, strictly on a personal level. He's a member of my gym."

"You own a gym too?"

Jon nods his head in amusement.

"Well, damn, you are the man of many talents. Which one?"

"Not really, I just like to keep my money flowing, that's all. It's the only venture that I am in without my brother."

"Oh, okay. So which one?"

"Bruno's Run & Jump Fitness Center."

"Wow and all this time, I thought Bruno's was an Italian-owned spot. How did you come up with that name?"

"Bruno is the name of my five-year-old boxer."

He refills his glass. I extend my glass before he could offer, which probably makes me look like a lush. But, I could care less. I hope he fills it to the rim because I will never have Dom again unless I hit the lottery. "I've been to your fitness center before."

"Oh, are you a member?"

"Nope, strictly on a visitor's pass," I laugh. "Too expensive for my budget."

Jon reaches inside his gray wool tweed overcoat, pulls out a billfold and extends me a card. "When you want to work out, call me and I will put you on the VIP list."

"Thanks!"

I'm feeling warm and bubbly inside and I don't think it's because of the Dom. Damn, could I actually be developing the urge to get freak nasty with a man after all these years of not wanting to be bothered with a man? Actually, I forget what it feels like.

"Well, here we are." Jon announces our arrival at the Red Dog.

"Great. Jon, thank you so much." I wait for Robert to open the door and let me out, while fighting off the urge to tell Jon to drive off, take me to his place and scratch my itch.

"It was my pleasure," he says, looking at me with contemplation. "Jade, I would like to see you again. Would you consider having dinner with me?"

"Jon, I think there is something that you should know about me."

"Well, straight people don't hang out at the Red Dog. That much I do know."

"Yes, well, I've been hurt by men before and I'd rather not go down that worn-out road again. I appreciate the offer though. Thank you and take care." I make my way out the car and into the Red Dog.

There is simply no other way to describe the place. The Red Dog is a hole in the wall that continues to exceed the Fire Marshall's capacity. Walking through the front door, I immediately begin to rub unfamiliar asses and dicks willing to mingle with other unknown dicks. The bar is flanked with bodies covered with designer attire with the matching stank attitudes. I hate this place, but Joy loves it. The eggplant-painted walls have matching light sconces. There are three retro 1970's disco balls hanging from the ceiling, exposing the pipes and sprinkler system. With the exception of the disco ball, the Red Dog has an artsy feel. Tables with no more than four chairs surround the dance floor — the width of an oversized jail cell — with folks packed like sardines, snaking and grinding.

Joy is waving at me as if she's guiding in a plane. All that's missing are those huge earphones and those orange beams of lights to direct me to the table. Damn, can she be just a little more noticeable?

"Hey, baby!" she exclaims like a trick excited as hell to see her period. She embraces me tightly and gives me a kiss on the neck.

"Hey you, been here long?"

"Nope, about twenty minutes. I ordered some Buffalo Wings."

Shari approaches the table with her usual perky demeanor and a smile as wide as the Atlantic Ocean. Shari is one of the sweetest people you will ever meet. She cracks me up when she gets her flirt on and bats her doe-like eyes with long, butterfly wing eyelashes. She's quite attractive. If it weren't for Joy, I am sure I would enjoy her company.

"What's up, Jade? Girl, I saw that big ass limo. What's up with that?" Shari laughs, with her nosey ass. Shari is my girl, but she is always in my business. "Humph, let me find out you big pimpin'." We both fall out with laughter. Joy, on the other hand, doesn't find any of this funny. "Whatcha' drinkin'?" Shari asks, retrieving her pencil from behind her ear.

"My usual."

"A shot of Jose Cuervos and a salty-rimmed Margarita, comin' up," she sings, turning on her Witchy Pooh boots and pushing her way through the crowd to the bar.

"Dang, it's packed in here," I say, looking around the bar, taking in the sights and glancing at Joy. She doesn't look too happy. "What's wrong, Joy?"

"What limo, Jade?"

"Oh, it's nothing."

"You're right, it's nothing. After all, you ride around in limos all day, every day," she says sarcastically.

Oh shit, here we go. I am not in the mood for her whining. "Joy, get a grip. It's not that serious."

"Well, if it's not that serious, why can't you tell me about the limo?" she whines.

Joy is a brat, very insecure and overly protective. Warning: You had better not get too close to me or you might get your eyeballs clawed out. She's always telling me that she and I make wonderful music together and that there is no one else out here for her. Believe me when I say, she will fight to the death to keep me. Now, that's some scary shit, which is why I won't tell her about Jon Meadows. Besides, there isn't anything to tell.

"Okay, well, I wanted to tell you later. I got a promotion today!"

Joy sits across from me with her arms folded across her chest and smiles. "That is wonderful, baby. Congratulations," she says, finding her new seat beside me. "What's the position?"

"Director of Human Resources," I say, stumbling on my words, with a faint smile.

Joy's smile fades. "Jade, what about the limo?"

"What about it, Joy? Damn, why are you so insecure? This shit is riding my fuckin' nerves."

"Because, this…," she says, slipping her hand under my skirt and palming my crotch, "…belongs to me, Jade, and I want to make sure you understand that. Don't be giving my shit away, bitch," she snarls.

"See, Joy. Your ass is trippin'." I gather my belongings. "This is exactly why I don't want to be out in public with you." I head for the door.

"Where are you going, Jade?"

"I am going somewhere away from your ass," I say, turning to walk out of the Red Dog. Joy is stomping on my heels, calling out my name. She catches up with me and grabs me by the arm, yanking me to face her. "I don't believe this shit, Joy. I give you all of me, inside and out, and I get this shit from you. I'm tired, Joy. Tired of not being trusted and tired of always feeling like I have to walk on eggshells around you just so you won't accuse me of fucking someone else," I snap.

"Jade, baby, I love you and I am afraid of losing you. Please, don't go. Come back to the table and let's celebrate your promotion." She forces a phony smile.

"I don't know, Joy. Look, the limo came with the promotion," I lie, diverting her off the scent of someone else. "Now, can we just drop it?"

"Yes, and I'm sorry. It's not that I don't trust you…"

"Save it, Joy. I need to go to the ladies room." I leave her there, looking like a damn fool, as I push my way through the crowd.

Flushing the toilet and adjusting my clothes, I step outside of the stall to meet Joy's gaze. "Is this a meeting in the ladies room," I chuckle. I brush by her and begin to wash my hands.

"Jade, I really am sorry."

"Yeah, okay, let's just forget about it." I reach around her, grab a paper towel and wipe my hands.

"No, I really am sorry, Jade." She kisses me on my lips as her hands roam up and down my body.

"Oh Joy, baby, its okay, really." She kneels down before me, lifts up my skirt, pushes my panties to the side and tastes my sweetness.

Joy never fails to amaze me, and because she is always pulling shit like this, I only wear stockings, making it easy for her to please me anytime, anywhere. I let her make it up to me by propping my leg on the sink while she tastes me with force. She rises to her feet, faces me and forcefully kisses me, her tongue playing with mine. With my leg still propped on the sink, Joy strokes my clit with her thumb and at the same time, strokes the inside of me with her finger, wiggling her finger around. She does this all the time. She calls it the Fuck Test. She claims that she can tell if I've been dicking a man. Now, she's a licensed Ob/Gyn.

"Jade, I'm so sorry, baby," she pants in my ear. Not being able to say a word, succumbed by the movement of her fingers, I grab her around her neck and thrust myself onto her fingers. "I do trust you. I just don't want to lose you," she says, still teasing me with her thumb. My body tightens, gripping her fingers as the trembling of my body tells her that I am about to reach my climax. Joy bends down and flutters her tongue over my clitoris.

"Oh shit!" I exclaim. "Don't stop, Joy! Don't stop!" I yell, shaking uncontrollably and releasing my juices.

Joy looks into my eyes and kisses me softly on my inner thigh. "You forgive me, baby?"

"Yes, I forgive you." This shit is getting old.

"Well damn, this is a public bathroom, you know?" A sistah, who is carrying a beige Louis Vuitton handbag and wearing matching shoes, stands inside the doorway.

Joy smacks my leg off the sink and adjusts my skirt. I've never been as embarrassed as I am at this particular moment.

"We thought we were alone," Joy responds.

"How could you think that? This is a public restroom."

"Okay, well act like you didn't see anything," Joy barks, her body stiffening as she prepares to attack. Down girl, I think to myself.

"Y'all are just two nasty. . ."

"Fuck you!" Joy yells.

"Joy, let's just go, baby. Let it go."

"Look, I ain't trying to fight. I'm beyond that. You just need to be a little more discrete, is all I'm saying," the intruder states.

"Do you think we give a fuck about what you think?" Joy muses.

"Well, we will see what the Manager has to say. It smells like ass in here!" The intruder storms out of the restroom and into the crowded restaurant.

I adjust my skirt and take a glance at myself in the stained mirror. "Joy, I'm outta here." I grab my things and make a hasty exit.

"Fuck that ho! She's just jealous."

I stop in my tracks, with my back toward Joy. I take a deep sigh and lower my head. "Jealous of what, Joy?" I ask, so sick of this shit.

"Jealous I wasn't between her legs. . ."

I toss my head back in disgust. "Joy, don't nobody want your ass but me, and even I am having second thoughts. . ."

"Hold up, what the hell you mean by that?"

"Nothing. I have an early day tomorrow. I'm gone." I hold my breath, open the bathroom door, step across the threshold and wait to hear the door slam behind me. I don't hear Joy coming behind me. Just go, Jade. Get away while you can, I think to myself. I haul ass into the crowd, bumping into the manager, followed by the intruder pounding on his heels in a huff.

Just as I thought, by the time I reached my apartment door, Joy was damn near on my heels. I quickly stick my key in the door and attempt to get inside before she could catch up with me.

"Jade! Jade!" she yells through the corridors. "You hear me, bitch!"

With the door open, I turn to face her. "Bitch? Must we resort to name calling?"

"Baby, I meant that in a good way," she smiles.

"Whatever," I say, slamming the door in her face.

"Open the door, Jade."

I don't respond.

"Jade, open the fucking door!" She begins to pound on the door. "So what, you want me to act a fool out here, for all of your neighbors to hear?"

I fling open the door. "Get in here and cut out all that damn yelling!"

"What is your problem?" she asks.

Now I'm confused. "Problem? I always assumed that you're the one with that small problem called insecurity."

"I am not insecure. I just protect what's mine."

"That's just it, Joy. I'm not yours. How many times do we have to have this conversation?"

Joy walks toward me. "Listen, babe. . ." I step to the side, making my way toward the kitchen. She takes a deep sigh. "I don't want to argue."

"Then let's not," I snap, heading toward the bathroom.

"Where are you going?"

"To take a hot bath. I need some time to myself."

"Care if I join you?"

"What did I just say that you're having a problem comprehending?"

Inside the bathroom, I bend over the tub, insert the stopper and turn on the faucet. Joy comes up behind me, slips her hand beneath my skirt and caresses my right ass cheek. I take a deep sigh and shake my head. This is unbelievable, I think to myself. I pull myself upward and turn to face her. She caresses my face with the palms of her hands, drawing me close to her. The sweetness of her kiss sends chills throughout my body, but this really is not what I want to feel now. But, as usual, left up to Joy, I don't have much of a choice. I return the sweetness. She unbuttons the single button on my sea foam-colored skirt, unzips the zipper and allows it to fall down around my stocking-covered French pedicured toes. She tugs at my lime green knit, sleeveless sweater. I raise my arms and allow her to pull the sweater over my head and tossing it onto the floor.

"You're so beautiful," she whispers, pulling me closer in to her and wrapping her arms around my back, unfastening my bra. She lowers her mouth to my hardened chocolate drop nipple and swirls her tongue, outlining the quarter-sized areola. "You're so beautiful," she whispers again, taking my hardened nipple between her teeth.

"Oooh," I coo, throwing my head back, her suckling bringing me to moisture and causing the knot between my thighs to swell.

Spreading my legs apart, Joy finds her way to the throbbing between my legs and gently sucks on the knot, gently grazing it with her teeth. Tears form in my eyes, not from pleasure, but from knowing that this will have to cease. I can't continue to live like this. I can't continue to be in a relationship where so much jealousy and insecurity festers.

"Uh, why, Joy?"

"Why what?" she mumbles, with me between her teeth.

"Ohhh, Jesus!" I pant. "Why. . .don't. . .you. . ."

"Shhh, Jade. You're messin' up my concentration. Just hush and enjoy me giving you what you need."

Joy gave me what I needed all right, but it certainly wasn't what I wanted.

Free

I've been trying to call Maya for three days and I'm not getting any answer. I have left a dozen messages, and it's unlike her not to return my calls. Did I do something to make my baby sister not want to be bothered with me? I doubt it. Something is wrong. I can feel it. I wonder if Jade or China has heard from her. They probably haven't since I am the only one who maintains some type of communication with her.

Jade and China were not too happy about Maya moving to Hollywood to follow a pipedream of becoming an actor. Between you, these four walls, and me that girl can't sing, dance nor act her way out of a wet paper bag. She has been in Hollywood long enough for her to have made a name for herself by now. But, she had determination and that is something that neither China nor Jade possesses. Instead of being happy and supportive of her, since we are the only family that she has, they are just plain jealous and it burns me up.

I walk over to my desk and flip through my Rolodex for China's phone number. I can't remember anyone's phone number these days, especially when I have to keep so many numbers in my head.

"Hey Sis, how are ya?" she answers on the first ring. I can't imagine life without caller ID. When you do not want to speak to someone, you do not have to.

"I can't complain. Just tired, that's all," I sigh. "How are the kids and Ron?"

"Everyone is doing just fine. What about the business, you still putting flowers on folks' gravesites?" she chuckles.

"It pays the bills," I snap, not liking her comment one bit. Not everyone is as fortunate as she is to stay home all day long and not have to do a darn thing. "China, you talk to Maya lately?"

"Not since we were all on the three-way a few weeks ago. Why?"

"I've been trying to call her for three days and she hasn't returned any of my calls. I'm getting worried."

"Free, you know how Maya is. She doesn't think about anyone but herself and will go off on a venture without saying squat to anyone."

"I don't know, China. It's not like her not to return my calls. It worries me that she is so far from reach. We can't get to her if need be."

"Well, I think she is doing fine. But, if it will make you feel better, I will give her a call, okay?"

"Thanks, I would appreciate that."

"No problem. So, how's your love life?"

"What love life?"

"Free, you are a successful business owner and you are far from being an ugly woman, so why don't you have a man?"

"Let's just say that I don't fit the criteria for men in these parts."

"What do you mean?"

"Girl, I don't know if you've noticed, but I am not exactly what you would call the perfect color?"

"Huh?"

"I'm too dark, China. Men are stuck on a woman's complexion and I am too dark. No one wants me and I've learned to accept that. I've accepted the fact that I am to be single and I'm happy with that. Maybe I will follow in Jade's footsteps and find me a woman."

"Okay, now you are talking like a jackass. Jade has issues any damn way."

"Maybe, but she is happy."

"No, she's not."

"How do you know?"

"Free, after a while, a woman will get tired of the kissing, pecking and touching and will want something that only a man can give her."

"And that is?"

"Penetration."

"Well, if I don't find someone to penetrate me soon, I will be penetrating myself." We both fall out with laughter.

"Have you ever thought about a dating service?"

"Oh no, China, I don't want to pay to get a date. I might as well stand on a street corner. At least then, I could rack up on dollars and penetration."

China laughs hysterically. "Girl, you gone make me pee myself."

I take a deep sigh. "I don't know, China. I just don't get it. Why are black folks so color struck?"

"Honey, that dates back to slavery when the light-skinned slaves were kept in the house and the…"

"Slaves with my complexion were kept in the fields to get darker," I close.

"Yep, and it's sad too," she sighs. "Try the Internet. Every time I turn that thing on, there is always a damn ad popping up in my face advertising a dating site. Try it. What do you have to lose?"

"My life, maybe?"

"Free, why are you so negative?"

"China, I am not negative. I just don't believe that meeting men through the Internet is safe, that's all."

"Well, I think you should do it."

"I'm not that desperate," I snap.

"No, you're just lonely."

"China, I am far from being lonely. I may be alone, but never lonely. I am happily single, thank you very much!"

"But what about sex?"

"What about it?" I ask, sitting on the wooden stool in a huff.

"Don't you yearn for the touch of a man?"

"There is nothing that a man can do for me that I can't do for myself."

"Penetration?"

"I have a vibrator."

"Goodbye, Free."

"Call Maya, okay? And give my love to Ron and the kids."

"I will. Give my love to the plants," she giggles and hangs up before I can respond.

I gaze out the picture window, across the street, at the American Café and I realize that, once again, China is right. What could it hurt? What do I have to lose? My dignity. I am lonely. Maybe I could sign up for a date on the. . .hell, I'm not even going to go there. There are too many psychos stalking around the Internet, looking for naïve souls to prey on. I refuse to be one of them.

Jade

Becoming acclimated to my new digs, I lean back in my leather executive high-back chair and prop my feet up on my desk. I peer out of the twelve-foot-wide picture window that extends from one wall to the next. I take a deep sigh. "This is all mine," I say to myself as I stretch my arms over my head. I think about the different types of artwork that I would love to have on the walls. This is my office and I plan to make it comfortable because I know that I will be spending many late nights here. I have so much to learn and I am just getting started. I need to get my sound system up in this joint too.

"Jade, there is a Mr. Meadows holding for you," Sherrell announces over the intercom, startling me. I hate when she does that—no buzz, just her husky, irritating voice.

"Thank you." I'm a little apprehensive about talking to him. Why is he calling me? I thought I made it clear that I didn't swing that way. I press the speakerphone button, take a deep sigh and here we go.

"Hello, Mr. Meadows. What can I do for you?"

"Have dinner with me."

"I thought we've already been through this."

"We have?"

"Yes, we have," I chuckle, enjoying the soothing affect Jon's voice is having over me.

"Well, I have a five-no rule."

"A five-no rule, what's that?" I ask, searching through my desk drawer for a Chiclet.

"That's when you say no to me five times before you say yes."

"Mr. Meadows. . ."

"Jon."

"Okay, Jon." I am smiling from ear to ear. "As I made it very clear to you the other day, I am not interested in men. I have a friend."

"Friend? What the hell does she mean by friend?" Joy thinks to herself as she stands with her ear plastered against the cracked office door.

"I only want dinner. Nothing less, nothing more," he begs.

"Yeah, right."

"Jade, you have my word. I just want to get to know you better."

"And why is that? Of all the straight women walking up and down the streets of New York City, why do you want to get to know me, a lesbian, better?"

"You strike me as not being like all of the women walking up and down the streets of New York City. Besides, there is nothing lesbian about you." Jon is making me blush and has me feeling warm between my legs. "Are you going to make me beg?"

"Ha! Well, you do what you have to do, right?"

"Okay, if you want me to beg, I will beg." Jon clears his throat. "Please, please, please," he attempts to sing, ripping up James' song.

Jon has me laughing so hard, I bend over and put my head between my knees to keep from peeing on myself. "All right, all right, James! Get up off of your knees." I can barely catch my breath. "Your cape is still in the cleaners!"

"So, does this mean that you will have dinner with me tonight?"

"Tonight? Well, I don't know."

Jon starts that damn singing again. "Please, please, please!" He sounds like a cat in heat.

"All right, tonight it is. Goodness, you don't give up, do you?"

Seductiveness sets in his voice. "Not when it's someone I want." His comment catches me off guard. There is five seconds of silence that feels like an hour. "I'll have my car pick you up at six o'clock from your office."

"Oh…oh, okay," I stutter, taken aback by his take-charge demeanor.

"Just beautiful," he says. I can hear the smile in his voice.

I want to make certain I will be appropriately dressed because, if tonight will be anything like that limo ride with the Dom Perignon, I want to make sure I am looking the part. "Where will we be having dinner?" I inquire.

"It's a surprise."

"But, is there a dress code? I moved into my new office today, so I am wearing jeans."

"Come as you are."

"Jon, where are we going?"

"Hush now, no more questions. See you this evening." Jon disconnects the call. I listen to the dial tone, hoping it will give me the answer to my question since he sure as hell did not. However, I must admit, I do like him being secretive.

Standing and facing my window overlooking New York City's skyline, the excitement of drinking more Dom Perignon overwhelms me. I let out a tiny, "Weeeee," and fall into the chair. I may leave the office early, head home to freshen up, change and be back here by six to meet the limo. Although I don't date men, having dinner would be harmless. Right?

For a quick minute, I catch an eerie feeling, sending a slight chill throughout me. Not giving it a second thought, I inhale, stretch my arms wide, close my eyes and exhale. I swing myself around to face Joy. "You startled me, baby!" Standing, I straighten my shoulders and clear my throat. "I didn't hear you come in," I stutter.

"What's up, Jade?" she asks, dropping herself down in the chair positioned in front of my desk. Her eyes are burning a hole through me and out of the window.

"How long have you been here?" I ask.

She tilts her head to one side. "Long enough." Her fine, arched eyebrows rise inquiringly.

"What?"

"Nothing," she snarls.

"Is everything okay, Joy?"

Joy forces a smile on her face that she obviously is not feeling now. "Everything is just fine." She slowly takes her eyes off me and scopes out my office. "So, this your new office, huh?"

"Yep, you like?"

"Yes, I love it and I love your view." She pushes herself to her feet and walks around the office, taking in the view. "You won't get any work done for leaning back in your chair, looking out the window and talking on the phone," she states with sarcasm.

Ignoring her sarcasm, I walk over toward the wall. Joy is undressing me with her eyes and I don't like it one bit. She is making me feel uncomfortable in my own office. I hold a Vanna White pose, focusing on imaginary letters. "My Charles Bibb piece will go perfect on this wall, don't you think?" Joy's nostrils flare like a bull ready to charge after the Matador. I drop my hands to my side. "Joy, what's wrong now?" That green-eyed monster never fails to reveal itself at the most inopportune time.

"Jade, we need to talk. Can you close the door so we could have some privacy?" I hesitate, not sure, if I want to be behind closed doors with here with her. "Please, Jade. Close the door," she insists.

Before closing the door, I inform Sherrell that I did not want to be disturbed. "I'm all ears, Joy." I take a seat on the leather sofa.

Joy walks toward me and hovers over me. "Who were you talking to on the phone?" she asks in a possessive manner.

"I beg your pardon?"

"I don't stutter, Jade."

"When? I've been talking to people on the phone all day. It is my job."

"Don't be a smart ass, Jade," she lashes out, taking a step closer, bringing me eye level to her crotch.

"Look, I am too busy and I don't feel like this today, Joy." I hop to my feet and rush over to my desk. Joy's piercing stare stops me in my tracks. "Joy. . ."

"Jade, I suggest you sit your ass down." She spits out the words contemptuously.

I am all too familiar with Joy's temper. Two years ago, she gathered a wad of saliva and hurled it in my face, while we were having dinner with friends. Why? Because I was sitting too close to Vivian, a former coworker. Before that, in a crowded club, she pinched my nipple as hard as she could because men were fixated on me and were asking me to dance. Last year, when we were visiting Free, she was upset because I went to the grocery store without her, so she tied me to the bed and performed her Fuck Test, poking and prodding inside me, looking for semen or other clues that I'd been with a man. She even did an anal exam, insinuating that I was hip to her Fuck Test and that I must be getting it in the ass.

I don't want anything to jump off at my place of employment, so, I take a seat. "What Joy? What's with the interrogation?"

"Jade, all I want you to do is answer my fucking question. It's not that fucking difficult."

"Joy, don't cuss at me and I don't know what phone call you are referring to."

"Okay, Jade, I'll let you dance around the question, so long as I get my answer." She folds her arms across her chest, resting her foot on the sofa and near my crotch. "Who were you talking to right before I walked in?"

"I was talking to a client."

"Since when did you start having dinner with clients?"

I smack her leg to the floor. "Since I was promoted." I stand to meet her glare. "This is ridiculous, Joy!" I walk behind my desk and flop down in my chair. "Why are you so damn jealous?"

"I'm not jealous, just protective when it comes to what's mine."

"Joy, I am not a piece of property. You don't own me. I don't belong to you or anyone else, for that matter!"

"You are my woman, Jade!"

"No! I am my own woman and if you keep up this insecurity bullshit, I will be my own woman, alone! Now, would you kindly leave? I have work to do."

Taking my hands in hers and kissing each palm, Joy kneels down before me. "Baby, I am just. . ."

"Just what?" I snatch my hands from her clutch, turning my head away from her.

"Jade, I don't know what I would do without you."

"You would survive, just as you had before you met me."

"Baby, please don't be mad at me," she pleads, standing to her feet and positioning herself between my legs. She softly strokes my dreadlocks. "Jade, you are the best thing that has ever happened to me. My life has been like a dream. I can't have anyone take my dream away from me."

"Joy, have I ever given you any reason not to trust me? I spend most of my nights sleeping next to you. Most of my mornings are with you. At least ten times a day, I am talking to you on the phone. I don't give my love to anyone else, but you. You have no cause to be this way. It hurts that you don't trust me."

"I know, baby, and it's not you. I don't mean to hurt you. It's other people who are jealous of what we have and want to see it destroyed."

"Other people? What other people?"

"Jade, there are people who wish they had what we have."

"Oh, you are being ridiculous and I can't take this anymore."

Joy strokes my face. "Look, I'm sorry and too bad you aren't wearing a skirt," she teases. "My tongue can be very apologetic." She bends down and softly kisses me. I don't return her kiss. "I love you, Jade."

I look past her, out of the window, not knowing what to say. At one time, I was so in love with Joy that I couldn't see straight. But now, I don't know. Her insecurities and lack of trust in me has caused my feelings for her to dissipate. "Me too," I mumble, forcing a smile.

"Well, I'll let you get back to work. What would you like for dinner tonight?"

"I have plans this evening."

"Well, I don't mind being a third wheel."

"Damnit, Joy, I told you that I have a dinner meeting with a client," I snap, my angry retort hardening her features.

Joy straightens and rounds her shoulders. "Yes, that's what you claim." She quickly turns herself around, her ponytail smacking her in the eye, and walks out of the door with not so much as a goodbye. I take a sigh of relief.

This relationship is too stressful and my encounter with Joy has left me stressing, so I decide to head home early to give myself time to relax and freshen up before my dinner date with Jon. That way, I won't have to rush, and I'll have plenty of time to make it back to the office before the limo arrives.

This is not a date-date. It's just two people getting together for food, drinks and conversation. Shit, whom am I trying to fool? This is a damn date and I can't believe that I am about to go down this tired, worn-out road again! He gets no pussy tonight!

Two years before meeting Joy, I was heavily into men. I was running a marathon to see how many I could bed in one week. Each week, I tried to break my own record. It was something about being with different men that I enjoyed. The different flavor, motions, sizes, you name it I had to have it—especially one in particular. His name was Marcus Graham. I swear, I can't stand that bastard and if the day ever came when I could just ram his nuts into his stomach with my foot, I wouldn't hesitate doing it. Marcus and I were dating heavily. I couldn't breathe unless I was around him. I ate, slept and shitted Marcus, until I found him eating pussy that didn't belong to me. Afterward, he turned the tables, saying it was my fault that he had his head buried between a funky snatch. He started feeling his oats and decided to put his hands on me. I guess it wasn't until after I clamped a mousetrap onto his dick that he realized he put his hands on the wrong woman.

Now I am about to be wined and dined by one of the richest black men in New York City and, I won't lie, I am as happy as a fag with a bag of dicks. Knowing my sisters, especially Free, they will start planning the wedding.

When I broke the news to them about Joy, Free took it the hardest. She told me that I had Mama twirling in her grave. "God created Adam and Eve, not Eve and Eve," she said. China couldn't understand why I would choose pussy over dick. Maya wanted to know what it was like to "go down on a woman." They don't understand I am not like them. I don't follow false dreams. I don't have insecurities and I don't allow anyone to steal my self-esteem. I love my sisters dearly, but I can't live by their definition of how I should be or whom I should love. I refuse to let life pass me by. I don't consider myself a lesbian, homosexual or whatever the "in" word is. I just want to give my love and receive love in return. I will date a German Shepherd if it treats me right. Okay, that was far fetched, but you get my point.

I enable my 'do not disturb' on my telephone and grab my purse. As I prepare to leave, once again, Joy makes her presence known. "Hey, I thought you were gone," I smile nervously.

"I was, but then I decided to come back. You are going somewhere?"

"Yes, going home."

"In the middle of the day? Are you not feeling well?"

Now I am irritated with her ass. "Joy, I am feeling fine. I don't want to wear jeans to a business meeting, so I'm going home to change."

Joy pushes her way into my office, slams the door behind her and locks it. She walks toward me, her finger ferociously shaking at me. "Jade, let me make something very clear to you."

"Oh come on, Joy, not again. Damn, this shit is getting old."

"I love you and I am not letting you go."

"Yes. I know this, Joy."

"I mean it, Jade."

"I've got to go, Joy. Let's discuss this on the way to the elevator." Her cheeks are turning crimson, which means that she is about to act a fool. I am not trying to become a leaf on the McAfee grapevine.

"It won't take long," She gripes, snatching my purse off my shoulder and tossing it onto my desk, causing papers to slide on to the floor. "Come here, baby." She grabs me by the hand and escorts me to the sofa. "Lie down," she instructs.

"Joy, not here, please. Someone may walk in on us."

"I locked the door. Besides, I think you need to have the fact that I love you and will go to any lengths to keep you, re-enforced." She unzips my jeans.

I shove her away from me. "Joy, stop it!"

"Come on, Jade, you know you want this as much as I do." Joy pushes me back onto the sofa, piling all of her weight on top of me.

"Joy, stop it!" The blood running through my veins rapidly approaches its boiling point. "I asked you to stop. You are having your way with me. You are raping me, Joy!" I try to wiggle free from her grasp. Joy is taller than I am, weighs more than I do and her body is crushing me.

Joy forcefully shoves her hand inside the opening of my jeans. "Raping you?" Her fingers wiggle inside my underwear. "Raping you?"

"Yes! Please, not like this, Joy!"

Her fingers stroke me fiercely. "Damn, you want this," she smirks. The Jack Nicholson grin on her face is freaking me the hell out. I flinch when she grabs hold of my clitoris. "I can feel your clit swelling. Just relax and enjoy me giving you what you want," she quietly chuckles between clenched teeth as she pins me to the sofa, grinding herself against my thigh.

"Ouch, Joy! You're hurting me," I whisper, trying to keep my voice down. These walls are like onion paper, except you can't see through them. "Why are you doing this to me?"

"You like it rough."

"Joy, you are squeezing too hard. You're hurting me! Please, get up. I can't breathe. You are too damn heavy!" My struggling to break free and her having her way with me just seem to excite her more. Anger rises within me. "Bitch, get your dike ass off of me!" I yell. Joy stops. "I don't want this, bitch! Get the fuck off of me!" I holler. "I don't want you anymore."

Joy still has her hands inside my pants with her fingers tightly affixed to my swollen clitoris. "Bitch? Dike?" Her grip tightens.

"Bitch? Dike?" she repeats angrily.

I continue to wiggle, wanting to break free. I can't stand confinement. It stifles me—makes me feel helpless and vulnerable. "Joy, you're hurting me!"

"Keep the fuck still," she growls. "What do you think you are, Jade?"

I'm tired. I cease my fight. "Joy, I can't do this anymore." Tears roll down my cheeks. "You say you love me. This is not what you do to someone you love," I state, my voice fragile and shaky.

Joy removes her hand from my pants, her cold brown eyes peering through me. She pulls herself upright. "You selfish, ungrateful cunt!" she sneers, giving me an open-hand slap across my face.

I gasp in astonishment. "What the fuck? You are crazy! It's over, Joy."

Joy stares down at me, with red-hot flames shooting from her eyes. She takes the form of Damian reincarnated. "I do love you," she growls from deep within, "I love you more than you will ever know. How dare you question my love for you?" she growls from deep within.

This bitch is possessed. She reminds me of that chick from the Exorcist. I just know that any minute, her head is going to do a three-sixty and white shit is going to start foaming from her mouth and fly all over my new office.

"If you love me," I whisper through salty tears, "let me go."

Joy gives me a deranged smile. "Nope, I can't do that, baby. If I can't have you, no one can." She grabs my neck with her hands and forms a chokehold around my throat. She leans in close. "I will kill you first," she whispers, breathless with rage.

With all my strength, I try to unleash her hold. Joy's strength and determination defeats me. I scream for help, but words fail to escape. Joy is choking the life out of me. I'm tired. I surrender, allowing my body to go limp. Joy panics and loosens her grip from my neck. "I'm sorry, Jade. I don't mean to hurt you. I love you. But you make me act like this. Why do you make me act like this, Jade? Huh?" She lowers her face to mine and softly kisses me on the lips. "I need you, Jade." She kisses me again. "You need me too, baby." A tear falls from her eye onto my bottom lip. She strokes the side of my face. My mind is racing at warp speed. My eyes roam the room, scanning for something, anything that I can use to knock her ass the fuck out. She kisses me again, parting my lips with her tongue. The juices from her kiss intoxicate me but I can't let her win, not this time. "Baby, I want to taste you. Pull your jeans down," she whispers, kissing my eyelids. She moves her body to the side. "Come on baby, let me help you." She tugs at my jeans. I grab her wrist. "What's wrong, Jade?"

"Not here," I whisper through clenched teeth, trying to maintain.

"Why not?"

"Someone may walk in on us. This is where I work, Joy."

"No, they won't. I locked the door."

"Please, not here. At home, tonight, okay?"

A forced wide smile appears on her face. "Does this mean that you aren't mad at me anymore?" At this point, I will say or do anything to get away from her. "I'm glad. We are good together, Jade." She leans in and kisses me on my forehead, then my eyes and down to the tip of my nose. She finds her way to my lips, parting them with her tongue, stroking the inside of my top lip. She grabs hold of my tongue and sucks it the same way she sucks my clit, with force. I close my eyes and place myself anywhere but here. I try to think of white sandy beaches, but the smell of her Cool Mint Listerine Breath Strip knocks me back to reality. I open my eyes to see her passionately kiss me, her head moving from side to side, her moans soft and inviting, but I refuse to accept the invitation. She thinks I am enjoying this, but she is sadly mistaken. Something comes over me. I wrap my arm around her neck and bring her closer, causing her to press her mouth harder against mine. I vigorously stroke my tongue around the insides of her mouth, grabbing hold of her tongue. I close my eyes tight and suck as hard as I can, allowing my teeth to graze her tongue. I bite down. Joy releases a deep-throated scream while I'm still holding on to her tongue. Joy is smacking me in my face, trying to get me to release my hold. No can do, this bitch doesn't know who she's fucking with. I open my eyes and smile like a crazed lunatic, still affixed to her tongue. I feel something between my butt and the sofa. I ease my hand beneath me and grab tightly to the ink pen that is puncturing my ass.

"Fuck you, bitch!" I yell, stabbing her in the side of her face with the Uniball ink pen.

"Arghhh!" Joy screams to the top of her lungs, holding the right side of her face and falling to the floor. Her bloody, severed tongue dangles out the side of her mouth.

I roll off the sofa, landing on top of her, straddling her and cupping both sides of her face with my hands. Don't. . .you. . .ever. . .put. . .your. . .fucking. . .hands. . .on. . .me. . .again!" I holler with every pounding of her head against the gray-speckled Berber carpeted floor. Joy lies there in a daze.

"Jade?" Sherrell stands in the doorway in shock at what is taking place before her.

"Sherrell, how did you get in here? I thought the door was locked?"

"I have a master key to all of the offices. . ." her voice trails off.

"Sherrell, call security and have this bitch thrown out on her ass. I don't want to see her face in here again." I stand to my feet, zip up my jeans and stroke my fingers through my auburn-colored dreadlocks. "I am going home for the day. If security doesn't get here in the next sixty seconds, call the police and have the bitch arrested."

"On what charge?" Sherrell asks, picking up the phone to dial security.

"Rape. Enjoy the rest of your day, Sherrell." I gather my things. "Oh, and Sherrell?"

"Yes."

"If I hear so much as a word of my business through the grapevine, you will be out of a job. Understand?" Sherrell nods her head.

I take one last look at Joy lying on the floor, holding the side of her face, with blood oozing between her fingers. "It's no wonder men don't want to fuck with black women. Y'all got fucking issues!" I slam the door behind me, washing my hands of Joy, and probably all women, forever.

Well, let's not be too hasty.

China

"Ron, did you speak with André?" I ask, trotting down the steps.

"Yes. Everything is fine, China. There's no need to worry."

"So, he's not having sex?"

"No, he's not," he responds irritably as he reaches for his Orlando Magic brimmed cap from the top of the hall closet. What is his problem? He is always snapping off my head, as if I am bothering him or something. He really needs to get a grip.

"Well, that's good," I sigh, resting my hands on my hips that are too wide. I really need to diet, exercise or stop eating so damn much. "Then what is he doing with condoms?"

"Water balloons."

"Huh?"

"Yeah. Listen, don't worry." He kisses me on the forehead. "I've got to run. I won't be home for dinner."

"Where are you going?"

"Hanging out with the fellas tonight. You know, have some beers, smoke a few cigars, shit like that," he says, feeling his pant pockets. "You seen my keys?"

"Yeah, they are where you left them, Ron, on the table by the front door."

"Okay, thanks."

"Have a good…" The door closes before I could get my words out.

Water balloons? André is not interested in no damn water balloons. All he knows is Nintendo and Sony Playstation. And where would he get the idea to use condoms for water balloons? Wouldn't you use a damn balloon for that? Nope, I don't buy that shit for a second. Either Ron did not have the father-son chat or André is lying his ass off. Ron is gullible as hell when it comes to the kids. He believes their bullshit. I guess that is why he doesn't possess the roll of disciplinarian.

"André!" I yell from the kitchen, up the stairs and into André's bedroom.

"What?"

"Boy, don't you what me. Come down here."

"Ma, I'm doing my homework."

"Bullshit. Get down here now."

"Ut oh, somebody is in deep doo-doo," Ashley yells from her room.

"Shut up!" André yells at Ashley.

"Ashley, mind your business and stay in your room."

"Aw Mama, why come I gotta stay in my room? I ain't do nuffin."

"You have to stay in your room to study your grammar book!" I yell.

It is a damn shame we are spending an arm and leg on private schools and she doesn't speak correct English worth a damn. If she paid more attention to her books and less to that damn mirror, she might pass to the eighth grade next year.

"What did I do now, Mama?" André whines, standing in the archway of the kitchen.

I pull a chair away from the kitchen table. "Sit down, baby. Mama needs to talk to you." I walk over to the refrigerator and open the freezer. "You want some ice cream?"

André raises his brow and looks at me with uncertainty. "Before dinner?"

"Sure," I smile to myself as I speak. "I'll make an exception, this time."

"Okay," he says, excitement glowing all over his face.

Smiling at my sweet, innocent child, I scoop out a couple of balls of strawberry ice cream from the carton and spoon them into André's favorite Winnie the Pooh bowl. André has always loved ice cream. It doesn't matter what the flavor. He will eat the entire carton if you let him.

Every morning, André has to have his cereal in his Winnie the Pooh bowl. He claims the milk has a funky taste coming from a different bowl. I just can't believe that a boy, who sleeps with a nasty blanket, that he's had since he was a year old, would know anything about condoms.

I return the carton of ice cream to the freezer, sit the bowl of ice cream in front of André and take a seat across from him. While glaring at him, I think how Ron and I have made two beautiful demon seeds. André is so pretty, he could put on a dress and pass for a little girl.

"What's up, Ma?" he asks, inhaling the ice cream.

"I need to talk to you about something really serious, okay?"

"Yeah."

"André, did your father speak to you about sex?"

He concentrates on his last few spoonfuls of ice cream. "Nope."

"Did your father talk to you today?"

Taking down the last spoonful, he slides his bowl toward me. "Nope. Can I have more?"

"It's may I, and no. You'll ruin your dinner. Are you sure your father didn't talk to you today?"

"Ma, tap your needle," he laughs.

"What?"

"You sound like a broken record, Ma."

"I'm serious, André."

"Ma, Dad ain't talk to me today 'bout nuffin."

"What kind of language are you speaking? Next year, you and your sister are going to stop wasting my money. You are going to public schools."

"Good, 'cause I can't stand those stuck up folks at that school."

"Never mind that, I have something I need to ask you."

"What?"

"André, are you having sex?"

"Aw, Mama, why you ask me something like that?" He frowns up his face as if he smells something rotten. "I don't even like girls."

"Are you sure?"

"Yes, I'm sure I don't like girls."

"Okay, so what do you know about water balloons?"

"I don't know."

"Do you play with water balloons?"

"Nope."

"Do you know how to make water balloons?"

"I guess you make them with water and balloons," he laughs. André cracks himself up with that one.

"Funny. Okay, well if you don't play with water balloons, then you want to tell me why I found a pack of condoms in your bottom dresser drawer?"

André's body stiffens. "They ain't mine!" he exclaims, his eyes wide and big as golf balls, about to pop out of his head.

"If they aren't yours, who do they belong to, André?"

He relaxes his shoulders and slumps over the table. "I thought they were yours."

"What?" I ask, looking puzzled.

"I found them in your bedroom. I thought they were yours."

"You found them in my bedroom?"

"Yeah."

"I see." My son has just awakened me from a long sleep of stupidity. "Where in my bedroom did you find them?"

"In your closet."

"In my…boy, what were you doing in my closet?"

"My new shoes were too tight. I wanted to stretch them with that wooden thing that Dad uses…"

I wave him quiet. "Where in my closet did you find the condoms?"

"They were in Dad's shoe. They fell out when I knocked the shoe over when I was reaching for that wooden thing…Ma, am I in trouble?"

"No, baby, you aren't in trouble. But, I don't want you playing with those again and keep your ass out of my closet, okay?"

"Okay."

"Good. You can go back to your homework," I smile. "Dinner will be ready shortly."

As André puts his bowl in the sink and leaves the kitchen, a tear drops from my eye onto the kitchen table.

Free

I took China's advice and joined one of those free dating services on the Internet. I have a date tonight with Samuel Meeks. Samuel is forty, single, no kids and a maintenance man for an apartment complex in Augusta—about one hundred miles from Atlanta—which is a good thing. If I don't like him, I won't have to worry about bumping into him on the streets. After talking with him for hours on the telephone, and feeling like a giddy teenager, I decided it was time for us to meet. So, we made a date to have dinner at Captain John's, here in Atlanta. He didn't want me making that drive to Augusta, which says a lot about his character.

"Hey, Free! How ya doin'?"

I look up from my bank ledger and remove my reading glasses. I really hate these things. They make me look like an old school teacher.

"Hey, Ms. Ethel, I'm doing great. How are you?"

"Oh, well, I can complain, but I won't. It won't do me no good no way."

"I know what you mean. Care for a drink? I've got some cold iced tea in the back."

"That sounds good."

"Great. I'll be right back." I close the register drawer and head toward the back. "Keep an eye on things for me, Ms. Ethel."

"I surely will, baby," she smiles, walking around looking at the plants. "You sure got some pretty flowers, Free. Where you be getting these flowers from?"

"Most of them I grow myself. I have a solar house in the back of the shop," I yell from the backroom. I pour the iced tea, reach under the counter and pick two mint leaves from my secret stash of mint plants that I grow. I love the way they smell and folks are always requesting fresh mint for their parties and restaurants.

My shop is more than a business to me. It's a place of solitude. It's a place where I can think. I love running my hands through the rich soil. I only use the best soil for my babies. Yes, I call my flowers my babies because I take care of them as if they are my children. I plant the seeds, nurture them and watch them grow. Once they reach maturity, I send them out into the world. Flowers have meaning and they will never betray you. Flowers are the best friends anyone can have. The Acacia Blossom, Ambrosia, Lilies, Hyacinths, Petunias, Roses, Tulips, Orchids and the many plants throughout my shop are my best friends. The Wandering Ivy surrounds the shop, keeping me warm and making me feel safe. My favorites are the Gladiolus and the Lilacs. The aroma in this place is intoxicating and reminds me of Mama. Her fragrance was Tea Rose, smelling like a bed of roses. I could never get enough of smelling her.

A bell rings twice. There is a bell over the front door that rings every time someone enters and exits the shop. I had it installed since I spend so much time in the back of the shop.

"Hey, Free! How ya doin'?" Ms. Ethel yells from the front of the store. "Are you here today?"

"Ms. Ethel?"

"Yep, it's me. Whew, it sure is hot today. Sorry I'm late, but my son stopped by to visit with me for a while this morning."

Feeling very confused, I place the two glasses of iced tea on a wooden tray and carry them to the front of the store. I place the tray on the counter. "Ms. Ethel, but. . ."

She clears her throat. "My throat sure is dry. It's a long walk from my place to here." She glances at the two glasses of iced tea, with mint leaves dangling from the rim. "You expecting company?"

I extend the cold glass toward her. "All right now, Ms. Ethel, I don't know what's going on, but here is your drink you asked for. . ."

"Free, I ain't asked for no drink. Chile, I just got here." She looks at me like I am the crazy one. "Might be the heat gettin' to ya." She takes a sip of her iced tea. "Hmm, this sure hits the spot."

Now, either I am losing my mind or Ms. Ethel done lost hers, and I do believe it's the latter. "Have a seat, Ms. Ethel." I bring the wooden stool from behind the counter. "So, you said your son stopped by this morning?"

Ms. Ethel tilts her head to the side and looks at me funny, like a puppy dog looks at you when he doesn't understand a thing you are saying. "Naw, I didn't say that. I ain't seen my son in. . .God only knows how long."

"But you just told me that your son came by for a visit."

"Free, I do believe you been working too hard. I think you need a vacation. Why don't you go and visit one of them sisters of yours?"

"Okey dokey then," I smile, removing the ball of confusion from my face. I think I need to change the subject before the men in white suits come through that door, strap me in a little white jacket, with my arms folded across my front, and tied tight as my girdle in the back. "Guess what, Ms. Ethel?"

"What?"

"I have a date."

"Oh Lord, help us all. The sky is 'bout to fall," she cackles.

"Ms. Ethel, that isn't funny," I frown. I take a sip of my iced tea and cut my eyes at this old woman.

"Oh, I think the fact that you have a date is quite funny," she cracks up with laughter.

"Ms. Ethel, that's mean."

"I'm sorry, baby. Go 'head and tell me 'bout the lucky fella'."

"Well, his name is Samuel and he is forty, single, with no kids. . ."

"What he look like?"

"I don't know."

"What you mean you don't know?"

"Well, I haven't seen a picture of him yet."

"A picture? Chile, how can you make a date with a man you haven't met? Is this one of them blind dates?"

"Well, sort of. I met him through an Internet dating service."

"Through the Internet?"

"Yes, and…"

"Do you think that's safe? I mean, these folks in this world are crazy. I wouldn't be meeting no man from no computer."

"Well, I am comfortable with meeting him, Ms. Ethel." I feel like I am holding a conversation with Mama.

"Well, I don't like it. It ain't natural for folks to meet like that. . ."

"I am a grown woman, Ms. Ethel," I snap. "No disrespect intended."

"None taken. But I still don't like it. Has your mama and daddy met this boy yet?"

"Huh?"

"This boy met your mama and daddy yet?"

Okay, she is totally gone. "Ms. Ethel, now you know my mama and daddy are no longer with me."

"Really? Where'd they go?"

Tears create a puddle on the brim of my eyes. "No, Ms. Ethel. My parents are in Heaven."

"You didn't tell me," she gasps, placing her hand over her chest. "I would've gone to the funeral."

Good Lord, I sure do hope she cuts her visit short today because my patience is running short. "Ms. Ethel, I lost my parents years ago. . ." I trail off, feeling sad and missing Mama and Daddy something awful.

"Oh?" She looks confused.

"So, what about you, Ms. Ethel?"

"My parents been gone."

"No, that's not what I mean. . ."

"Well say what you mean, chile. My days are numbered."

"I wish you wouldn't talk like that, Ms. Ethel. You've got at least eighty years left," I smile, desperately wanting to change the subject. Death scares me and is not my favorite topic of discussion. "I was asking what about you. . ."

"What about me?"

"Mr. Perry. He still in the picture?"

Ms. Ethel stands to her feet and props her hand on her round hip that extends past anything else on her frame. "Free, that man tried to make a pass at me, but I wasn't having it."

"Are you kidding me?"

"Nope, and I told him that it wasn't no point in him trying to feel my stuff when he wouldn't know what to do with it."

"I hear that," I chuckle.

With the glass in her hand, she walks over to the roses and strokes each petal. "Do you know about the birds and the bees?"

"Well, I think I do. Not unless you know something that I don't."

"I know that if you feel the urge to give it up, then do it."

"Ms. Ethel, I don't give it up on the first date."

"You ain't gettin' no younger. Your stuff gone start sagging soon. Don't no man want to dibble dabble in no saggy. . ."

"Ms. Ethel!"

"What?"

I can't believe that I am having this conversation with this old woman. But I must admit, it's been quite some time since I've had a man interested in my goods.

"Ms. Ethel, I don't care if it sags to the pit of hell. I am not having sex with a strange man on the first date. That is totally out of the question."

"There's nothing wrong with it."

"I should say that it is."

"Free, there ain't nothing wrong with having sex on the first date. When I was your age, I wouldn't date a man if he didn't know what he was doing in the bedroom."

"Ms. Ethel, my mama didn't raise me like that."

"I bet your mama didn't waste any time either."

"Can we not go there, please?"

"Well, suit yourself. But you can't build a relationship on just talking and kissing."

"I'm well aware of how to build a relationship. . ."

"Uh huh, that's why you single now. What about oral sex?"

I gasp, not believing my ears. "What about it?"

"Men like oral sex," she says, biting her lip to stifle a grin. My mouth hits the floor. "That's it. Depending on his size, if you open a lil' wider, you can fit the whole. . ."

"Just never mind!"

"Why are you in such a huff? Oral sex is a natural thing. Everybody's doing it."

"Well, I'm not everybody."

"So, you telling me that you wouldn't want a man to eat you out?"

"Ms. Ethel," I say calmly. "You know I have the utmost respect for you."

"Yes, I know this."

"And you know that I love you just like a mother."

"Yes, I know. Where're you going with this?"

"Well, just like my mother, I will not discuss this topic with you either."

"Humph, humph, humph," she moans, shaking her head in disbelief. "Free, you are an Old Maid and you better break out of that. Listen to what I'm tellin' ya."

The blaring ring from the telephone breaks my glare with Ms. Ethel. "Whew, saved by the bell," I mumble, walking behind the desk to tend to the ringing telephone. "Excuse me, Ms. Ethel."

"Handle your business, baby."

I think she watches too much TV. "Free's Floral Design Boutique, how may I help you?"

"Free, it's China."

"Hey Sis, how are you?"

"I'm okay, I guess."

"You don't sound so hot. What's going on? Are the kids all right?"

"Yes, they are fine. How's business?"

"Business is great. I filled a huge order yesterday and, of course, folks are dying off like flies. I've had to fill six orders for sprays and the week isn't over yet." I glance toward Ms. Ethel and whisper into the phone. "I am having a very bizarre conversation with Ms. Ethel. All that's missing is the theme to the Twilight Zone."

"Oh, tell Ms. Ethel I said hello."

"I sure will." I take a deep sigh. "Okay, something is wrong. I can hear it in your voice."

"I just need to talk, but if you are busy. . ."

"I am never too busy for my family. Besides, I have something to tell you. Girl, you won't believe it. I have a date tonight. . ."

"I think I have wax build-up. I could've sworn I heard you say that you have a date tonight."

"Well, you may have wax build-up anyway," I laugh. "Yeah girl, your spinster sister has a date. Can you believe it?"

"Yes, I can believe it. I have a beautiful sister. Why wouldn't any man want to date her?"

"You know why."

"Will you please get off of that? Who is he and where did you meet him?"

"I know you didn't call to talk about my date."

"You're right, I didn't. But I want to hear about him anyway. Spill it, girlie."

"Well, his name is Samuel Meeks. . ."

"Is he single?"

"Yes, and. . ."

"Any kids?"

"No, and. . ."

"Wait, a single man with no kids?"

"Yep, and. . ."

"He lives with his mama, right?"

"Nope, and would you please let me finish? He lives in Augusta, alone."

"How old is he?"

"Forty."

"Okay, let me get this straight. He's single, no kids and forty years old?"

"Yep."

"What's wrong with him?"

"What do you mean? Ain't nothing wrong with him."

"Uh huh, something's gotta be wrong if he's that damn eligible and don't have a woman." China sucks her teeth. I hate when she does that in my ear. It's so annoying. "Is he employed?"

"Yes, he is employed."

"What does he do?"

"Damn, China!"

"What?"

"He does maintenance for an apartment complex."

"Free rent."

"Huh?"

"Free rent. Typically, if you work maintenance for an apartment complex, you live there for free or your rent is subsidized."

"I don't know. I didn't ask him all of that."

"If he isn't paying any rent, he shouldn't be a cheap date. Where y'all going?"

"To dinner."

"Where?"

"Like you're gonna know if I tell you."

"You're right. Okay, so what does he look like?"

"I don't know."

"You don't know?"

"That's what I said."

"Well, how can you. . ."

"I met him through a dating service."

"You took my advice, good."

"Yeah. I signed up for one of those free Internet dating services."

"Okay, but you can swap pictures on the Internet."

"Yeah, well we didn't. But, we do talk on the phone all the time, as if he lives around the corner."

"Well, I am happy for you, Free. Just have fun and call me tomorrow morning to fill me in on all of the details."

"Thanks. I hope to have fun, and no, I won't call you and fill you in on my business."

"Fine, I'll call you!" she exclaims as we both fall out with laughter.

"Okay, so what's your problem?"

"I don't know where to start."

"Wow, it's that heavy? Wait, that bastard isn't putting his hands on you again, is he China? So help me, I'll shoot him!"

"No, it's nothing like that. Calm down, Assassin."

"Then what? You are making me nervous."

"Well, let me take you from the beginning…"

"No, get to the point."

"Okay. This morning, I found a pack of condoms in André's dresser drawer."

"You aren't serious, are you?"

"As a heart attack."

"What does a ten-year-old boy know about condoms?"

"Free, I'm going to head back now. I will talk to you later," Ms. Ethel interrupts.

"Hold on, China." I balance the receiver on my shoulder. "Okay, Ms. Ethel. What are your plans for the rest of the day?"

"The usual. Going to watch my stories. *Young & The Restless* will be on in thirty minutes. You know that Shemar Moore just makes me hot in the pants. He sure is pretty," she laughs uncontrollably. "If I were fifty years younger…whew!"

"Okay, Ms. Ethel," I laugh. This old woman never fails to catch me off guard with her off-handed comments. "Well, I'll see you tomorrow?"

"Yep, and I want to hear all of the details too," she snickers.

"I bet you do. Take care and be safe."

"I will baby. Have fun tonight." Ms. Ethel waves her hand in the air as she starts out to make the two-block walk home.

"China, I'm back."

"Girl, I don't know what to do."

"Well, it sounds to me that Ron needs to have a heart-to-heart with his son."

"Yeah, well, that's another story."

"I'm all ears."

"Ron told me that he would talk to André."

"Okay. . ."

"And when I asked Ron if he had spoken with André, he told me that he had and that it was all innocent, that André was using the condoms to make water balloons."

"I thought you used balloons for that?"

"Yeah, last I checked, and you know I didn't buy that shit for a minute. So, I talked to André myself."

"Good. What did he say?"

"He says the condoms aren't his."

"If they aren't his, then whose are they?"

"They belong to Ron."

"After fourteen years, y'all are using condoms?"

"Hell no, I haven't seen a condom since before Ashley was born. Hell, we weren't using condoms when we were dating."

"Well, I don't understand. . ."

"Ron is fucking around. Can you understand that?" she snaps.

"Well, China, maybe he's. . ."

"He's what? Making water balloons? Nope, there's no maybe. Why does my husband need condoms? He isn't using them on me, so he must be using them on someone else," she hesitates. "Aren't I enough for him?" I can hear China sniffling.

"China, now don't go getting yourself worked up over something that you haven't confirmed."

"Free, how much confirmation do I need?"

"What are you going to do? See China, I hate to say that I told you so, but. . ."

"Then don't. I really don't need to hear that shit right now."

"Sis, I just wish that you hadn't given up your career. . ."

"Free, I didn't give up my career. I just put it on hold."

"For over twelve years."

"Yes, to raise my babies."

"Well, you need to take the motherfucker for all his black ass is worth."

"Free! Oh my word, did you just cuss?"

"I know," I laugh. "It sounded just as funny to me as it did to you."

"What am I doing wrong, Free?"

"What do you mean?"

"What is it that I am not doing to make him want to go to another woman?"

"It's not your fault, Sis."

"I just don't understand why men cheat."

"Ask Michael Baisden, he wrote a book about it," I chuckle, but China didn't find it the least bit funny. "Listen, it's not your fault, and I don't want you blaming yourself."

"We have a great sex life. I mean, we make love all the time and. . ."

"China, you are sharing too much."

"For real, Free. I don't understand. It's not like I don't do everything I need to do to satisfy him. Hell, I suck his. . ."

"China!"

"Damn, Free. Stop being so damn prudish. Ain't nothing wrong with sucking your man's dick."

"If it ain't in the Good Book, I don't practice it."

"Free, you ever had your pussy eaten?"

"What? Good Lord, China!"

"Girl, you haven't experienced anything until a man has tried to suck the skin off of your man in the boat."

"Okay, China. You are being very offensive toward me and I don't like it." I take a deep sigh and shift my weight. "What is a man in the boat anyway?"

"Free, please. I don't know why you insist on acting like you're the Virgin Mary. You've opened your legs a time or two."

"China, that's my business. Thank you very much."

"Uh huh, and a man in the boat is your clitoris."

"All right, I know I am going to regret this, but why is that thing called a man in the boat?"

"Clitoris, Free, it's called a clitoris. Come on, say it with me. . .cli-to-ris," she chuckles, enunciating each syllable.

"Shut up, China!"

"Well, you asked."

"Look, you need to think about what you are going to do. You are going to leave him, aren't you? You aren't going to stay with a man who is messing around on you, are you?"

"I haven't decided what I'm going to do."

"What is there to decide, China? Your husband is a cheat and once a cheat, always a cheat."

"I need to find out who she is and why Ron feels the need to leave his mark in someone else's bed."

"Why would any woman mess around with a married man?"

"Usually, the woman doesn't know that the man is married."

"How can you not know if a man is married?"

"Free, it's not like they're walking around with a sign pasted to their foreheads that reads 'married'."

"Men who are married wear wedding rings."

"Not all of them. Too many men have approached me, who were married, and didn't have on ring the first."

"I do know one thing. I wouldn't stay with him. That's for sure."

"I have to think about my kids, and I have to get myself on track, financially, before I make a move. I don't want to be ass out in the cold. You know what I mean?"

"That's true. When you do decide to leave, you and the kids have a place to stay."

"Thank you, Free," she says, blowing her nose. "Well, I won't keep you. I know you have a business to run."

"Okay, and hey, did you get a chance to call Maya?"

"She hasn't called me back yet."

"Something isn't right, China. I can feel it in my bones."

"I am sure she is fine. I will call her again, and I will talk to you and your bones tomorrow to get the scoop on your date."

"Okay. Take care." I hang up the phone and open the register to count my money for the third time today.

That is exactly why I am single. I can't deal with all the stuff that China takes from Ron. If he isn't pissy drunk, tossing her all over the place, he is screwing around with other women. If I were China, I wouldn't have sex with him anymore. For all she knows, he may slip up and decide not to use a condom and bring home a sexually transmitted disease, or worse AIDS. China is playing with fire. I pray she doesn't burn herself.

Maya

"Maya, you there? Pick up if you're there. I guess you aren't there. This is your sister, China. I was just calling to check on you. Call me as soon as you get this message, okay?" Beep.

"Okay," I whisper, with tears streaming down my cheeks. I attempt to move my legs. My mind is telling me that I am moving my legs, but I don't feel anything. "Jonah, what have you done to me?" I sob. I don't know how long I've been lying here—one, two, three days—and the phone continues to ring and I can't get up to answer it. Free has called here at least twenty times and I know she, more than the others, is worried sick about me. I'm so hungry. My mouth feels like sand paper—rough and dry. I can feel the dried, crusty blood around my lips. "How did I get myself into such a mess," I mouth. Sound refuses to escape me.

China and Jade were right. I haven't done anything but chased a pipe dream. Ever since I was a child, I wanted to be an actor. I wanted to be the next Ruby Dee or Diahann Carroll. I auditioned for every play from elementary school to high school and even while attending community college…although, I never did finish college. I can still see the look on Mama's face when I told her that I wouldn't be continuing my studies. "I'm going to Hollywood to become a movie star, Mama," I said. Yeah right. Mama cried for days. Her heart had been broken and I was too selfish to see beyond my wants. China and Jade will never let me forget the pain and anguish that I caused Mama.

After graduating from Spelman College, Free decided to make her home in Atlanta. China graduated from Howard University, married Ron and his job relocated him to Orlando, Florida. Jade went to New York to attend Columbia University and she's been there ever since. I was all Mama had left at home, and what did I do? I packed my bags, traveled three thousand miles with only one hundred dollars in my pocket and left Mama to fend for herself. It would've put Mama in the hospital if she knew that I hitchhiked to Hollywood. It's been four years and hundreds of auditions, cattle calls and rejections, and here I lie on the floor, probably paralyzed from head to toe, all because of my selfishness. I guess I am reaping what I've sown.

It took me a month to get to Hollywood. I thumbed rides to wherever people were headed, hanging out in this town and that town for a few days, even weeks, and getting a piece of a job to make a couple of dollars to hold me over until I could catch my next ride. I met many different people from different cultures and backgrounds. It was truly a learning experience and somewhat of a fantasy come true because I've always wanted to travel. But, once I got to Hollywood, the fantasy was over and reality bit me so hard. I can still feel the numbness when I sit. It was nothing like I had expected. On TV, they don't show you the dark side of Hollywood—drugs, prostitution and the wild nightlife. There is no point in stepping foot on Rodeo Drive if you can't afford to buy a pair of simple bangle earrings, and forget about taking a stroll through Beverly Hills, unless you own one of those million-dollar mansions.

Mama would've loved Hollywood. She was crazy about Louis Gossett, Jr. and Robert DeNiro. I wanted her to come out for a visit, but I couldn't let her see that her baby girl was a wanna-be-actor by day and a whore by night. Once I got my life together, I was going to move her out here. When I called and told her that I wanted her to live in Hollywood with me, she got so excited.

"Oh my word, Maya!" she exclaimed. "I've never been that far from home before. What do I pack?"

"Everything, Mama. You are moving out here. You're not going back. . ."

"Really? Lord have mercy. Wait until the girls hear about this. I knew my baby would make me proud. Chile, let me get off this phone and start packing. When do I come?"

"Next month, Mama. I will send for you next month. I love you, Mama."

"I love you too, baby. Be careful out there and I'll see you next month!" she said. Little did I know that would be the last time I'd hear Mama's sweet voice.

The week before her arrival, Mama died of a heart attack. I was unable to go back home to Emporia, Virginia, for the funeral. I was flat broke and my pride wouldn't let me ask my sisters for plane fare, giving them the chance to say, "Maya, we told you so." I regret not going to Mama's funeral. The guilt eats at me every single day. Because Free was the only one who would talk to me after the funeral, she told me Mama went home in style and with a smile on her face. She said Mama looked peaceful and rested.

"I'm so sorry, Mama. If you can hear me, please forgive me," I cry.

I met Jonah after three days of being in Hollywood. I was broke, hungry and had made my bed in front of Groman's Chinese Theater. But that didn't last too long. The cops arrested me and I ended up spending the night in jail. It was better than the cold concrete though. I was released on my own recognizance and given a court date. I had no money, no place to stay and, most of all, I was terrified of going to court.

After my release from jail, I was peddling on the streets for half the day. I was able to scrounge up enough money to get me something to eat, and I was seriously craving a hamburger. While counting my change and walking in a daze trying to find a burger place, I turned the corner and bumped into Jonah—tall, handsome, dressed to a tee and smelling wonderful. I guess he could look at me and tell that I was in desperate need of help and a hot bath. He introduced himself and told me that he could help me, if I wanted it. I was so taken by him that I agreed to go with him to his place. He fed me, cleaned me up and took me shopping. I don't know what he did or whom he talked to, but the charges of my loitering in front of Groman's were dropped and I was free as a bird. At least from the California judicial system, that is. Little did I know that I would leave one jail and enter into another.

I didn't know it then but Jonah was my first love. I wasn't in love with him. I was in love with being around him. Jonah was very popular and admired by many. When I started with Jonah, he had twenty-five whores vying for his attention. Jonah insisted that his women were classy and always in style with the latest fashion trends. He even went as far as to send us to finishing school.

I was the Queen Bee and, out of the harem of whores, I was the only one he would take into his bed. He preferred fucking me to the other girls. "They are good tricks and give the clients what they want but, for me, they don't know how to work the dick like you do, Maya," he said. "I keep the sweet stuff for myself."

Being the Queen Bee, I was never took appointments. Instead, I scheduled them. After new pimps started showing up with better propositions and taking Jonah's tricks off the track, I was all he had. I tricked ten, sometimes twenty, Johns a night, which didn't leave any time for me to make auditions. My dream of becoming an actor was placed on hold while I nurtured my new career of being a classy ho. Threesomes, blow jobs, anal sex, role playing, sexing other women, S&M, you name it, I did it all.

In the beginning, I loved all of the attention and flattering compliments I would receive from my Johns. I would have dinner in the best restaurants, was given expensive jewelry and I was getting the best sex that I've ever had. That was when Jonah was being very selective about who he would put me in contract with. But now, it's all about the money and he doesn't care who goes between my legs, so long as he is paid.

All of the Johns are horrible tippers. They are big spenders but small tippers. That is how I earn my living, off my tips. If they don't tip, I don't eat. But, he has really fucked up now. I am definitely no good to him. He's out of tricks.

I want to go home. I want my mama.

Ron

"Reservations for Douglas," I say to the desk clerk at the White Dove Inn, located on the outskirts of Orlando. It's close enough to home in case of an emergency, but far enough to take care of my business.

"One night?" the clerk asks.

"Yes."

"Shall I put this on your credit card, Mr. Douglas?"

"No, I'll pay cash. Fifty-five, right?"

"Yes, Sir."

I retrieve my wallet from my back pocket. While fumbling through my wallet, a strip of sensitive latex condoms falls out and onto the counter. The desk clerk shoots me a dirty look, takes my money and gives me the room key. "Thank you," I say bashfully.

"Do you need help with your bags, Sir?"

"No. I'm fine, thanks."

Heading toward the elevator, the desk clerk calls out to me. "Mr. Douglas." I turn to see the clerk nonchalantly waving the strip of condoms in the air. "You forgot these."

I am too embarrassed from the disapproving stares coming from the patrons sitting in the lobby of the Inn to go back for the condoms. Hopefully, Marion will come prepared. "You can toss them. I don't need 'em."

At the elevator, I press the call button and wait for its descent. I glance over my shoulder to see the clerk's eyes affixed to me.

"Hello," came a seductive feminine voice from beside me, much like the voice I'd hear whenever I'd call the 900-SEX-TALK line when China wasn't in the mood. I know it's sick, but a man has to do what he has to do. Shit, I have to get mine somehow, and now that I have Marion, I have the best of both worlds.

I glance her way and smile. "Hello to you too."

"Slow elevator, huh?"

"Very."

She extends her hand with a warm smile. The hairs on my neck stand to attention. "Imani Oku," she says, introducing herself with a warm, inviting smile. The glare from the rock on her finger damn near blinds me.

I take her soft, warm hand in mine. "Ron Douglas." Either she doesn't do any work or she has daily manicures, because her hands are as soft as the down comforter that China keeps on the bed, year-round.

"It's nice to meet you, Ron Douglas."

Imani has a beautiful deep Godiva chocolate complexion with a smidgen of cream. Pinned-up tresses with tendrils seductively sweeping her brow. She smells of sandalwood and her beauty is natural, not hidden behind layers of foundation and rouge. Her lips are tinted glossy rose. Her figure is petite and very shapely in all of the right places. She has legs for miles.

"Likewise, Imani Oku. You have a beautiful name."

"Thank you. So, are you on vacation or are you from this area?"

"I'm from this area. . ." Her stunning beauty and poise causes me to speak too fast, forgetting why I'm here in the first place.

"I mean, I am not from this area, per se, but I am from Florida, and you?"

"I live in Orlando."

"Oh?" I ask, hoping like hell that she doesn't know China. "Well, what brings you here, if you don't mind me asking?"

"No, I don't mind at all. I am coordinating my family reunion that will take place in the banquet room. I'm trying to tie up a couple of loose ends."

"Sounds nice," I smile.

I want to see her teeth. Something about a woman with pearly, white teeth that turns me on. When China and I were dating, I had to send her to the dentist because her teeth were yellow-stained from the coffee and cigarettes. I think it says a lot about a woman who doesn't keep her mouth clean and free from cavities, but I married her anyway.

Imani looks as though she wants to say something but doesn't quite know how to say it. "Ron, would you like to come to my room and have a drink?"

Stunned by her request, I stand motionless and speechless. I check the time on my Rolex. "I have an hour to play around with before I have to set things up, so it wouldn't hurt to have a drink with a beautiful woman." Well, I do have some time. Sure, I would like that." The doors open and I motion for Imani to step inside the elevator. She presses four on the elevator panel and we ride in silence. I guess she is wondering what she just got herself into; I am wondering the same damn thing.

The elevator ascends to the fourth floor and I exit after Imani. I admire the bounce in her stride, the swing in her hips and her, what looks to be a size eight, booty sway from side to side. Damn, what a juicy sight.

Imani glances over her shoulder and flashes me a smile. "Well, here we are," she announces while sticking the key in the door. "After you this time," she smiles, motioning for me to enter. I feel like a spider about to become entangled in Charlotte's Web.

"Thank you. You are such the gentleman," I chuckle, and she did the same.

"Well, I try. What are you drinking?" The door closes behind her as she tosses her purse on the bed.

"Whatever you have is fine." The mound of clothing has given the chair a new look, so I take a seat on the disheveled bed.

"So, are you married, single, divorced or widowed," she asks, pouring us both a glass of Hennessy.

"Married," I respond, twisting my wedding band around the finger that China claimed twenty years ago.

She extends the snifter of Hennessy. "Oh, I see." Her deep onyx eyes are drinking in every ounce of me. This isn't good.

I try not to meet her gaze, but her eyes are irresistible. "I'm sorry, I should've told you."

"Don't be sorry, I prefer married men, Ron."

"Why is that?" I inquire, hoping to hear an excuse that will erase the dirty thoughts that are running laps through my mind.

"You see, I am married myself. Married men do not come with ties and I prefer that. I prefer a different flavor from time to time. You know what I mean?"

"Yes, I do." I smile at her and think that this is truly a good move on my part—non-committal booty. "So, do you sample different flavors often?" I ask with a smirk.

"Whenever I can, but not too often. I must keep things in perspective."

"Right, right."

"What about you? You obviously are not here with your wife."

"And what makes you think that I'm not?"

Imani chuckles and then takes a sip of her drink. "If you were staying here with your wife, you wouldn't be in my room, sitting on my bed and drinking up my Hennessy."

"Yeah, well, you've got a point there."

"So, who are you here with?"

I'm beginning to feel uncomfortable. She's asking too many damn questions. "Me, myself and I."

"Aw, secretive, huh? I like that," she teases. "It's okay. I don't need to know." She takes a seat next to me. "How's your drink?"

"its fine, thanks."

"What do you do for a living, Ron?"

"Marketing Executive for an advertising firm. You?"

"I teach thirty-two bad ass sixth graders."

"I bet they can be a handful. I have a son who is ten and a daughter that's twelve, and they are definitely a handful."

"Are you happily married?"

"I'm married." I smile and take a sip of my drink. "So, what are some of your interests?" I ask, trying to remove myself from scrutiny.

Imani inches closer and whispers in my ear. "You are one of my interests."

I unbutton the top button of my polo shirt. "Oh, I see." I feel a little suffocated.

"Ron," she whispers with her lips slightly touching my ear, sending an electric shock throughout me. "I have something to tell you."

I feel my loins beginning to rise. "What is it?" I nervously ask.

"I want to fuck you."

There goes my dick, hard as Chinese algebra. If Marion smells another woman on my dick, that would be the end of us.

"I think I'd better go." I stand to my feet and walk toward the door.

"No, please don't leave me here alone," she begs, briskly stroking her crotch like two sticks rubbing together, trying to get a spark. "You won't be disappointed. See, look. . ." She holds a finger in the air and waves it around. "Smells good, doesn't it?"

"Smells more like piss and vinegar," I think to myself. "Imani, I am flattered, really, but I don't bone women I don't know."

"Well, come and get to know me," she says, sitting upright.

"I'm sorry, I can't do that." I open the door.

"Listen, baby. I'll suck ya dick, Daddy."

"What?"

"Come on, Daddy. For fifty dollars, I'll suck ya dick real good."

"You are a prostitute?"

"I can be whatever you want me to be."

"I don't believe this shit!"

"Okay, I'll suck ya dick for twenty and toss your salad for ten," she begs. "You like being tossed, right Daddy?"

Heat rises within me. "You are a whore!"

"I gotta make some money, Daddy," she pleads as the door slams behind me.

Power walking toward the elevator, I contemplate the situation I fled. I can't believe she was a prostitute. She didn't look like a prostitute. She didn't look like she was hurting for cash either. School teacher? Married? That was all a lie. Damn, am I that naïve?

Maya

I tune out the shrieking cry of the phone.

"Oh God," I sob. "What did I do to deserve this?" I ask, hoping He hears my cry. "God, please, give me some kind of sign that I will be okay."

"Hey Maya, it's Jade. I was just calling because I haven't touched bases with you in quite some time. I don't know if you got my email, but I got a promotion and, girl, I have a date with a man! Can you believe that? Girl, he is fine too. Joy started trippin', so I had to let her go on about her business. Anyway, I love you and miss you very much. Call me." Beep.

"Jade, don't hang up," I weep. She can't hear me. "I love you too."

I can't believe Jonah did this to me. I can't move my legs and how can I smell like piss when I don't remember having the urge to use the bathroom? I can't feel anything from my waist down to my toes. I think I'm wiggling my toes, but I don't feel my toes wiggling.

"Dear God, if you help me, I promise to make things right with my sisters and my life. I promise to change my ugly ways. I won't deal with Jonah anymore. I will clean up my life. Dear God, please help me," I pray.

I can see the phone cord. I have to try to reach it. I raise my arms above my head, attempting to grab the cord, but I'm unable to reach it. I try to raise myself on my elbows and slide myself toward the phone cord, but nothing happens. I still can't move.

I collapse to the floor in defeat. "Oh, dear God, please give me strength," I silently pray. Again, I attempt to raise myself on my elbows and slide toward the phone cord. "You can do it, Maya. Keep going, girl. You can do it," I motivate myself, as I continue to use my arms to slide my weight toward the table where the phone sits. Just then, the phone begins to ring again, giving me the extra boost of motivation I need to pick up my momentum. "I'm coming." I actually hear my voice! "I'm coming!" I yell to the top of my lungs. With the phone on its third ring, I yank at the cord and the phone hits the floor, knocking the receiver off the hook. "Hello. Hello, please don't hang up. I'm coming!" I yell with laughter. "Thank you, God!"

"Maya?" The sweet sound of my sister's voice is music to my ears.

"Free, I'm coming. Please don't hang up."

"Maya, what is going on?"

"Free! Oh, sweet Jesus, it's you!" I exclaim with my ear to the receiver, gasping for air.

"Maya, where have you been? Is everything all right? We've been trying to reach you for days. . ."

"Free," I sob. "Help me, please!"

"Maya, what in the hell is going on?"

"Free, call 911 and have them come to my apartment. Please, tell them that I can't move. I think I am paralyzed."

"What? Oh my God! Oh my God, Maya, what are you talking about?"

"Free, please! Just do it!"

"Okay, okay, hold on."

While Free has me on hold, tears of joy and gratitude stream down my face. "Thank you, God. I promise to keep my word."

"Maya? I have the 911 operator on the line. Tell them what's going on."

"My pimp, Jonah Edwards, beat me up. I have been lying on the floor, unable to move, for more than three days and I need help, please. I think I am paralyzed. . ."

"Pimp? Paralyzed? Maya, what…"

"Please Ma'am, I need your address and someone will be there within minutes," the operator interrupts.

"My address is 267 Pico Boulevard, apartment three. Please hurry!"

"Okay, Ma'am, calm down. I have dispatched the police and an ambulance to your residence."

"Oh thank you, thank you, thank you."

"You're welcome. Would you like me to stay on the phone with you?"

"That won't be necessary. I am her sister," Free responds. "I will stay on with her until they arrive. Thank you."

"All right, I wish you both the best," the operator says, then disconnects the call.

"Maya?"

"Yes."

"Help is on the way. I am taking the next flight and will be there as soon as I can."

"No, Free. I will be fine."

"Maya, how can you say that? You've been lying on the floor for more than three days and you may be paralyzed. No, I am coming, and I am going to call China and Jade and let them know what's going on."

"No! Free, please don't call them. They won't understand."

"Maya, baby, I don't understand. Has it been that bad for you that you. . ."

"Free, I don't want to talk about it now."

"Okay, we will talk about it when I get there."

"Free, please don't come. I will be fine."

"I don't know, Maya. Paralysis is a serious issue."

"Free, I don't know if I am paralyzed or not."

"Maya, you couldn't get up off of the damn floor!"

"I know! I know!" I cry. "Why did he do this to me, Free?"

"I don't know, baby girl. He is a sick person. However, I'll respect your wishes and do it your way. You will call me tonight and let me know what is going on, right?"

"Yes, I promise."

"Okay. If you can't reach me at home, call me on my cell."

"I will. I've gotta go. The police are here."

"How are you going to open the door?"

"Free, everything will be fine. I will call you tonight. I love you, Free."

"I love you too, Maya. Don't forget to call me."

Jade

Standing outside of McAfee & Associates, I am freezing my ass off and Jon's limo is nowhere in sight. It's after six o'clock and I am reminiscing on why I don't mess with men. They aren't reliable. As I turn to enter the building, I hear a car pull up behind me.

"Ms. Howard," Robert, Jon's driver, calls out through the opened passenger window.

"It's after six o'clock and I don't appreciate being made to stand out here in the cold waiting. . ."

"I'm sorry, Ms. Howard," he says, getting out of the limo and rushing to open the rear passenger door. "There was traffic back up," he claims. "Please accept my apology. It will never happen again."

"Okay, well, you are only ten minutes late. Besides, you don't have control over the traffic," I smile. Robert extends his hand to assist me into the limo. "Thank you, Robert."

Robert peeks inside the limo. "Would you care for a drink to warm you up, Ms. Howard?"

"Yes, I would love one, but I can fix it myself. Thank you, Robert."

"No problem, Ms. Howard." Robert closes the door, makes his way to the driver's seat and I make a beeline to the Dom Perignon. Before pulling into traffic, Robert looks into the rearview mirror. "Is everything all right? Would you care to make a quick stop anywhere?"

"Yes, everything is perfect and no, I don't need to make a quick stop." I am really digging this whole limo scene. "Robert, where are we going?"

Robert, who is still looking in the rearview mirror, smiles at me. "Sorry, Ms. Howard, Mr. Meadows has sworn me to secrecy." He rolls up the tinted window partition and pulls into traffic. A few moments later, Phyllis Hyman's *Betcha by Golly, Wow* flows through the Bose speakers as her angelic voice wraps me tight. I take a deep sigh, kick off my black Enzo pumps and prop my feet up on the leather seat to the left of me. "I could get use to this shit," I say to myself, while taking a sip of my chilled Dom Perignon and singing along with Phyllis.

I must've dozed off because before I knew it, Robert had opened the door for me to exit the limo.

"Where are we?" I inquire.

"LaGuardia Airport, Ms. Howard."

Sitting up and slipping on my Enzo pumps, I peek my head out of the car, taking a quick glance around at my surroundings. "What are we doing here?" Robert doesn't answer. Instead, he extends his hand. "Robert, I asked you a question." I take his hand and step out of the limo and onto the runway. "What in the hell. . ."

"Ms. Howard?"

"Who are you?" I retort, just about fed up with this secretive bullshit. "What am I doing at the airport?"

"I'm Veronica Chandler, Jon's Personal Assistant. Will you come with me, please?"

"Come with you where? What's going on?" I ask, looking at Robert for some type of explanation.

Robert looks at me and flashes his pearly whites. "You are in for the time of your life. Trust me," he winks.

Reluctantly, I take Robert at his word and follow Veronica to a leer jet that has *JonAir* inscribed on the side. Get the fuck out of here! I don't believe this shit. This brother has his own jet.

"Ms. Howard, please, watch your step," Veronica says as she leads me up the stairs and onto the jet. Once inside, she tells me to have a seat wherever I feel comfortable and she would be back to check on me in a moment.

To hell with this, I want to know what is going on. "Where is Jon?"

"Jon will greet us at our destination."

"Which is?"

"Oh, I'm sorry, Ms. Howard, but I am not at liberty to say."

"Not at liberty. . .well, *Veronica*, I am at liberty to tell you that I am getting off of this bitch, unless you tell me where you are taking me! I don't take kindly to someone kidnapping my ass!"

"Ms. Howard," she chuckles.

"And cut out that Ms. Howard shit. My name is Jade," I snap, irritated as hell.

"Okay, Jade. You have my word that you are not being kidnapped and you will not be disappointed. Please, take a seat and relax. We will be taking off shortly. Would you care for a drink?"

I hesitate for a moment and then relax my posture. "Yes, a strong one, thank you." I take the first seat I see. "Veronica, um, will we be returning tonight?"

Veronica takes a deep sigh, smiles and shakes her head. "Okay, I will tell you if you promise not to say anything to Jon."

"I promise," I smile, now sitting on the edge of my seat.

"He would have my head if he knew I let the cat out of the bag."

"Okay, I won't say a word," I promise, giving the double peace sign. "Scouts honor!"

"Well, the jet is not due back here, at LaGuardia, until Sunday evening."

"Sunday evening? How am I going to get back home? I have to be at work in the morning."

"I've already taken care of that for you. . ."

"You've what?"

"Yes, I telephoned Mr. McAfee. . ."

"You did what?" I yell. "Have you lost your fucking mind? Girl, you gone get my ass fired and I just got the damn promotion!"

"No, no, no. Calm down, Sistah, everything is fine," she laughs. She finds this shit funny, but I don't. I do not have a problem with knocking her the fuck out. "Jon has already spoken with Mr. McAfee and he isn't expecting you until Monday morning."

I slide back into my seat. "Well, ain't this a bitch." I hear the jet engines ignite. The 'fasten your seatbelt' sign flashes. "Well, Jade, I guess you are about to take the adventure of your life. Best sit back and enjoy the ride," I mumble, taking a sip of this dry ass martini that Veronica prepared. A personal assistant, yes, but a damn bartender, she is not.

I have to pee, so I wait for the sign to stop flashing. It doesn't look like it's going to stop any time soon. "Veronica, when will the 'fasten your seatbelt' sign stop flashing? I need to use the little girl's room."

Veronica waves her hand in the air. "Don't pay any attention to that sign. You can go now. We are high enough where you can walk around." She points her slender finger toward the back. "The bathroom is in the rear of the jet."

I unhook my seatbelt and find my way to the bathroom, maintaining my balance by holding onto the softest leather seats I've ever felt. They feel like butter. "Well, I'll be damned," I whisper, opening the door to the bathroom.

This is not your typical commercial airline bathroom in which you have to stand to pee, because if you were to sit, your legs might become stuck between the four walls. This is a full-size bathroom with oak paneling, gold-plated fixtures, cream-colored wall-to-wall plush carpeting and an eight-tier chandelier. This is truly a shitter's paradise. There's this little dispenser above the toilet that releases a fragrance of fruits and berries every two minutes. On the sink, sits a basket with all kinds of lotions, soaps, mouthwash, unopened toothbrushes and little moist towelettes.

I must be spending too much time in here, because Veronica is knocking on the door. "You all right in there?"

"I'll be out in a minute."

"Yes, well, it's not your usual toilet, is it?" she chuckles. "I've got to admit, I love it in there too."

I open the door to face Veronica. "All that's missing is a wet bar and you'd be good to go."

"You've got that right." She playfully taps me on my shoulder. "Are you hungry?"

"Yes, kind of."

"Good, me too. Let's see what's in the kitchen."

"Kitchen? This jet has a kitchen too?"

"Yep."

"Well, if that bathroom is any indication of what the kitchen will be like, I can't wait to see it." I follow on her heels like a kid in a candy store.

"Yes, well, this jet is something."

"Something is putting it lightly."

"This is Jon's taste."

"So I see." We turn a slight corner and I do not believe my eyes. "Damn!" I blurt out.

"I told you," she chuckles.

Veronica is petite, with an athletic build and a golden bronze complexion. She looks like the 'pamper me' type, with freshly manicured nails, Oprah hair and she dresses sharp too. It's obvious that Jon pays her well because old girl is decked out in Versace. I would definitely do her. I wonder which way she swings.

"What in the world does someone need with so much kitchen on a jet?" I query.

"Jon stays in the air," she says.

"Yeah, but this is ridiculous. The bathroom I can barely grasp, but this kitchen. . .the jet doesn't look that big from the outside."

The kitchen is too immaculate to be on a jet, in my opinion. It's not like one of those little cubbyholes that flight attendants have to try to squeeze in two at a time. Instead, you could house an entire cooking staff in this place. There is an island in the middle of the kitchen, with matching knotty pine paneling and wood flooring. A chrome refrigerator stands between the matching chrome stove and sink. Veronica opens the refrigerator, exposing tons of food, enough for an army.

"Why is there so much food?" I ask.

"Jon likes for his guests to have an assortment. What would you like?"

"Well, what do you have?"

"Probably, whatever you want," she chuckles. "You name it, I'm sure it's in here."

"Okay. I want lobster," I say, just for shits and giggles.

Veronica pulls out a bin from the bottom of the refrigerator. "Lobster it is." She reaches in the bin and pulls out a live lobster, with its claws tied with thick rubber bands.

"Oh, this is too much," I jump. "That thing is still wiggling! I thought you had to keep lobsters in salt water in order for them to stay alive."

Veronica points toward the bin. "Look. There's salt water in there."

"Well, stick me with a fork because my ass is done." I throw my hands in the air. "If I didn't see it for myself, I wouldn't have believed it."

"I think I'll have one too." She pulls out another live lobster. "I usually don't ask, but could you please give me a hand? Both of mine are full."

"Sure. What do you need me to do?"

"Could you grab the lobster pot from the pantry?"

I look around for the pantry. "Where is the pantry?"

"Over there," she nods, "beside the doorway."

I open the pantry and can't believe my eyes. This pantry is a walk-in closet. More narrow than your standard walk-in closet, but big just the same. The pantry has everything you would have in your home. It is filled with every spice from All Spice to Wasabi Powder, whatever that is. I bet you a dollar that his ass doesn't know what it is either. In the rear of the closet is a stocked wine rack that holds twenty bottles. I shake my head in disbelief and grab the lobster pot, carry it over to the sink, fill it with water and sit it on the top of the stove.

"Veronica, if we hit turbulence, this pot of water will be all over the floor."

Veronica lights the stove and pulls up the guardrail around the stove. "See, it won't fall."

I am too outdone now.

She opens the refrigerator and pulls out two bottles of Dom Perignon and a tray of cheese, fruit, smoked salmon, smoked oysters and crackers. "Come on, let's go rest our feet. I am dog tired," she says, handing me the bottles of Dom while she carries the tray. I follow her into a miniature dining area and plop myself in the leather, high-back reclining chair that's bolted to the floor. Veronica can sense my surprise. "Speechless, huh?"

"Uh, yeah," I nod.

"Most are, especially the white folks." Veronica kicks off her beige and black Versace pumps and props her freshly manicured feet in the chair across from her. "They can't believe that a black man has so much clout, power and his own jet," she muses.

"I bet. How long have you been Jon's assistant?"

"Ten years."

"You like being his assistant? Okay, that was a dumb question," I laugh. "Hell, who wouldn't love traveling in a jet such as this?"

"Yes, I love it and it's not just the traveling. It's meeting all kinds of interesting and powerful people." She pops the cork on the Dom and pours us both a glass. "What line of work are you in?"

"Director of Human Resources for McAfee. . ." I cross my eyes at her. "Well, you already know who my employer is." I help myself to the smoked salmon.

"I'm sorry about that. However, Jon can be persistent when it comes to something, or shall I say *someone*, that he has his mind set on." She winks at me. "You are a very lucky woman, Jade Howard, and obviously, a special one. In the ten years that I've been with him, I can count the number of women, on one hand, that he's had on his baby."

"His baby?"

"Yes. He calls this jet his baby," she chuckles. "It is his pride and joy. Jon is so in love with this big hunk of metal. Before he boards, he has a forklift to raise him to the nose of the jet. He rubs the nose and makes baby noises."

"You have got to be kidding me."

"Nope, I wish I were. I think it's sick, but then again, he works very hard to be able to purchase anything he wants. He cherishes everything and everyone in his life. He takes nothing for granted."

All I can do is shake my head. I could never begin to fathom having my own house, let alone my own jet.

"Jon doesn't date a lot of women?" I inquire.

"Nope, dating is hard for him."

"How so? I would think that he can have any woman that he wants."

"He can, and that's the problem."

"I don't follow you."

"Okay, let's talk sistah to sistah."

"Okay."

"Now you know as well as I do that, with the exception of a handful, a sistah will jump all over a black man with money out the ass."

"That's true, especially those who don't have much going for them."

"Exactly. That's why he doesn't date much. It's hard to find a woman who is genuine and sincere, who doesn't see the dollar signs and who is capable of bringing fifty percent to the table. You have to capture him intellectually too. He is far from being a stupid man and he doesn't want a stupid woman."

"How do you know so much about his likes and dislikes?"

"Well, I have been with him for ten years and I date his brother, Paul."

"For real?"

"Yes, and I love that man's dirty drawers," she smiles, while shaking her head in disbelief of loving someone that damn much. When it comes to the dirty drawers, I draw the line.

"Ooh, now that's a serious love jones you got going on there," I tease. "That is some serious love, girlfriend."

"Yeah, I know. But girl, he is so good to me, whew! He is truly a good man."

"Were you working with Jon before or after you met Paul?"

"I got this job on my own merit," she snaps.

"I wasn't insinuating that you. . ."

"It's cool. I had been working with Jon for about a year when Paul and I hooked up. At first, I didn't want to have a thing to do with him. He always acted as if his shit didn't stink, if you know what I mean. So, I wouldn't give him the time of day. Girl, he would send me flowers every single day. I wasn't budging. One day, he showed up at my front door with an entourage of men dressed in tuxedos, each holding a dozen of red roses."

"Damn, he bought out the damn florist, didn't he?"

"Girl, that's only half of it. Why did Paul start singing Luther's *If This World Were Mine*? I was too through and totally taken. And as you can probably guess, I gave in. We've been dating for the past eight years."

"Eight years? No wedding?"

"Next year."

"Really? That's wonderful, congratulations."

"Thank you." Veronica displays a smile of happiness and contentment. "Oh, let me go check on the lobsters. Be right back." She returns with the lobsters and two Caesar salads.

"Where are we headed?" I ask, with my jaws stuffed with lobster. "Oh, this is heavenly."

"Glad you're enjoying it. I put on two more just in case you want another one."

"There goes my diet!" We both chuckle.

"I can't tell you where we are headed," she says.

"Why not?" I take a hard swallow. "Sistah to sistah, remember?"

"Girl, Jon will kill me."

"How would he find out? I won't tell him."

She looks at me with skepticism. "Okay. But, if you say one word, I will tell him that you. . .you. . .I don't know, but I will think of something," she giggles.

"Okay, it's a deal. I won't say a word. If I do, you can tell him a big fat lie on me."

"You better believe I will." She laughs so hard at herself that her lobster goes down the wrong pipe, causing her to choke. She pounds her chest with the palm of her hand.

"Are you okay? Raise your arms in the air."

She does as I suggest, clearing the clog in her throat. "Thanks, I'm fine." She gathers her composure and drinks the last of her glass of Dom.

"So?"

"We are going to Jamaica."

"Jawho?"

"You heard me," she chuckles. "Paul is meeting us there, so you will get to meet him too." She flashes a bright smile, bright enough to light up the friendly skies.

Veronica is a very beautiful and classy woman. Although I haven't met Paul yet, I can see why he, or any man, would be so taken by her. To be honest, I am a little taken by her myself. But, after Joy, I'm staying away from cats for a while.

"Some first date, huh?"

"Well, I wish he had told me. I would've packed a suitcase. I don't have a toothbrush. . ."

"Oh honey, please. When you are with Jon Meadows, you don't have to worry about any of that. I can guarantee that you will have a full weekend wardrobe waiting for you in your room. "Yeah," she smiles, "that's one classy dude."

"Well then, I can't wait to get there. I hope he got the right size," I frown.

"Not to worry. He'll get the right size." She takes the bottle of Dom to the head. "God, I love this stuff," she sighs, wiping her mouth with the back of her hand.

"Me too," I giggle, popping the cork on the second bottle of Dom and taking it to the head. "This is truly the good life." I follow suit by wiping my mouth with the back of my hand, and without warning, I let out a huge belch. "Oh, excuse me!"

Veronica and I laughed so hard she had to excuse herself and go to the bathroom because she peed herself. And me, well, let's just say that I didn't make it to the bathroom either. I hope Jon doesn't hold it against me.

Free

Despite what she says, I should be with Maya. But, I will respect her wishes. I can't believe my baby sister is a prostitute. I didn't know that she was having that hard of a time in California. I thought she was going on auditions and getting small parts to keep food on the table. I don't dare tell China and Jade about this, although, it will be wrong for me not to tell them that she has been beaten up. Knowing Jade, we all would be on the next plane to California, looking for that Jonah character and whipping on his black behind.

I don't get the weak men who use their women as punching bags, or the women who stick around to be punching bags. That 'no account' Ron used to beat on China's tail like there was no tomorrow. It seemed like every other day he would hit the bar after work, drink himself into a stupor and then head home and take out his frustrations of the day on her. It's sad that the children had to witness that mess. Ashley, poor child, would jump on her daddy's back, trying to keep him from beating on her mother. I just hope that André doesn't grow up to be like his sorry daddy. They say children emulate their parents. Well, I sure as hell hope he doesn't emulate Ron. He isn't worth the change in my pocket.

It's been almost three years since Ron has put his hands on China. His cheating must be his diversion. I swear, China needs to leave that sorry, good for nothing, probably can't screw, so-so looking, husband of hers. She could've definitely done better.

I just hope that she had sense enough to put money to the side throughout their twenty-year marriage. Still, China has her education and that's one thing can't nobody take from her, not even that sorry son-of-a-biscuit-eater she calls a husband.

I am to meet Samuel at six o'clock and it is now four-thirty. I haven't a clue as to what I am going to wear. I want to look cute and sexy, but I don't want to look easy, because he isn't getting any tonight, that's for sure.

I look through my closet for something nice, but conservative, and decide to wear my black slacks, leopard print blouse with the matching shoes and handbag. I will wear my hair up off my face because I look good with short hair. I'd been thinking about getting my haircut. However, I refuse to sit in a beauty salon for eight hours on a Saturday, under a hair dryer, while conditioner cooks in my hair, until the beautician finishes with the four clients she overbooked before me. Folks don't run their businesses like back in the day, when customer satisfaction was a priority. Now, it's all about, how you say, the Benjamins?

I refuse to tell Samuel where I live, so we are meeting at Captain John's. I love seafood, which is why I ate a light meal earlier. I don't want to look like a glutton. I've heard that on the first date you should eat like a bird, so the guy, especially if you are digging on him, won't think that you are a pig and he can't take you anywhere. Thank goodness, Captain John's is an all-u-can eat restaurant. I won't have to worry about the prices on the menu when I place my order.

China gave me advice about dating, as if I have never been on a date before. She said that I shouldn't order the most expensive thing on the menu. And, if my nose begins to itch, I should excuse myself and go to the ladies room to scratch it. She also told me not to do a lot of popping. I have a bad habit of popping my bra because for one, I don't like wearing them, and two, the underwire drives me up the wall. A man must've invented the bra. That would explain why it is the most uncomfortable garment a woman has to wear, along with the girdle. It's claimed that the underwire keeps your breast from sagging. I know that's a lie too. I can't seem to find a bra anywhere that does not have an underwire, and I've seen more sagging breasts than I care to see.

Samuel and I decided that, since we didn't exchange pictures, we would both wear red. That way, we would be able to recognize each other. China told me to wear a different color, which I am, because if I see him before he sees me and don't like what I see, I can drive off and leave it at that.

I arrive twenty minutes early and am sitting in my car, looking at all of the size 'twenty-two' folks going in and out of an all-u-can-eat buffet. Just because it says all-u-can-eat doesn't mean you eat all you can.

A red 2002 Jaguar X-type pulls into the parking lot of Captain John's. The brother sitting in that ride is gorgeous, and he's wearing red too. Oh my goodness, that can't be Samuel. How can a maintenance man afford a brand new Jaguar? Lord, I have gotten myself mixed up with a drug dealer or something. But, then again, China did mention that he probably doesn't pay any rent doing maintenance for an apartment complex. I slide down in the seat, because I don't want him to see me before I get a real good look at him. This welcome sight steps out of his ride wearing black slacks and a red crew neck top that, from a distance, looks like silk. He reaches inside the backseat, pulls out a red blazer and slips into it. He wears a blazer well. I make sure to pay close attention to his shoes. Maya has always said something about never dealing with a man who wears run over shoes. From where I'm sitting, his shoes look brand new. I think it is Samuel. I hope it is Samuel. I roll down the passenger window and try to call out his name as lady-like as I can. He turns in my direction. Yes, it's Samuel.

"Free?" Samuel walks toward my car. I am so glad I went to the car wash today.

"Yes, it's me," I wave, looking a little too excited.

Samuel leans inside the car. "Hey, Lady," he greets in a silky voice.

"Hi," I say, smiling bashfully. "It's good to finally meet you." I extend my hand.

Samuel looks at me as if I have said something offensive. "Lady, you better get out of this car and give me a hug."

"Okay," I thought to myself. "Sure, let me grab my things and lock up."

Samuel walks around to the driver's side of the car. He opens the door, reaches for my hand, helps me out of the car and embraces me as if I was a long lost friend. His embrace is intoxicating. I don't want this to end.

Samuel is six-foot-one, bald and physically fit. His almond complexion and chestnut eyes makes for a mesmerizing blend, along with that lush, thick mustache sitting on top of his full, delicious lips. He is truly a black prince. After tonight, he won't want to see me anymore because I probably do not fit in the category of the type of woman that he prefers. I am too dark. I think Mama was a chain smoker when she carried me for nine months.

"You are as beautiful as your voice," he smiles, gazing into my eyes.

"Thank you. But I know you are just saying that."

"No, I mean it. You are exactly how I pictured you."

"Really?"

"Yes. You are stunning. You are truly an African queen. . .high cheekbones, sculptured body. . ."

"Okay, you must've had a drink or two before you left home," I chuckle.

"What? Don't you believe that you are a beautiful woman?"

Samuel takes my hand and we walk toward the entrance of Captain John's. Oh Lord, that food smells so good. The sign on the door says that they are offering 'all-u-can-eat' blue crabs and Alaskan King Snow Crab legs tonight. Darn, what did I do to deserve this? I love crabs and it is so hard for me to pass them up. Well, Samuel will just have to see the real Free tonight because I am going to eat me some crabs.

"Samuel, you don't have to flatter me."

"I'm not flattering you. I'm telling you the truth." Samuel opens the door for me. "Free, I thought. . ."

"Hi, and welcome to Captain John's. How many?"

"Two. No smoking, please," he says, flashing his warm smile.

"Sure." The hostess removes two menus and two sets of silverware, wrapped in white linen napkins, from the bin beside her podium. "This way, please."

Once at our table, Samuel pulls out my chair, unwrap the silverware and places the napkin in my lap. "Thank you, Samuel."

"Free, call me Sam."

"Okay, Sam. And you can call me Free," I laugh.

"You're silly."

"Just a little."

"I wasn't aware that you had such low self-esteem, Free." Sam unrolls his napkin-wrapped silverware, placing the silverware on the table and the napkin in his lap.

"I beg your pardon?"

"You obviously have some self-esteem issues."

"And what makes you think that?" I snap, ready to get up from this table and take my behind home. I do not appreciate being offended, especially on a first date.

Sam senses my discomfort with his comment. "Free, I didn't mean to offend you, sweetheart." Sam grabs my hand. "I only meant that when I told you that you were stunning, you acted as though you didn't believe it."

"Sam, I don't need you to tell me that I am stunning. I know that I am a beautiful black woman and I have enough self-esteem for you and me both. But, I also know that your type prefer women who are light, bright and close to white. I don't fit that mold."

"What exactly is my type, Free?"

"The expensive cars, nice clothes and good looks. I've never seen a man who is as handsome as you are with a woman who is dark chocolate. As you can see, I haven't a bit of cream."

"Oh, so now you are sitting in judgment of me because of the car I drive and the clothes I wear?" he snaps. "That's very shallow of you, Free." He rises to his feet. "I think I was wrong about you and maybe we should end this evening before we end up having regrets." He tosses his napkin on the table.

"Sam, please don't go. I was wrong. I've been single for so long and have been passed up many times by men because of my complexion. I guess it has made me a little insecure."

"I doubt if they've passed you up because of your complexion. I am sure it has to do with your negative attitude. You need to get that in check." Sam looks at me with disgust and walks away in a huff.

Before I could form my lips to call his name, the waiter approaches and asks if we would care for a cocktail. "Could you give us a few minutes, please?"

"Sure. I'll be back shortly. Take your time."

I sprint for the door, out of the restaurant and into the parking lot to see the tail end of Sam's car.

"Sam!" I yell to the top of my lungs. "Sam!" I am not letting this one slip away. The car's brake lights illuminate. "Sam, please! I am so sorry. Please, come back!"

I look and feel a mess. My underarms are sweating and the weatherman screwed up, it's raining buckets. Sam sits in his car, looking at me through his rear-view mirror. He probably thinks I am the world's biggest jackass. I stand here, looking like something the cat drug in, hoping that he will turn his car around and forgive me for being such a fool. The car door opens, Sam hops out and turns toward me. I look so pathetic.

"You look a beautiful mess," he chuckles.

"I'm sorry."

"I accept your apology."

"Thank you." My pinned-up hair slightly falls down around my shoulders.

Sam gets in his car and backs up toward me. "Get in. You're getting wet."

I jog around to the passenger side, where Sam has pushed the door open for me from the inside. I wipe the rain from my cheeks, trying not to smudge my eyeliner. "Were they calling for rain today?"

Sam stares at me with a smile. "You are a beautiful woman and I love your chocolate complexion." He leans in toward me.

"Sam, I. . ."

Sam places his index finger over my lips. "Shh. Let me bask in your beauty for a minute." He gazes at me apologetically. "I am so sorry about questioning your level of self-esteem. It was wrong and I was being judgmental."

"It's okay," I whisper. Sam leans in closer. I close my eyes as he softly caresses my lips with his. I don't resist, feeling a warm glow flow through me. "That felt nice," I say with my head tilted to the side and my lips slightly parted. Sam kisses me again, this time his tongue comes out to play. I allow my tongue to play too. All of my defenses begin to subside from the sweetness of his kiss.

"I want some crabs," he says, pulling away from me with a smile.

"Yeah, so do I." I feel like a kid about to get on a merry-go-round.

"Great, let's go back inside." He parks the car in the front so that I won't have to walk in the rain. What a gentleman. His mother raised him right.

"Okay, let me get myself together. I can't go in there looking like I've been through a car wash."

"You look beautiful. You don't need to touch-up a thing." Sam removes the hairpins from my hair, allowing my tresses to fall down around my shoulders. "There. That's perfect." He runs his fingers through my hair, his eyes raking boldly over me. "Stay put." He uses his car's remote to pop the trunk. He gets out of the car and retrieves something from the trunk. He opens my door. "Come on, baby." Sam holds an umbrella over me.

Getting out of the car, I stare into his eyes and give him a big kiss on the lips. "Thank you, Sam. Thank your mother for me too."

Sam smiles. "My mother will love you."

Sam escorts me into the restaurant and back to our table, pulling out the chair for me to have a seat. He places the napkin in my lap and motions for our waiter.

"Hi, my name is Rodney and I will be your server this evening. Can I get you a drink or an appetizer?"

"I will have a Courvousier, straight up, and this beautiful lady will have a Long Island Iced Tea." Rodney jots down the order and trots away.

"You remembered!" I exclaim.

"Of course," he smiles. "I am glad I got it right. I wasn't sure if it was the Long Island Iced Tea or the Peach Martini that you said you loved so much."

"I love them both."

"So, Free, tell me, what exactly are you looking for?"

"What do you mean?"

"What do you expect from me?"

"I expect nothing from you," I respond with confusion.

"Don't sell yourself short."

"Really, I am not looking for anything from you. All I want is your friendship."

"That's it, just friendship?"

"Should there be more?" I inquire. It's early in the game. I think homeboy should pump his brakes a little.

"Yes."

"Okay, well, why don't you tell me what you are looking for and then I can tell you if I am looking for the same thing," I chuckle, passing the buck, removing myself from the spotlight.

"For starters, I am a very passionate man and I like to show my affection to the woman that I am involved with."

"There's nothing wrong with that," I smile.

"I want my woman to know and feel that she is the center of my universe."

"She would be one lucky lady," I say, now feeling uncomfortable.

"I want to hold her, caress her smooth skin and kiss her gentle lips."

"Um, well. . ."

"I want to take long walks in the park and have evenings cuddling, watching a movie and listening to soft music."

"I like movies. . ."

"I want to take her to her favorite places to eat and then dance the night away."

"I love to dance. . ."

"I want to bring her a red rose every day and I want to give her sensual massages, take warm showers and soothing baths with her."

"I can sell you those roses," I laugh, trying my best not to have an orgasm right in this man's face. It's been too long and his words are working on me, big time.

"I want her to be my queen and I her king." He takes my hand in his. "Free, I want to prepare your favorite meals and, in the morning, serve you breakfast in bed. I want to make love to you in a way that will take your mind, as well as your body, to a place where only the two of us can go. . ."

I pull my hand away. "Oh my!" I exclaim. "Where is that Rodney guy with our drinks?" I exhale. I can feel the sexual magnetism that makes him so self-confident, that same sexual magnetism that will have my panties on the floor if I'm not careful.

"Baby, I want your heart to be mine and know that the bond between us is as unbreakable as the bond between a man and a woman can be."

"I get the picture, Sam. Can we please change the subject?"

He ignores my request. "I want to love you and you love me." He rises to his feet and kneels before me. "Free, you took hold of my heart the first time we spoke on the phone. Your laughter, kindred spirit and the warmth and kindness that exuded from you captured me. I know that I can love you the way you deserve. Tell me, Free, can you give me the love that I need and deserve?"

I am speechless and embarrassment is showing all over my face. "I don't know what to say, Sam." I'm not good at this. I can't tell if he is full of mess or if he's sincere. Dang, I wish I could call China right about now. She would know.

"Here we are!" Rodney sings. "Here are your drinks." Sam, not taking his eyes off mine, makes a gesture to Rodney to wait for a minute.

"Free, is this what you want? No, am I what you want?"

"I don't know if I am capable of loving you that hard, Sam. I've never loved or been loved like that before."

"Baby, right here, right now, I pledge my promise to you that I will love you as much and as hard as you will allow me to. I won't hurt you, Free. All I want to do is love you. I feel, in my heart, that you are the woman for me."

I force a smile, "Sam, please, get up," and look around at all of the smirks coming from the onlookers. I feel so embarrassed. How can he pledge his love to me when he doesn't know me from a hole in the wall?

"Not until you give me an answer."

"Goodness, Sam. You are not proposing, so please get up."

"Is that what you want?"

"This is ridiculous!"

"You want me to propose to you?"

"What? Oh, this is nonsense!"

"Free, let me love you for the rest of your life. I want you to be my woman. I want you to be my wife."

"Okay, now you are being silly. Man, get your crazy ass up off of the damn floor!"

"Well, Free, what's it gonna be?" Rodney butts in.

"Don't you have some tables to wait?" I snap. "Go mind your business." Rodney rolls his eyes and walks away with a switch in his hips. "I think he's funny."

Sam caresses my face with his hand, turning my attention from the waiter to him. "Free, I am not getting any younger. The longer you keep me down here on my knee, the harder it will be for me to get up." We both fall out with laughter.

"All right, all right already. Yes! Yes, I can love you and you can love. If you are still around five years from now, we'll talk about marriage. Now get up!"

Sam jumps to his feet, bends down and kisses me. "We have to celebrate!" he exclaims as the entire restaurant begins to applaud and Rodney returns with much attitude.

"Sam, what am I going to do with you?" I smack him on his hand. "Sit!" I demand.

"Ahhh, a bossy woman. Just what I love," he chuckles. "Robert, can we. . ."

"Rodney," he retorts with much attitude.

"My bad, man. Rodney, can we get a bottle of champagne?"

Rodney nods and skips off like a kid in a candy store. "I think you're right, Free. He is just too jolly," he chuckles and then exhales a long sigh of contentment. "Thank you, baby."

"For what?"

"For wanting me."

"No, thank you for wanting me. I blow a kiss at my new man. "Okay, so since we are a couple now, when can I get the keys to the Jag?"

Sam breaks into laughter. He reaches into his pocket and tosses the keys onto the empty plate sitting in front of me. "There ya go. Now, I am going to need transportation, so will I have to rent a car or will you give me the keys to the Beamer?"

Three hours later, Sam and I full of crab and champagne. The giggle bug has bitten me, thanks to the four glasses of champagne and two glasses of Long Island Iced Tea.

"Sam, I am so embarrassed," I say with a tongue thick as New York style cheesecake.

"Why?"

"I am too drunk to drive home," I pout.

"Aww, baby, don't worry about that. I will make sure you get home safe."

"But you can't drive two cars at one time, can you?"

Sam chuckles, leaves his chair and motions for me to get up as well. "No, baby. Your man can do many things, but driving two cars at one time is beyond his capabilities."

"I'm so sorry, Sam." Tears begin streaming down my face. Sam is looking around at the patrons and probably wondering how fast he could get me out of this place before I embarrass him further.

"You have nothing to be sorry for, Free."

"Yes, I do," I cry, sounding like a retake from *I Love Lucy*.

"Baby, come on. Get your purse and let's go. I will drive you home and have a cab to bring me back to pick up your car, okay?"

"You would do that for me?"

"Yes, and then some."

I burst into laughter and yell, "You said dim sum!" Sam escorts me out of the restaurant and to his car. "I ain't never rode in no Jaggywire before." I stumble over my words like a bumbling idiot.

Sam puts me inside the car, closes the door and attempts to get in on the driver's side. "Baby, I need you to move over so I can get in," he says, moving my head from the driver's seat to the headrest behind my head. "Are you going to be okay, baby?"

I nod my head, mumble "yes" and fall off to sleep.

Two traffic lights later, the gurgling of my stomach awakens me. My head is spinning and my stomach is killing me. I can tell from our location that it would be at least forty minutes before we get to my house. "Sam, I need to use a restroom. Do you think you can stop somewhere?"

"Sure, babe. I believe there's a Days Inn up the road. As soon as I can get out of this damn traffic jam, I'll stop there. I think there's an accident up ahead."

I feel like I have to break wind. "Sam, I don't think I can wait until we get to the Days Inn. Can you pull into that McDonald's over there?"

We are still inching in traffic. "Let me see if I can. . .baby, where are you going?"

"I can't hold it." I jump out of the car and dash through the traffic jam, dodging oncoming cars. Once out of harms way, I dart inside McDonald's and make a beeline to the bathroom. I don't have time to line the toilet seat with paper towels and I barely have time to get my pants down before bending over the toilet and taking a sigh of relief.

This happens to me all of the time with seafood, especially crab. When I eat too much of it, I get sick to my stomach and end up in the bathroom all night. I was hoping that I would be in the privacy of my own bathroom by now. Using the Wet Ones moist towelettes that I keep in my purse, I cleanse my backside. After freshening my behind, I stand in front of the sink, splash water on my face, wash my hands and look at the fool in the mirror.

Sam is leaning against his car in the McDonald's parking lot. "I sure feel sorry for whoever has to clean that bathroom," I think to myself while walking toward the car.

"You okay?"

"Yes, I'm fine. I feel better now."

"Good." He turns the radio to smooth jazz and pulls out of the parking lot into thick traffic.

I recline the seat and rest my head on the headrest. Miles Davis injects me with the tranquilizing, melodic sounds of his saxophone. About ten minutes later and twenty minutes from home, my stomach does an encore. My eyes pop open as if jolted from a deep sleep. "Sam, I've got to go to the bathroom!"

"Again?"

"Yes, I'm sorry."

"What's wrong? Is everything okay?"

"Yes, everything is fine. I am so embarrassed. I ate too much crab. When I eat too much, my stomach gives me a fit."

"Okay," he chuckles. "So, seafood gives you the shits, huh?" Sam's chuckle has turned into hysterical laughter.

"It's not funny, Sam," I whine, trying to put my head between my legs. "I need to get to a toilet before I mess on myself and your leather seats!"

"Okay, okay! As soon as this light turns green, I will pull into the Exxon station."

This light is taking forever to turn green. "Why are there so many damn traffic lights?" I whine with irritation.

Holding my breath and trying to keep my mind off having to use the toilet, I look out of the passenger window and notice a Port-O-Potty across the street. Without warning, I hop out of the car and, once again, dodge through traffic and oncoming cars, sprinting for the Port-O-Potty.

Once inside, the stench is far from intoxicating and it's dark. I can't hold it any longer. I take off my pants because I don't want them touching the floor. I bend over the toilet and take a sigh of relief. The smell of the Port-O-Potty, in combination with what was coming from me, makes matters worse. I regurgitate in the corner of the Port-O-Potty. I search with my hands, in the dark, for toilet paper. There isn't any.

"Shoot! You left the damn purse in the car," I scold myself.

I am too embarrassed to ask Sam for tissue. So instead, I use my underwear to wipe my behind, flushing it down the toilet with the rest of the waste. Then, I remove my bra and use it to wipe my mouth, tossing that down the toilet too. I wish I had a piece of gum for my breath.

Sam is leaning against his car and smoking a cigarette. "I didn't know you smoked," I say, exiting the Port-O-Potty. I can smell the stench of that funk box in my clothes. I stand in place for a minute, gazing at Sam's fine behind, allowing the funk to escape my clothes before I advance any closer to him.

"And I didn't know you were a little shitter," he laughs at me. "Are you okay or do we need to hit another toilet on the way home?"

"Shut up, Sam!" I pout, walking toward the car.

"I think we need to get you home. You look and smell awful," he laughs, as he flicks his cigarette butt into the street.

"Go to the devil, Samuel Meeks!"

"I love you too, baby," he chuckles.

Sam laughs all the way to my house and, fortunately for me, we didn't have to make any more stops. I don't think my behind could take any more releasing.

Maya

"Ms. Howard, I am Dr. Stewart and I will be your attending physician during your stay here at Mercy Hospital," he says, pressing the cold stethoscope against my back. "Take a deep breath, please."

"Am I going to be all right?"

"Ms. Howard, the X-rays show that you have sustained bruising to your lower spinal chord, which led to you experiencing temporary paralysis."

"But, I still feel a little numbness."

"Yes, and you will for a while. You are badly dehydrated. You were lying on the floor for several days with no water or food. Your body needs nutrients. But, not to worry, we will take very good care of you."

"When can I go home?" I ask through tears.

"We would like to keep you for a couple of days for observation and until you recover feeling in your lower body extremities."

"Okay. I need to call my sister and let her know what's going on."

"You should be in your room within the hour. There will be a phone in there for you to use."

"Thank you. Will I be able to get anything to eat?"

"Sure. I'll place an order for you."

"Thank you, Dr. Stewart."

He nods with a smile and returns back to the chaos of the Emergency Room.

A young man, riddled with bullet holes and covered in blood, is wheeled into the Emergency Room on a gurney. The woman in the room next to me sounds like she's coughing up a lung. An old man walking by my waiting area has his gown on backward, showing entirely too much of his business. The nurses are carrying on conversations, as if they have nothing else to do.

Two hours later, I'm still in the Emergency Room. My butt is getting sore from lying on this hard, plastic gurney and I am starving.

"Ms. Howard?"

"Yes."

"Your room is ready." the orderly says, covered from head to toe in mint green scrubs and rubber gloves. "Do you have all of your belongings?"

"Yes, they are under the gurney."

"Great. Let's rock and roll," he says, swinging the gurney from the waiting area and into the chaos of the Emergency Room, bumping into everything that stood still.

I am beyond irritation at his lack of concern for my safety. "Do you think you could take it easy? This isn't the Indy 500," I growl.

"Yeah, sure," he casually says, still bumping into shit.

Once inside my room, I eat my cold dinner and call Free. Beep. *"Free, it's me. I am at Mercy Hospital. I am doing just fine, but they are going to hold me overnight for observation. Don't worry about me. I will call you tomorrow. Love you."*

China

"Baby, please! Let's work this out."

I stand in the doorway of the family room, eavesdropping on his phone call.

"Marion, I didn't mean all of those things that I said. Please, can we meet and talk? I can't make it without you."

Ron is holding a phone call, in my house, with that bitch that he's fucking, without regard for the children or me. I can't believe what I am hearing. He is actually begging to see another woman.

"Okay, yes. I love you. Is that what you want to hear?"

I gasp at his words, placing my hand over my mouth. Tears begin to well, my heart is in my throat and my legs feel wobbly.

"I miss you so much, Marion. Let's meet tomorrow night at the same place," he begs. "Great. I'll make the arrangements and when I can, I will call you back with the room number. I promise to make it up to you real good, baby." Ron hangs up the phone and turns to face me standing in the doorway. He shows no emotion.

"Who was that, Ron?" I ask, my voice breaking miserably.

"Nobody." He is nonchalant, acting as if he doesn't care that he has been caught with his hand in the cookie jar.

"You love and miss nobody?" I ask, choking on my words.

"What are you doing, spying on me, China?"

"I wasn't spying on you."

"No? Well what do you call it?"

"Ron, those condoms I found in André's drawer belong to you, don't they?"

"You need to shut your mouth!"

"You need to answer me!" I yell, my tears subsiding and anger taking over.

Ron steps to me. I can smell his breath. He's been drinking. "I don't have to tell you shit!" he yells. "You got that? Now get the fuck out of my face!"

"Am I not pleasing you? Why are you fucking someone else?"

"China! Lower your voice before the kids hear you."

"You are the one who's yelling, and I hope they do hear me so that they can see you for the no good motherfucker that you are!" Ron strikes a blow to my face that lands me into the wall, knocking over the trophy that André received for playing junior league football last year. "Ron, you promised!" I whimper. "You promised you would never do that again!"

"Woman, you're going to make me hurt you. Now move!"

"How could you do this to me? How could you do this to your children? Who is she?"

Ron stands before me with his hands balled into a fist, his head hung low and his eyeballs rolling up and aiming toward his brow. "China, I tried to talk to you. I tried to tell you that I was unhappy with you. . ."

"But, I don't understand. You've never told me. . ."

"No, of course you don't understand because you never shut the fuck up long enough to listen." Ron points his finger in my face. "Now, I said to move out of my way, or do I need to move you?"

I step to the side.

With his back toward me, I pick up André's junior league trophy to put it back in its place. But instead, I throw it at the back of his head. "You motherfucker! I hate you!"

"What the fuck?" Ron gasps, his hand caressing the back of his head. "Bitch! Have you lost your fucking mind?"

"Mama, what's wrong?" Ashley yells from her room. "What's going on?"

"Stay upstairs, Ash," I yell. "Baby, don't come down here. Mama and Daddy are having an adult discussion."

"Okay!" she yells, closing her bedroom door.

"Your discussion sure is loud," André yells, following Ashley and closing his bedroom door.

"China, it wasn't necessary for you to do that," he growls, looking deranged.

"Who is she?"

"Mind your business."

"Mind my business?" I gasp. "You are my fucking business, motherfucker!" I grab another trophy from the mantel.

"Don't you throw that!" Ron leaps toward me and snatches the trophy from my hand. "What the fuck is your problem, woman?"

"*You* are my fucking problem. My husband! You are out here fucking some crack head, dick-suckin' bitch and then you come back into our fucking house, into our fucking bed and stick your fucking dick in me! That's *my* fucking problem."

With this back to the family room's door, he uses his foot to slam the door shut. "China, I don't want to talk about this."

"No, you don't have to talk about it because you are going to pack your shit and get the fuck out!"

"No, I'm not going anywhere. This is my house. I pay the bills!"

"Fuck you! You are getting the fuck out of this goddamn house!"

"No, I'm not," he snarls, using the back of his hand to strike me across my left cheek. "I think your ass need to know who runs this fucking house." Ron smacks me upside the head.

"Ron, stop hitting me!" I form a fist. "You said you wouldn't hit me anymore." I strike a mighty blow to the side of his face, knocking him off balance.

Ron shoves me into the wall. "Naw, you wanna run ya fuckin' mouth," he growls between clenched teeth.

"Ron, please. Just leave!"

"I told you I wasn't going anywhere." Ron grabs me by the arm and tosses me onto the sofa. He uses his knee to place all of his weight on my stomach.

"Ouch, Ron, you're hurting me!" I try to push his knee off me.

Ron grabs me around the neck. "I told you to leave me alone," he shouts, slapping me in my face.

After repeated cries for him to stop, I reach under his crotch, make a fist and slam it into his testicles.

"Arghhh!" Ron loosens his grip on me, hunches over and rolls off me and onto the floor. "You bitch!" he cries.

I look down at him with disgust. "Get the fuck out of my house, you two-timing son-of-a-bitch!" I grab a clump of his hair and snatch his head back. I feel like snapping this fucker in two. I glare into his partially opened eyes. "You make that the last time you put your fucking hands on me," I snarl, carefully enunciating each word then connecting my knee with his chin.

He falls backward, hitting his head against the sofa. Staring down at him, I begin to feel sorry for him. "Ron, you are pitiful. Go be with your slut. She can have your weak ass. I don't want you, I don't want you, I don't want you!"

The knot in my stomach reminds me of the years that I put everything on hold to be the kind of wife that he wanted me to be. All of the black eyes, bruises and visits to the Emergency Room because he took his frustrations of the world out on me. Twenty years down the fucking drain and I haven't a thing to show for it, except my two babies.

"You fucked up my life, you bastard. That bitch you are fucking will never be me." I step over the pile of shit that lies before me and, with my head held high, I strut into the kitchen and fix myself a cup of coffee.

Sitting at the kitchen table, sipping on a cup of almond cream-flavored coffee, Ron limps past me. "China. . ."

I look around the kitchen, snatch the butcher knife from the chopping block and point it in his direction. "I know you aren't saying shit to me, are you?"

Ron shakes his head and mumbles, "Crazy bitch." He limps out of the kitchen through the garage door.

"I didn't think so." I toss the butcher knife into the sink, making a loud thump. "Go and whip on her ass, Ron. I quit." I pull out a pen and pad from the kitchen's miscellaneous drawer, and proceed to write down my plan of action.

1. *Find a black, female lawyer first thing in the morning and take that motherfucker for all that he is worth, which isn't much.*

2. *Change all of the locks, because he will not see the inside of this house again.*

3. *How am I going to tell André and Ashley?*

4. *Find a job with no experience.*

I lower my head in the palm of my hands. "I gave that bastard twenty years of my life."

"What's wrong, Mama?"

"Nothing, baby." I wipe the tear-stained residue from my face. "It's nothing. You want some ice cream?"

"Yes, please! Will you have some too?"

"Yes, I'd like that," I smile.

I scoop a few balls of ice cream from the carton and spoon them into André's Winnie the Pooh bowl. I sit the bowl of ice cream in front of him and stroke my fingers through his naturally curly tresses. "Dré?"

"Yeah, Mama."

"Will you do your mama a favor?"

"Sure, Mama. What's up?"

"Promise me that you will never, ever treat a woman the way you would not treat your mama. Okay?"

"Okay, Mama."

I bend down and give him a kiss on his forehead. "I love you, baby."

André nods his head and continues to inhale his ice cream. "Mama?"

I take a seat across from him, scoop a spoonful of butter pecan straight from the carton and shove it between my bruised lips. The coldness soothes the ache.

"Why does Daddy beat on you like that?"

I slowly pull the spoon from between my tightly pursed lips and take a deep sigh. "Well, baby, Daddy is dealing with some demons right now. He doesn't mean to hurt me. . ."

"The next time he puts his hands on you, I'ma pop a cap in his ass."

I look shockingly at my baby. "André," I say calmly, "where did you learn that talk from?"

He shrugs his shoulders and replies, "I dunno."

"Do you know what that means?"

"Yep."

"Tell me what it means."

"It means that if Dad don't stop putting his hands on you, I'ma put a bullet in his ass."

"I see. Well, thank you for wanting to protect me. But, popping a cap in someone's ass is not the answer. I don't want to hear talk like that from you again. Is that understood?"

"Yeah, Mama, but. . ."

"No buts, Dré. I don't want to hear you talking about killing someone," I snap. "I hope that I am raising you better than that."

"Aww, Mama. I ain't say…"

"I didn't say."

"I didn't say. . ." he pauses, taking a sigh of irritation, "that I was gonna kill him, just put a bullet in his butt," he pouts.

"Well, that goes for bullets in people's butts too," I laugh. "You want more ice cream?"

"Yes, please!"

"How did I know you would want more?"

"I want some too!" Ashley exclaims, gleefully walking into the kitchen.

"Dang, I can't have anything to myself," André pouts. "Go back upstairs. Me and Mama is having an adult-like conversation." I grimace at his grammar usage.

"Shut up, you pussy!"

"Ash, what did I tell you about your mouth?"

"Mama, pussy is not a bad word," she says with the roll of her head.

"No?" I swear, one of these days, I am going to smack her head clean off that lil' skinny neck of hers.

Ashley grabs a bowl from the cupboard and flings it onto the kitchen table, watching it slide into André's favorite bowl. "No, it's not."

"Cut it out, Ash!"

"And why is pussy not a bad word?" I ask, anxious to hear what her explanation will be.

"Well, it depends on how you use it," she says studiously.

"Do tell," I smirk.

"Well, you have pussy cat, pussy willow, Pussy Galore. . ."

"Pussy Galore?"

"Yep. That's a lady's name."

"It is? What lady do you know with that name?"

"She so dumb, Mama. She talking 'bout that James Bond movie we saw the other night on TV."

"Shut up, she ain't ask you nothing," she snaps, cutting her eyes at her brother, who obviously annoys her to no end. "Mama?"

"Huh." Ashley knocks me out of my trance. "Yes, baby, what is it?"

"Mama, do you really not know who Pussy Galore is and how come you have a bruise on the side of your face?"

"It's nothing, baby. No, I don't know who Pussy Galore is, but I am sure you are about to tell me."

"Uh huh, Pussy Galore is James Bond's woman."

"No she isn't!" André teases.

"She is too!"

"Is not!"

"Is too!"

"Okay, cut it out. Finish your ice cream and get ready for bed. André you need to take a bath."

"Hahahaha! Mama said you stink!" Ashley taunts.

"I did not and you need a bath too," I taunt.

"Mama, that ain't funny."

"Whatever, Ashley."

"Ooh, Mama just dissed you!"

"Oh shut up, you pussy, before I toss your funky bowl in the trash!"

"Mama! Did you hear what she just said?"

"Y'all are getting on my damn nerves." I walk out of the kitchen.

"Where you going, Mama?" asks Ashley.

"To mind my own business."

"Dang, she just dissed you again!"

"Shut up!"

"You don't tell me what to do, Ashley. You ain't my mother."

"I wouldn't want to be your mother, you crying pussy!"

"I am not a pussy!"

While jogging up the spiral staircase to my bedroom, I yell, "If you two don't cut it out, you both will be pussies when I finish with you!"

The kids fall out with laughter. I close my bedroom door behind me, lock it and fall backward onto the bed. I close my eyes and reminisce on the best years of my life.

"Oh well," I sigh, "I can't turn back the hands of time."

I raise myself off the bed, unzip my sundress and watch it fall to the floor. I take inventory of the woman in the mirror. Sure, I have a bit of cellulite here and there, but it's nothing major. Humph, what he doesn't want, someone else will.

I step out of the sundress and head for the bathroom to draw myself a warm bubble bath. I light my candles, pin up my hair and immerse myself in another world for at least an hour. "God, I need a life."

Jade

JonAir landed at the Sangster International Airport in Montego Bay, Jamaica. Veronica and I were tore up from the floor up. During the flight, we consumed three bottles of Dom Perignon, several shots of Jose Cuervos and three lobsters apiece.

"Girl, what we s'pose to do now?" I ask, stumbling over my thick tongue.

"Boss, we s'pose to get off d'plane," she says in her weak Tattoo impersonation.

"Girl, you are silly." We both fall out with laughter. "I've gotta go to the bathroom."

"Okay. I'll wait right here until you get back," she says, plastered to the chair. I attempt to stand up. The feeling of being on a boat comes over me. "Girl, why are you wobbling like that? Are you okay?" she asks.

"I don't feel so good."

"You don't look so good either."

"No, seriously, I need to get to the bathroom, but my feet won't move."

"Oh shit. Girl, don't you puke all over Jon's jet. He will have a fucking fit!" Veronica hops to her feet and stumbles to the floor. "Ut oh."

"Oh shit," I laugh, holding my stomach. "Girl, you okay?"

Veronica pulls herself up onto her knees and crawls toward me with her head hung low. She extends her hand. "Here, take my hand," she says.

"And do what? Walk you like a damn dog?"

"I am going to help you to the bathroom," she hiccups.

"How are you going to help me? You can't help yourself right now."

"Do you ladies need any help?"

I turn to face my knight in shining armor. I attempt to straighten myself in an upright position. "Oh, hello, Jon," I slur.

"Hello, Jade." Jon kisses me on the cheek and then looks down at Veronica sprawled out on the floor of his million-dollar jet. "Veronica, are you all right?"

"Yes, I am fine." Veronica attempts to pull herself up from the floor. "I just need to

get. . ."

"No, don't move. I'll get someone to help you." Jon walks away laughing so hard, he's unable to walk upright. "I don't believe this." He found his way to the front of the jet and yells out of the door. "Paul, man, come get your woman!"

"Ut oh. Girl, he done called Paul on you. Here, let me help you get up." I bend over and grab her by her arms. "Girl, I can't let a sistah go out like that." Veronica doesn't budge. "Girl, come on. Here comes Paul." I try to pull her by her arms again, but she refuses to budge. "Girl, come on. . ."

"I ain't scurred of Paul," she giggles. "Shit, he ain't gone do shit. Humph, all I gotta. . ."

"Girl, stop running your mouth and get up!" I tug at her again. "Veronica, you're gonna be in deep shit." I stumble backward into Paul's arms.

"You must be Jade." Jon is standing behind Paul, full of laughter.

I point toward Veronica. "I think something's wrong with her. She won't move."

Paul releases me and walks toward Veronica's sprawled, drunken body. "Get up, Ronnie." He bends down over her. "Baby, come on now." He rolls her over to see her eyeballs rolled back in her head and the wad of saliva streaming out of her mouth and onto her chest. "Ronnie, quit playing and get up."

"Oh no!" I cry. "Jon!" Jon takes me in his arms and plants a kiss on my forehead.

"Man, is she all right?" Jon asks. "Jade, what were y'all doing?"

"Nothing. I mean, we were just having fun."

"What did you drink?" Paul asks, trying to lift Veronica to her feet.

"We had three bottles of Dom. . ."

"Three!" Jon snaps.

I flinch from his arms. "Yes. . .yes," I stutter. "And some shots of Jose Cuervos and lobster. I'm sorry. I didn't mean to hurt her. Is she dead?"

Paul is able to get Veronica to her feet. "No, she's not dead," he says with a sarcastic tone. "She's fucked up!" Paul lifts her in his arms, cradling her like a baby, and carries her off the jet.

"Jon, I am so sorry."

"For what? You didn't do anything. Ronnie is always getting drunk and passing out. It's not your fault."

"Really?"

"Yes. Now, let's get your things and get out of here. It smells like a brewery in here," Jon chuckles.

"Okay, but I have to go to the bathroom first." I cover my mouth and haul ass to Shitter's Paradise. Closing the door behind me, I drop to my knees, put my face in the commode to heave up the lobster, Caesar salad, and smoked salmon.

"Jade, are you all right?" Jon asks from the other side of the door, still laughing. I don't respond.

After rinsing out my mouth with the trial-size bottle of Listerine, I gather my composure and open the door. Jon is still laughing. "What the hell is so funny?"

"I see you and Ronnie had a blast, huh?"

"Kiss my ass, Jon!" I snap, irritated with him.

"Ooh, anytime, anyplace, darling."

He is still laughing and getting on my damn nerves. I whisk by Jon, brushing up against him, making my way to the front of the jet.

"Jade, I'm sorry. Okay, I'll stop laughing." But, of course, he doesn't.

Once inside the limo, Veronica comes to her senses and is alert. "How ya doing, girlie?" I ask.

"I'm okay," she answers, smiling. Jon is still laughing.

Veronica cuts her eyes at Jon. I know she wants to cuss him out, but he is her boss, so she must hold her tongue, but I don't. "Jon, do you think you can cut that shit out? You are getting on my nerves."

"Okay, but you've got to admit, y'all are just too funny."

"Ronnie, you make it hard for me to take your ass anywhere. You are always getting fucked up," Paul snaps. Jon bursts into laughter again.

I cut my eyes at Jon. "It was probably the altitude," I say, sounding like a damn fool.

"No," Jon laughs. "It wasn't the altitude. It was more like the three bottles of Dom…"

"Shut the hell up, Jon!" I roll down the window and stick my head out of the car like a French poodle, allowing the wind to blow in my face.

"Don't throw up again!" Jon yells. I use my foot to kick the hell out of his shin. "Ouch, Jade!"

Road debris pops me upside my head. I come back inside the car and whisper in Jon's ear. "I have a bone to pick with you."

"What did I do?" he mouths.

I lean in close. "You took it upon yourself to contact my boss and request days off for me. I don't like that."

Jon covers his mouth. "You need a breath mint," he laughs.

"You know what, Jon? Why don't you just go to hell? I swear, you are acting like a simple motherfucker!"

"Ooh, wait a minute. Are you getting upset with me?"

"Yes, you are. . ."

"Jade, I am the one who should be pissed. My baby smells like throw up and a damn brewery."

"See, I told you that plane was his baby," Veronica interrupted.

I look at Veronica in disgust and couldn't say a word. He was right.

"I didn't tell you about the trip because I wanted to surprise you."

"Yeah, well, you surprised me all right."

"Jade, what's the big deal?"

"The big deal is that I don't need my employer knowing my personal business," I snap. "You had no right to do what you did."

"Well, sue me, all right? What's done is done," Jon snaps. Damn he's a cutie when he's angry.

"Don't tempt me, damnit!"

"Ouch! Okay, no more surprises. Can we call a truce?"

"We're not at war, Jon. But, if you do that shit again, it will truly be World War III up in this piece."

Jon surrenders by raising his hands in the air. "Whatever you want, Jade."

"And he means that shit too," Veronica slurs. "Girl that man will get you anything your heart desires. Shit, he can afford it. Yeah, sue his ass and then give me half," she laughs.

"Veronica, you need to chill," Paul says calmly, looking out of the window.

"Whatever, Paul." Veronica waves her hand in the air and rolls her eyes at Paul. "Am I lying, Jon?"

Jon looks at Veronica with amusement. "Nope, you're not lying." Jon brushes his lips against my cheek, pulling me in to him.

"See, girl, I told you." She leans forward. "Girl, as long as you're workin' that ass right, that motherfucker will be wrapped 'round yo finger." She motions for me to give her a high-five. She looks at Paul, slips her hand between his thighs and grabs his crotch. "Ain't that right, baby?"

Paul grabs her hand and squeezes it tightly. "I am sick of this shit, Veronica. You are embarrassing me."

"Aww sugah wugah," she pouts in a whiney voice. "You'll be fine after I work that dick. . ."

"Veronica! That's it. You need help. . ."

Veronica leans in to kiss Paul but he pulls away. "Oh, don't be like that, baby."

I feel the need to change the subject. "Okay, Mr. Meadows, since you didn't give me advanced notice, what am I going to do about clothes?"

"Girl, he's got that taken care of. Don't you, Jon?" Veronica answers, while Paul looks over at her with disgust.

"Yes," Jon smiles, "I've got it all taken care of."

"See, I told you, girlfriend. That man doesn't miss a beat," she says.

The car's interior wreaks with the smell of alcohol that is spewing from Veronica and my pores. I feel like throwing up again. "Jon, can we please stop the car?"

"What's wrong?" Veronica slurs.

"She's not talking to you," Paul snaps. Hell, I wish she would shut the fuck up too.

"What the fuck is your problem, black man?" Veronica snaps at Paul.

"Veronica, stop! I am sick of this," he responds angrily.

"Sick of what? I don't do shit to you but fuck you when your ass get horny!"

"Oh my!" I exclaim. "Girlfriend, you are sharing too much."

"No, I want the truth to come out." Veronica leans forward. "Sistah girl, let me let you in on some shit." Inhaling Veronica's breath is like taking fire from a dragon. "This motherfucker here..."

"Veronica!" Paul is very brusque with her. "I have had all that I am going to take of your childish, drunken behavior." Paul yanks her back against the seat. "Now, sit your ass back and shut the hell up."

Veronica looks at me and smirks. "Girl, I'll tell ya later," she snickers and turns to Paul. "I like it when ya rough, Daddy."

The limo pulls up in front of a nineteenth century, twenty-acre estate. "What is this?" I ask Jon in astonishment.

"This is home," Paul answers.

"Yeah, girl, and you should see the one in Florida?"

"Get out of the car, Ronnie," Paul says, helping her out of the car.

"Florida. . ." With Jon's help, I get out of the limo and stand in amazement. "I have never seen anything more beautiful."

"I am glad it meets your approval," Jon says. "We will have the left wing and Paul and the lush puppy will have the right wing."

"I heard that, Jon," Veronica slurs. "You ain't cute!"

I face Jon. "I think we need to talk."

"We will. Let's get ourselves situated and talk later, okay?"

"Okay."

I follow Jon up the pebble stone-covered walkway. Jon stops in his tracks, turns to me and spreads his arms as wide as they can go. "Welcome to Meadowland."

"Meadowland? Sounds like an amusement park," I chuckle.

Paul and Veronica head for the house and Jon takes me by the hand and guides me toward the main house. "This place was built in the late nineteenth century and it has a spectacular view of Montego Bay."

"Wow, this is absolutely breathtaking," I say.

Jon points toward white sand and turquoise blue water, with snow-white waves brushing against the shore. "Over there is the beach. It's private. Feel free to run naked," he chuckles.

"In your dreams," I smile. "Private? You own the beach too?"

"Yep."

"You mean to tell me that no one else can come on this beach?"

"Nope."

"It's all ours. . .I mean, yours?"

Jon admires my forthrightness. "Yes, it's all *ours*."

Once inside, Jon begins his tour of the house. The marble flooring in the foyer glistens from the glare of the chandelier that expands across the width of the ceiling. In the middle of the foyer, a matching marble, never-ending staircase stretches from the front door to the landing of the second floor, where ten bedrooms reside. Across from the foyer is the living room that is heavily decorated with ethnic this and ethnic that, with a white baby grand that looks out of place. Across from the living room is the dining room, filled with beautiful palm trees and exotic flowers that spread the length of the oak-carved dining room table, which could easily seat fifty people. Behind the never-ending staircase is the kitchen that resembles the kitchen on *JonAir*, except it's larger, with restaurant-style silver appliances and shit hanging from the ceiling. You know pots, pans and those huge cooking utensils that no one ever uses because, lets face it, who in the hell would want to wash out those big ass pots? The tour of Meadowland concludes with the basement's wine cellar, the professionally manicured compound with the swimming pools (yes, there is more than one) and tennis courts (uh huh, like he really needs two of those), and the private beach.

"What in the world does one man need with this entire house?"

"I don't *need* this entire house. I'm only one man. It's more of an investment."

"Investment?"

"Yes. Times that I am not here, I rent it out. I have a cleaning service to come in weekly to maintain the property for me."

"How much do you rent it out. . ." I catch my nosey self. "Oh, I'm sorry. That's none of my business."

"No, I don't mind you asking. Fifteen thousand a week."

My bottom lip hit the floor. "Fifteen thousand a week what?"

"Dollars. . .that's how much I rent out the house for."

"Well, it must be nice. I wish I had that type of money to spend a week here."

Jon pulls me in to him. "Your money is no good here, Ms. Howard."

I take a step back from Jon, pinch myself and twirl around in a circle. I can't believe any of this is happening. I can't believe he is interested in me.

"Jon, we need to talk."

"You already said that and we will talk later."

"No, I want to talk now, before we go any further."

Jon takes me by the hand and leads me to the spiral staircase.

"Where are we going?"

"Upstairs."

I pull back. "Slow your roll, Casanova. I prefer to talk standing up."

"You silly goose, I am showing you where you will be staying and besides, we will have privacy upstairs."

"Privacy? Jon, there isn't a damn soul in this wing besides you and I."

"Okay, geesh. Let's go in the living room."

"That's better," I chuckle.

"Care for a drink?"

"What do you have?"

"Your favorite."

"Now, how do you know what my favorite drink is?"

"The three empty bottles. . ."

"Shut up!"

Jon is standing at the two-tier, trimmed in silver glass bar cart. "Okay, so let's talk. Baby, what's on your mind?"

I stare down at the white plush carpeting. "Jon, I don't believe in beating around the bush. . ."

"Yes, I gathered that much."

"Will you let me finish this without any interruptions, please?"

"Ooh, I'm sorry." Jon places my glass on the table in front of me, without a coaster. "Please, continue."

"Where are your coasters? You don't want to mess up your beautiful table."

"Don't worry about it. I can buy another one."

"Anyway, like I said, I don't beat around the bush and I like to get straight to the point. It's been a long time since I've been with a man. . ."

"Yes, the Red Dog, is it?"

"Jonathan!"

"Sorry."

"Well, for the last three years I was dating a woman."

"Was? Does that mean you two are no more?"

"You know what? I am going to kick your ass if you don't stop interrupting me."

"My bad," he laughs. "It's a habit."

"Well, you need to break that nasty habit." Jon is such a kid. He finds laughter in everything and that is what I like about him. He doesn't take every little thing so serious. "As I was saying. . ."

"Baby, what's your point?"

"My point is that it's been a while since I've been with a man and I am afraid that I won't know what to do."

"Is that it?"

"Yes."

"Whew, I thought you were going to tell me that you didn't want to see me anymore."

"Why would I do that? So you can leave me stranded here? No, it's the opposite. I like you, Jon. I would be lying if I said that I wasn't impressed by the lifestyle. . ."

"Oh, so it's the money?"

"No, it's not the money," I snap, my lips thinning with anger. "I can't believe you offended me like that. Let me remind you that you are the one who whisked me away, without my permission. You kidnapped me, damnit!"

"Your feistiness turns me on." His eyes grew openly amused.

Admittedly, I am enjoying the gentle sparring just as much as he is. "Kiss my ass, Jon. Be serious for one minute."

"Jade, relax. Life is too short. The only thing I am serious about is my money and my woman."

"Jon, that's what I'm trying to say. I can't be your woman because I don't have the type of money that you have. I can't bring fifty percent to the table. . ."

"Wait a minute. Who asked you to bring fifty percent to the table? I don't recall asking you to bring anything to the table."

"Veronica said that you only date women who can bring half to the table, and well, I just got my promotion and I know damn well it ain't half of what you make."

"Jade, don't be silly," he huffs, "and Veronica needs to mind her drunken business." Jon takes a seat beside me and rests his hand on my knee. "Jade, I am not interested in your money. I have enough money for the both of us, too much for one man. All I am interested in is what's in your heart. When I look into your eyes, I see so much love and compassion."

"Wow, I don't know what to say."

"Jade, I've been single for a long time. I've dated many women and I know a good woman when I see one. I'm no fool."

"But, I just don't know. I've been hurt so much by men."

"Jade, if I so much as look as though I am about to hurt you, I want you to turn your back on me. I would no longer be worthy of you, your love or your time."

"Are you sure you want me?"

"Do you want me?"

"Let's take it one step at a time."

"One step at a time is the only way I know how to love you, Jade." Oh shit, he's good. Folks sure do toss that *love* word around.

"Jon, love is just anther four letter word like shit, damn and fuck. People are too loose with the word as it is, not having a clue as to the real meaning behind it."

Ignoring me, Jon leans in and gently strokes my bottom lip with his tongue. Cupping my face, he covers my mouth and takes hold of my tongue, sucking, trying to pull it out of my mouth. To keep up with his rhythm, I inch myself closer to him and hold on tight. He releases my tongue and makes a saliva trail to my neck, moving his tongue in a circular motion behind my ear. "Oooooh, baby," I moan, "that's my spot." I stutter from the chills raging throughout me. He slips his hand under my blouse and finds his way to my breast, gently squeezing my erect nipples between his fingers. "Oh, Jon, we can't do this," I pant.

"Why not?" he asks, still tweaking my nipples, as if he were changing radio stations.

"Someone may come in."

"Nobody will come in."

Leaving an imaginary trail from my breast to the top of my hips, he gently eases me to the edge of the sofa where his tongue gently caresses my swollen, sensitive nipples through my blouse. I resist no further, allowing my body to heave in to him.

Unzipping my jeans, he slides his hand inside and wiggles his fingers in my warmth, tantalizing my bud, causing it to bloom to its fullest. "This shit feels so right, baby."

He can say that again. It feels too right. It feels too good to be true. I can't believe we are vibing so strong. I have one of New York City's wealthiest black men, with his hand down my pants. I guess this just goes to show that even the rich are normal folk and have needs too.

Jon pushes the coffee table out of the way with his foot, allowing him room to kneel down on the floor.

"What are you doing, Jon?"

Jon pulls my jeans, along with my underwear, down around my ankles. He starts to gawk between my legs. "Girl, your pussy is pretty as hell." He bends down, inhaling me like a breath of fresh air. "Aww, you smell sweet too," he exhales. "Let's see," he says, preparing for his diving expedition. "After three bottles of Dom, you should taste like a thousand bucks," he chuckles. I pop him upside the head. He parts me with his index finger and sticks out his tongue. In slow motion, Jon wiggles his tongue like a dancing snake, tickling me. I try to suppress my laughter. His tongue wiggles its way toward my bud, caressing it with light strokes.

His gentle strokes send currents of desire through me. "Oh!" I flinch.

"You okay?"

"Yes, just a chill, that's all."

Jon repeats the light strokes against my bud, using his finger to stroke my rectum. "Baby, how does this feel?" he asks, his breath warming me.

"Feels real nice," I pant, wiggling my hips against his face. "Suck me," I demand.

Jon sits back on his legs and pulls my hips closer to his face. "Wrap your legs around my neck, baby." I do as he instructs. "Don't let go of me, Jade." Jon gazes into my eyes. "Jade?"

"What?" I wish he would shut the fuck up. He talks too much.

"I'm serious. Don't let me go."

I cease the wiggle in my hips, unwrap my legs from around his neck and rest myself on the edge of the sofa. "What are you saying to me, Jon?"

"Just you and me, Jade."

"Exclusively?"

"Yes." Jon leans in to kiss me. He's right, I do taste expensive.

"Jon, how could you ask me to be exclusive when you don't even know me?"

"Well, for one, I am between your legs. I don't make too many trips between legs and two, you don't know me either. I can promise you that we both will have a wonderful time of getting to know each other."

"Exclusively, huh?"

"Exclusively."

"You are asking a lot of me, Jon."

Jon's shoulders slump. "I know and I'm sorry. I don't know what I was thinking."

"Jon?"

"You're right. I shouldn't ask you to be exclusive when we've only known each other for a couple of days."

"Jon?"

"But Jade, I am so tired of the single scene. I am ready to settle down."

"Jon?"

"What?"

"Are you letting me go?"

Jon smiles. "Not for a second."

"Good. I would hate for you to miss out on a good thing." For a split second, Joy flashed through my mind. She would literally kill me if she knew a man was deep sea diving on me.

I shrug my shoulders and lean back onto the sofa, wrapping my legs around his neck. "Let's get back to business." Jon laughs and happily obliges.

Two hours between my legs and ten orgasms later, I am dating a man. A fine, rich man too.

Free

"Good morning!" Samuel places the breakfast tray in front of me. "Rise and shine, pumpkin."

"Good morning," I yawn, barely able to open my eyes. My head feels like someone has been banging it against the wall all night long. "What time is it?"

"Eight o'clock."

"In the morning?"

"Yep!"

I take a deep sigh and raise myself up in the bed. "Yummy, this looks good. I need to brush my teeth before I eat though."

Sam lifts the breakfast tray, being careful not to spill the freshly squeezed orange juice and the array of fruits and cheeses.

I pull the covers back and feel a cool breeze waif between my legs. I look down and then up at Sam. "Where are my underwear?"

Sam places the breakfast tray on the dresser. "That's a good question," he smirks. "When I put you to bed last night, you didn't have them on. I just figured you didn't wear any."

"Don't be silly, I always wear. . ." Then it dawns on me what happened to my underwear. "Oh, well, never mind."

"And you didn't have on a bra either."

"Just never mind, Sam." I get up from the bed and walk butterball-naked to the bathroom. "You could've at least put something on me." I close the door behind me.

"I tried, but you weren't having it," he yells.

I open the bathroom door. "Did we. . .ah, you know?"

Sam smiles and asks, "Have sex?"

I bashfully nod my head. "Did we?"

"No. You were too intoxicated and I don't take advantage of women. I slept on your sofa."

"I appreciate that."

"Besides, after throwing up and shitting in Port-O-Potties, I had no intentions of going there."

"You ain't never lied!" We both fall out with laughter. "As a matter of fact, let me take a quick shower before I have my breakfast."

"You do that. I will go down to the kitchen and clean up the mess I made."

A man who cleans up behind himself. Mama always said you could tell a lot about a man by the way his mother raised him. "You do that and make it quick. I hate to shower alone." I can't believe I said that. Am I still drunk? I close the bathroom door and turn on the shower. Pew, I don't blame him for sleeping on the sofa. I do stink.

Ten minutes later, there is a knock at the bathroom door. "You still want some company?"

"Absolutely," I say, feeling a tingle between my legs.

Technically, the first date was last night. We are on day two, which makes this the second date. Besides, I am horny.

Sam pulls the shower curtain to the side and stands before me with a penis hanging a few inches above his knees and a chest full of curly, black hair.

"Oh my! Is that all you?" I ask, somewhat afraid. I've never seen a penis this large before.

"Care to find out?"

"I. . .I don't know. . .it looks painful." I turn up my nose. "And you aren't even erect."

"I guarantee you nothing but pleasure," he smiles, stepping into the shower and reaching for the soap. "You are so beautiful, Free." After lathering his hands, he palms my vagina, focusing on the lips. "You feel good, babe."

My body quivers. It's been a very long time since I'd felt the touch of a man. I move in closer, giving him a kiss on his lips. The deep yearning for him makes me turn my back toward him, slightly bending over and propping my foot on the ledge of the tub.

"Do you have a condom?" I ask.

He reaches outside of the shower and picks up the condom that he had dropped on the floor when he entered the bathroom. He had it all planned out, thank God for that. He rips open the package with his teeth, retrieves the condom and carefully rolls it onto his hardness, while at the same time searching for holes and making sure not to tear it. He moves closer to me and strokes his latex-covered penis against me. I release a slight moan and push myself into him. He eases inside me.

"Oh! Are you all the way in?" I ask, feeling like a virgin.

"No, not yet," he pants.

I reach down to feel the shaft of his penis. He is barely halfway inside me. "I think you are too big."

"It will be fine, baby." Sam leans on my back, latches on to my breast and inches himself deeper inside.

"Ouch, Sam, that hurts!"

"You need to relax, baby." He lets out a deep-throated moan. "You are so tight. Open your pussy for me, baby."

Sam presses the palm of his hand against my back, signaling me to bend over further. He continues to inch deeper inside, his shaft pulsating against my walls.

"Sam. . ."

"Hush."

"Sam. . ."

"Hush."

"No, Sam. . ."

"Free!"

With the yell of my name, Sam pushes himself inside me, causing me extreme pain. "Ouch! That hurts!" I can feel Sam's hardness swell inside of me. This is unreal. This is not how I expect my first time, in such a long time, to be like. "Samuel, that hurts!"

"Relax, Free. You need to relax your muscles. Stop tightening up on my dick, baby."

"That hurts! How many times do I have to tell you?"

"It won't hurt if you would just fucking relax!" he yells, giving me a hard thrust and causing me to bang my head against the shower wall.

"Ouch!" I holler. "Sam, you bastard! Why are you hurting me? Get out of me!" The warm stream of water washes away my tears.

Sam ceases stroking. "Free. . .I, oh no. . ." Sam pulls himself from me and leans back against the shower wall. "I don't know what came over me."

"Yeah, well. . .I don't know either. It's not what I had expected, that's for sure." I get out of the shower, throw on my robe and open the medicine cabinet. "I need a damn Tylenol. I have a headache, no thanks to you." I snatch the bottle of Tylenol, slam the medicine cabinet shut and storm out of the bathroom, toward the kitchen, for a glass of water.

Fifteen minutes later, seated on the sofa flipping through the latest issue of *Essence* magazine, Sam comes down the stairs and kneels before me. My eyes affixed to the Tampax ad on page fifty-three.

"Free, I don't know what came over me."

I don't look at him. "It's okay, Sam."

"I guess I wanted you that bad." I pop him upside the head with the *Essence* magazine. "Free, I don't want to ruin. . ."

I press my index finger against his lips. "Shh." I kiss his lips. "It's okay. We will be fine."

Sam smiles and plops beside me on the sofa. "What do you want to do today?"

"Get rid of this headache." We both laugh. "Nothing special, just relax."

"That sounds good to me."

"Sam?"

"Huh?"

"Thank you for not taking advantage of me last night."

"That is something I would never do to you, my love."

Maya

I am so glad to be back at home. I can't wait to get into a nice warm bath. Now that I have been given a second chance on life, I am going to straighten up and fly right. It has become apparent to me that I won't be the next Halle Berry or Angela Bassett. It's not like directors and casting agents are knocking my door down or ringing my telephone. Not to mention, my agent isn't good for shit either.

I notice the red light flashing on the answering machine. I press the 'new message' button and begin to undress in the living room. I can't believe I rode the bus wearing the same funky ass clothes that I've been wearing for the past week. I don't blame people for staring at me and not wanting to sit next to me. I look like a homeless person who peddled up sixty cents for a damn bus ride to nowhere.

"Maya, it's me. Where you at, bitch? I got some new clients. I need you to do what you do best. Call me ASAP!" Beep.

"Fuck you, Jonah," I say aloud. "I can't fuck with you no more. I am going to get my life together!" I yell at the walls.

As I walk to the bathroom, there's a knock at the door. I run to the bedroom and snatch my robe from the hook behind the bedroom door. The knock at the door is persistent. "Yeah, hold your horses!"

With the chain on the door, I crack it open. "Fuck me, huh, bitch?" Jonah blows through the front door like the tornado that whipped through Kansas and carried Dorothy's ass to Oz, causing me to stumble backward. The chain flew off the door, hitting me in my eye. "Is that right, Maya?"

"No, it's not," I squirm, with my hand covering my eye. The throbbing pain shoots to the back of my head. "I mean, I am just ready to turn my life around."

"What life? You ain't got no life. I own your fuckin' life!"

I feel weak and vulnerable in the face of his anger. "I'm not happy with the way that I've turned out," I whine, now curled into a fetal position on the floor.

"You're not happy? Oh, so now I don't make you happy?"

"No. That's not what I am saying, Jonah," I answer, crying into my knees and scooting myself into a corner.

"Talk to me, bitch," he yells, hovering over me. "Tell me what the fuck you saying."

"Jonah, I am very appreciative of all that you have done for me, but our last encounter made me realize that I need to make some changes in my life and. . .Oh my God!" I cry, grabbing my nose that just made an impact with Jonah's fist. "Not again, Jonah!" I sob, with a palm full of blood. "I think you broke it!"

"I'm 'bout to break your ass!" he hollers, with a slow drawl. "Bitch, you done lost your goddamn mind. Don't nobody fuck with my money. You got that, whore?"

"Jonah, get out!"

"Jonah, get out," he mimics. "Jonah, get out." Jonah yanks me to my feet and bends my arm behind my back.

"Jonah, you are hurting me again!"

"How the fuck you gonna tell me to get out of my goddamn apartment?" Jonah bends my arm further. "Bitch, I made you!"

"Ouch, Jonah, please!"

"Yeah, I like it when you beg. Get on your knees, bitch!"
Jonah forces me down to the floor, releases my arm and grabs a
handful of my hair. "I wanna hear you beg some more." He
bends down and leans in close. "You making my dick hard."

"Jonah, I'm sorry," I plea. I try to divert his attention from
another ass whipping. I can't stand anymore of that. "You want
me to suck your dick, Daddy?"

Jonah ponders my offer. "Well, I dunno. You didn't do a
good job the last time."

"I will take it all this time. I promise."

"I'll tell ya what," he says, his eyes conveying the fury within
him. "If ya don't take it all down ya throat this time, you will be
taking it all up in ya ass." His voice is quiet, yet holds an
undertone of cold contempt.

Unzipping Jonah's pants, I nod my head in agreement and
watch them fall down around his ankles, truly dreading this.
Jonah scoots himself closer to my face. He's been with someone
else. I can smell it. I slowly open my mouth and take him in. I
hold my breath and wrap my arms around his thighs. He scoots
in again until his hardness starts to tickle my tonsils; my body
heaves. He grabs the back of my head and pushes himself further
down the back of my throat, causing me to gag. I open my eyes,
look up at him, take a deep breath and say a quick prayer. I
close my eyes and clamp my teeth down around his shaft as
hard as I can. Jonah yells to the top of his lungs. His grip on my
hair tightens, almost pulling my hair from the roots. "You
fucking bitch, I am going to fuck you up!" he cries. "Let go!"
he cries. I nod my head no and sink my teeth deeper. Jonah is
still yelling to the top of his lungs. His knees buckle, but I refuse
to let go. I want him to feel the pain that I felt when he beat my

ass and left me to die. "Maya! Let go of my shit!" he cries. "You crazy bitch, let go!" Jonah's cries aren't heard. Feeling the warmth of his blood oozing out the sides of my mouth, I release him. Jonah grabs his severed penis, falls down to his knees and falls over on to the floor, crying like a newborn baby.

I stand over him as he lies in a fetal position withering in pain. "This will be the last time you put your hands on me, ever again!" In a heated rage, I grab the lamp that sits on the end table next to the sofa and release it from my grip onto Jonah's head. His cries cease. "Jonah?" I nudge him with my foot. He doesn't move. "Jonah?" I kneel down before him and place my finger under his nose. "Jonah," I whisper. He is breathing but isn't moving. He must be in shock.

Jonah partially opens his eyes. "Help me," he whispers. "I need a doctor."

"Well, I hope like hell you get one in the next four days." The table has turned. I am now the vulture and he is my prey, and just like a vulture, I hover over him. "Now, you've got some unfinished business." I raise my robe and squat over his face. "Open your mouth."

Jonah looks at me with questionable eyes. "Maya, I am bleeding to death. I need help," he cries.

"Ha! Do you think I give a fuck if you're dying? Motherfucker, please end all of my worries and die, you bastard!" I gather saliva from deep within and hurl a wad in Jonah's face. "You need to do as I tell you. Don't let me have to repeat myself, Jonah." Whoever said revenge was sweet damn sure wasn't lying. Jonah slowly opens his mouth. "Wider, open wider," I snap. "You better not move either." I drop my head back, release a deep moan and use Jonah's mouth as my toilet.

He begins to choke, trying not to swallow my urine, but he doesn't have any other choice. I hold his mouth shut. "Now who's the bitch, huh, Jonah?" Sitting all one hundred and thirty pounds of me on top of him, his body wiggles like an eel through water. His lips are turning blue. My urine trickles from his nostrils. Suddenly, his body stops wiggling. His eyes stare at me with coldness. "Jonah?" I release his lips and stick my index finger under his nose to see if he is still breathing; nothing. I stand to my feet, close my eyes and say a little prayer. I step over the scum and head toward the bathroom to indulge in a much needed shower. "You're lucky I don't have to take a shit," I mumble.

After taking my shower and packing a few things, I call Free at the shop. It's time for me to leave *Hollywood*.

"Hey Sis!"

"Hey baby girl, how are you feeling?"

"I'm feeling fine," I answer, staring down at Jonah and thinking how I've done the community a service by killing off the bastard.

"Are you home? What did the doctor say?"

"Yes, I'm home. The doctor says that I'll be just fine."

"Well, what about your legs? Can you walk? Are you in any pain?"

"My legs are fine, and yes I can walk. No, not feeling any pain."

"So what was wrong? Why couldn't you move?"

"Free, you ask too many questions. I'm fine."

"Well, good. I wish you were here so I could keep my eye on you."

Bingo. That was just what I needed to hear. "Really?"

"Yep. You need some guidance, girlie," she chuckles.

"Yeah, well, I do want to get my life back on track and nothing is happening here for me."

"Well, I have an extra bedroom."

"Free, I would love to come and stay with you, but. . ."

"But what?"

"I have no money," I sigh. "I am broke."

"I can send you the money. Better yet, I will purchase the ticket and have it waiting for you at the airport. How does that sound?"

"Sounds like I am going to get to visit my big sister, Free!"

"Great, when?"

"Tonight?"

"Tonight. . ."

"I need to get away from here, Free."

"Is everything okay, Maya?"

"Yes, I just need a change of scenery."

"Okay. Let me call my travel agent. I will call you back with the flight information."

"Great. Thanks, Free! I love you."

"I love you too."

I step over Jonah's 'corpse,' head to the bedroom and finish packing my things. Jonah was right. This apartment is in his name. The utilities and phone bill is in his name, although I paid them every month. Every stitch of furniture belongs to him. The only things I have are my clothes. After packing four suitcases of everything that I own, I pour myself a glass of wine. I take a seat on the sofa and peer at Jonah's lifeless body stretched out in the middle of the living room floor. A few minutes later, he flinches. Startled, I jump to my feet. "Jonah?" He doesn't move. He lies lifeless. I sit back down, thinking that maybe my mind is playing tricks on me, until he flinches again. I jump up, run over toward him, kneel down and stick my finger under his nose. I feel warmth exuding from his nostrils. "Oh shit! He isn't dead! Okay, I need to calm down," I think to myself. I pace the floor, knowing that if Jonah can get up from that spot, he will whip my ass until my skin peels off. The ringing of the telephone startles me. I try to keep my voice and hands steady. "Yes, hello," I whisper into the receiver.

"Hey, it's me, Maya."

I breathe a sigh of relief. "Oh, hey, Free."

"You're all set. You're booked on American Airlines, Flight Number 635, departing LAX at six o'clock this evening. Is that okay?"

"Yes, that's fine. You will meet me at the airport?"

"Yep! I can't wait to see you."

"Me too. Free, is there a return date?"

"Nope, I left it open."

"Great. Let me get back to packing, I will see you when I get there."

Placing the phone back in its cradle, I resume pacing the floor, doing a once over of the apartment and making sure to gather all of my belongings. I tower over Jonah, glaring down at him. Memories of years of mental and physical abuse blows around in my mind like a windstorm. The more I think about the black eyes, bruises and missed auditions, the angrier I get and the more I want to stomp the heel of my shoe into his eyeball. "I hate you!" I yell down at him. "You ruined my life and you will pay, you sonofabitch!"

It's time to put out the trash. I open the front door and look up and down the hallway, not a peep. I run down to the trash chute to check out the dimensions—too small for a body. Walking back toward the apartment, an eerie cold feeling surrounds me, sending a chill through me. I stop in my tracks and look down at my hands that are shaking like leaves blowing in the wind. The fear of going back into that apartment is overwhelming. Hell, I'm scared as shit. I slowly open the door to discover Jonah sitting upright, trying to get up off the floor. I panic. I quickly close the door behind me, take off my shoe and hit Jonah on the back of his head, knocking him out cold. I conduct the 'index finger' test and to my dismay, he's still breathing. Shit, this stubborn bastard won't die. Half of me want him dead so that he will not be able to ruin anyone else's life. But, the other half is relieved because my ass doesn't want to be anyone's bitch in a jail cell either. I glance at my watch and see that I have two hours to make my flight.

I gather my bags from the bedroom and sit them at the front door. I turn to see Jonah sitting upright once again. "Oh shit! I thought I had knocked your ass the fuck out. You're like that damn Chucky doll. No matter what I do, you keep springing back up."

"Where are you going, Maya?" Jonah looks like he's been tied to the rear of a car and dragged for miles. I really messed him up good. However, I am not done with him. "Help me out, Maya." As he tries to pull himself up off the floor, I fling my right leg toward his head. "What the. . ." He falls back onto the floor.

"Shut up, Jonah!"

"Why are you doing this to me, Maya?"

"You are finally getting what you deserve."

"I don't deserve this. . ."

"You do deserve this!" I can't believe my ears. "Motherfucker, you deserve to have something rammed up your. . ." A light bulb goes off. I rush to the kitchen, grab the broom and stand over Jonah, drunken with hatred.

"What are you going to do with that?"

"What you've been doing to me for years, fuck you."

"Ho, you are fucking crazy!"

"I might be, but you will never do to another what you've done to me."

"Maya, let's talk about this. I mean, what do you want? You want half the business? What you want? Anything you want, it's yours," he pleads for his life.

Funny, I can remember pleading for my life, but did he listen? Hell no. Should I listen to his pleas? Hell no. "Jonah, I don't want shit from you except freedom, peace of mind and the fact of knowing that you will *never* harm another." I kneel down before him. "Now, turn your punk ass over."

"Naw, fuck that shit," he cries. Jonah tries to move, but it's another case of what goes around comes around. Now he's the one suffering from temporary paralysis. Now he knows how it feels, the bastard. "You gone have to kill my ass right here," he says.

"Is that what you want?"

"No, Maya, let's work this out. You have my word, baby girl, I won't put my hands on you no more," he begs. His eyes are crimson from crying like the true bitch that he really is.

"You're right, you won't." With my hands tightly affixed to the broom handle, I raise it above my head. "This is for all of the missed auditions, black eyes and you leaving me to die."

Jonah's eyes are big as honeydew melons, about to pop out of his head. I close my eyes, "Maya, noooooooooooooooo," and ram the broomstick handle into Jonah's throat and through his windpipe, lifting his head off the floor because of the broomstick handle protruding from the back of his neck.

China

As usual, Ron makes his call and storms out of the house. Curiosity is getting the best of me and I wasn't blessed with nine lives. I need to find out about the woman who occupies so much of his time. I slowly approach the phone, having second thoughts. What will I say to her? What will this prove? Will he leave me for her? I reach for the phone. "What am I doing," I whisper. I step back from the phone and briskly wring my hands together. "This is ridiculous." I turn to walk out of the family room. "This won't solve anything," I mumble as I come to grips with reality—our wedding picture—Ron in his tuxedo looking dapper and me in my wedding gown, pledging our love to each other in front of two hundred people. She can't have him! I rush to the phone and press the redial button. My stomach is doing flips and my hands are shaking profusely. My knees feel weak and I have no clue as to what I am about to encounter. I pull a cigarette from the pack of Newports that Ron left sitting on the table next to the phone, light it and take a long deep drag. I don't smoke, but today I do. A male's voice on the other end makes me choke on my inhale. I quickly gather my composure. "Yes, may I please speak with Marion?" I ask sharply.

"Who's calling?"

"She doesn't know me," I snap.

"Who is this?"

I take a deep drag and exhale. "My name is China. . ." I clear my throat. "China Douglas." There is a long pause and then a dial tone. "What the. . .why did he hang up on me?" I press redial. The line rings six times before he answers. I'm pissed. I hate people to hang up on me. It's so damn rude. "Is there or isn't there a Marion at this number and are you her husband?"

"Yes, there is."

"Good. I would like to speak with her, please."

The man clears his throat and takes a deep sigh. "You're speaking with Marion."

"What?" My lit cigarette falls to the floor, along with my bottom lip. "Excuse me?"

"This is Marion, how may I help you?"

"I think I may have the wrong number."

"No, you have the right number."

I begin to cry. "No! Oh please, no."

"You shouldn't have called here, China."

I attempt to gather my thoughts. "Are you fucking my husband?"

"I think you should speak with Ron."

"Are you or aren't you dicking my husband?"

"Yes, Ron and I are intimate."

"Oh my God! Oh, dear God! I don't believe this!"

"I am sorry that you had to find out this way."

"What's wrong, Mama?"

Ashley startles me and I drop the receiver. "Go back upstairs, baby. Mama is fine," I order, scrambling to retrieve the handset from the floor before this idiot hangs up on me again. Damn, how much did she hear?

"China, we shouldn't be discussing this. You should really speak with Ron."

I close the door to the family room. With the phone's cradle in my hand, I pace the floor, trying not to break my neck by tripping over the phone cord. "Marion?"

"Yes."

"How long have you been having an affair with my husband?"

"China, don't do this to yourself."

"You've already done it. You've broken up my family. My husband is a pervert. My children's daddy likes to fuck men. No, you owe me an answer to every fucking question I ask you."

"Very well, Ron and I have been together for three years."

"Three years. . ." My voice trails off as calmness and the realization that the man that I love is actually a stranger in disguise. Anger and vengeance take over my God given senses. "How did you two meet?"

"China, I really don't think I should. . ."

"Answer me, you faggot!"

"Fine, but I will not be too many faggots."

"I call them as I see them."

"I am a human being, with feelings. I warrant respect, China."

"In my eyes, you are a perverted whore, a home wrecker, a sicko! You get no respect!"

"Fine, you want to know? No problem. Ron and I met in a movie theater."

"A movie theater?"

"Yes."

"I don't understand."

"We met at a porn theater."

"What? But. . ."

"When I first met Ron, he wasn't receptive. However, he was curious about the lifestyle. . ."

"So you tamed his curiosity, huh?"

"I didn't do anything that Ron didn't want me to do."

"Do you have AIDS?"

"I beg your pardon?"

"Do you have AIDS?"

"Do you think all homosexuals have AIDS?"

"Yes. Do you?"

"You are a small-minded woman and I can plainly see why Ron. . ."

"Skip the bullshit. Do you have AIDS?"

"No, I don't. I've been tested and I am very particular of who I get involved with."

"Is that why you chose a married man, so that you wouldn't get AIDS?"

"Look, this is getting ridiculous. I think we've talked enough. If you have any more questions, please direct them toward Ron and don't dial my number again. Thank you." He hung up on me, again. Oh, it's on!

A man? Of all the young booty walking around, why would he want a man? I don't get it. Was it something I did? Hell no, my shit is powerful and would turn a gay man straight. . .I guess all except my gay man. How can I tell André that his daddy is gay? I can't let my son continue to grow up around a faggot. The more I think about Ron and his infidelity with another man, the more the desire rises within me to call Marion back. Plus, I feel like fucking with his ass.

"Did you always use condoms with my husband?"

"China, please. . ."

"Please, I need to know."

"Yes, except once."

"All it takes is once."

"What do you mean?"

"I mean, all it takes is one time for you or him to contract a STD."

"Well, I am clean."

"Is Ron clean?"

"He says that he is."

Feeling vindictive and wanting to lash out at someone, I retort, "Do you always believe everything you're told?"

"Well. . ."

"I know that Ron has been having an affair for some time, I just didn't know with whom. Would you like to know how I knew?"

"Not really."

"You see, I went to see my Ob/Gyn for my annual exam and they gave me a Pap smear test. Do you know that is?"

"No, I don't. I've never visited an Ob/Gyn," he responds sarcastically.

"Well, I don't know when the last time you were tested, but my Pap smear test came back abnormal. Do you know what that means?"

"No, but I am sure you are going to tell me," he sighs, irritated as hell. Who gives a shit?

"That means that everything wasn't kosher in my pussy. . ."

"Okay, I've heard enough."

"No, you haven't. You see, Marion, I have been a faithful, devoted wife and mother for twenty years. I put my career on hold to raise our two beautiful children. You do know that Ron has children, right? Their names are Ashley and André."

"What's your point, China?"

"If you are so clean, then that could only mean that Ron has not been totally faithful to you. My Pap smear came back abnormal because I had contracted gonorrhea. Now, I know I wasn't fucking around, and if you were being totally faithful to Ron, then. . ."

"I have to. . ."

Click! This time, I slam the phone down on his ass. I sit back on the sofa and contemplate my next move. I give that bastard all of me and all I get in return is a couple of black eyes, a bruised up body and an occasional fuck with a bisexual. I light another cigarette and take a long, slow drag. I've always wondered why Ron's dick would smell funny when he would climb in bed after a night of 'hanging out with the boys.' That motherfucker let me go down on him after he pulled his dick from Marion's ass. The nasty fucker could've at least taken a damn shower first.

"All these years, he didn't care about me," I sob.

"Mama, is everything okay?"

"Yes, Ashley. Everything is just fine, baby."

"Why are you crying?"

"Oh, baby. These are tears of joy. Listen, how would you like to visit your Aunt Free?"

"Yeah!"

"Good. Why don't you go upstairs and pack a few things."

"How long are we staying, Mama?"

"We will see once we get there, okay?"

"Okay." Ashley skips out of the family room, through the kitchen and up the spiral staircase, taunting André as usual. "Hey, you pussy, me and Mama are gonna go see Aunt Free and you not going with us!"

"Stop calling me that and I am so going, you bitch!"

"Bitch? Who you calling a bitch?" Ashley snaps. "I've got your bitch, you pussy," she yells to the top of her lungs. That child is going to wake the dead.

Leaning my head against the wall, I take a deep sigh. "André, come here, now!"

"But, Mama…"

"Now!"

André mopes into the family room. "Mama, I get tired of her calling me a pussy."

"André, a bitch is a female dog and I didn't give birth to a female dog, understand me?"

"Yes. But, she acts like a bitch."

I jump from where I sit and slap André across the face. "If I ever hear you call your sister out of her name again, I will whip your ass! Now, go upstairs and pack a few things, we are going to visit your Aunt Free," I yell.

André presses his hand against his cheek, looks at me and starts crying. "Mama, you always getting on me! Ashley gets away with murder!" André storms out of the family room and into the kitchen, kicking over the kitchen chair.

I trail him. "Boy, have you lost your ever-loving mind? Pick up that damn chair and go upstairs and start packing!"

"Damn, Mama!"

"What the hell did you say?"

André holds his head down, kicking at imaginary dirt. "Nothing."

"Yes, you said something. I have had enough of both your nasty ass mouths! Ashley, get your ass down here right now!"

Ashley skips into the kitchen. "Yes, Mama."

"Have a seat." I pull the chair out for her to sit. "André, pick that chair up and sit your ass in it before I have to heat it up!" Ashley laughs at André. "Ashley, shut up," I snap, leaning on the kitchen table. "Now, you listen and you listen to me real good. I have had enough of the bickering back and forth between you two. You are brother and sister, not pussy and bitch. Do I make myself clear?" They nod in agreement. "Ashley, it's okay to learn new words, just know when to use them, got it? If anything ever happened to me, all you have are each other. So cut that mess out!"

"Yes, Mama. But. . ."

"Hush." I turn my attention toward André. "André, a bitch is a female dog. Do I look like a bitch to you?"

"No, Mama."

"You should never call any woman, or your sister, what you wouldn't call your mother. Understand me?"

"Yeah, but she ain't no woman."

"André, you heard what I said."

"Yes, Ma'am."

"Good. Now, please, for the umpteenth time, go upstairs and pack."

"Okay. Is Daddy going with us?" Ashley asks.

"No."

"Why not?" she asks.

"Ashley, do what I tell you!" Ashley flinches. André giggles and they leave the kitchen, starting up that bickering again. "I am not going to tell you again!"

The vision of Ron with another man keeps flashing through my mind. I find it hard to believe that my husband would have his pelvic bone meshed against some man's ass. Most importantly, I can't believe he would put me, as well as the kids, in harms way. Suppose he would've contracted something from this Marion character? Who is to say that this Marion can be trusted? Who is to say that his ass isn't burning up with AIDS or some STD? Well, if Ron is not going to concern himself with our safety, then I will.

I sure hope Free doesn't mind having some company for a while. I could stay there, clear my head and figure out my next move. I do know one thing…I am not staying in this marriage. I don't want no man who messes around with men. Poor André, I just don't know what I am going to do about him. If he ever finds out that his father is funny, he will be devastated.

I grab the phone and speed dial Free's number. "The kids and I are coming for a visit," I say before she could say hello.

"Really? Well, it will be a regular family reunion because Maya is here."

"She is? Why? Is everything all right with her?"

"Yep, everything with baby girl is just fine. She's decided to change her life around and start over."

"Well, that is so good to hear."

"So, why are you and the kids coming?"

"You wouldn't believe me if I told you."

"Ron has screwed up, huh?"

"Girl, and how." I look around to make sure the kids are nowhere around. "Free, my husband is a fudge packer."

"A what?"

"A fudge packer, a doo-doo chaser, he enters through the exit, a. . ."

"Okay, I get it, China. Ron is having an affair with a man?"

"What? Ron is having a what with a what?" Maya yells in the background.

"Tell Maya I said hey and I can't wait to see her. It's been so long."

"Yeah, I will, but first, back to the issue at hand. Ron is having sex with a man?"

"Yep."

"Oh, Sis, I am so sorry. How do you know for sure?"

"I spoke with him myself."

"Oh my word! I don't want to hear anymore."

"Well I do!" Maya yells. "Hurry up and get here, girl."

"You driving, China?" Free asks.

"Yep, me and the kids will be leaving in an hour."

"You're driving up tonight? China, that's at least a ten-hour drive. Do you think that is wise?"

"I will drive until I get tired and then stop at a hotel."

"Okay. We will see you some time tomorrow then."

"Yep."

"Well, come to the shop first. Most likely, I will be there, although, Sam might be here."

"Sam?"

"Girl, he is fine!" Maya chimes in. "Free has hit the jackpot. . .he's got big feet too!"

Free places her hand over the phone. "Maya, shut up and stop yelling in my house like you are out in the street."

"Sis, I will see you tomorrow," I say, interrupting Free's motherly chastising of Maya. "I don't know how long I am staying though."

"Don't matter, I have plenty of room. Can't wait to see my babies."

"Hey, Free?"

"Yeah."

"I love you, Sis. Thanks for always being there for me. . .for all of us."

"I love you, too, and if you can't depend on your family, who can you depend on?"

"Not a damn soul," I respond softly. "I feel sorry for Ron. He's not as fortunate. The children and I are the only family he has." I take a deep sigh. "See you soon."

Jade

Despite my 'let's get to know each other first' speech, Jon and I end up in the same bed after all. After a night of passionate lovemaking, I wake up thinking about Joy. I feel bad about the way things ended between us. Aside from being my lover, she was also my friend. She's always been there for me through all of the good and the bad. I am sure she hates my guts by now. But, truth is, I do love her and I miss her very much.

After last night, however, I can't go back to that lifestyle. I chose that lifestyle not because it was the life that I wanted to live, but because I no longer felt that men were good for me. . .that they couldn't love me the way that I needed to be loved. . .the way that I would love myself. Women possess a love that is sincere and genuine, a love that caters to our emotions. Men are totally the opposite. They don't care about your feelings. All they care about is *tappin' the ass* and scratching their musty balls.

It's only been a few days since I'd met Jon and here I am in Montego Bay, lying in his bed, with his body wrapped around me like a boa constrictor. I barely got any sleep. Hell, I can barely breathe. Yet, when I look at him sleeping and see how much at peace he is with himself, I feel that I've made the right decision. I feel like I have a new lease on life.

My sisters will be overjoyed, especially Free. She has been riding me for years about being involved with women. She says, "It's a sin. If God wanted women together, he would've created

Eve and Eva," or something like that. I haven't spoken to Free since that little nasty email she left me, asking me if I have a man yet. I must've really struck a chord with her. Oh well, she'll get over it.

Free is the strongest of the family. She's a regular Mother Hen. When things go haywire in our lives, we swarm to her like bees to honey. When Mama died, she handled everything. When Maya didn't show up for the funeral, I wanted to whip her ass. Free was the one who explained to me that Maya is lost and is desperately trying to find her way, that Maya was trying to prove something to her family, the ones who doubt her the most. Hell, I don't doubt her. I just think she lacks talent.

Jon's hold on me loosens. "Good morning, Angel," he yawns.

"Good morning."

"How did you sleep?" he asks, stretching.

"Well, I'm not used to being in a body lock all night but, other than that, I slept peacefully."

"I just wanted to make sure you didn't leave me."

"Where the hell am I going?" I chuckle.

"You know what I mean."

"Uh huh, and don't start that possessive shit 'cause that don't fly with me."

"Woman, you are a tough cookie. How about some breakfast?"

"Sure, I'm starving and not to brag, but I'm a great cook."

"You don't have to cook." Jon rolls over and picks up the phone. "I will call downstairs and have something set up for us on the beach."

"Who are you calling? I didn't see a soul in this house but us, Paul and Veronica."

"I have servants that will take care of all of that."

"Servants? Where they at?"

Jon chuckles at my use of Ebonics. "They should've arrived early this morning."

"But. . ."

Jon places his hand on my thigh. "Good morning, Gloria. How are you?" Jon puckers his lips and blows me a kiss. "That's good to hear. Gloria, could you please prepare something for two, beachside?" I lean over and kiss him on his shoulder. "Just one second." Jon places his hand over the receiver. "Baby, what would you like for breakfast?"

"Oh, well, nothing special. . ."

"Omelet?"

"Sure, that sounds good."

"Gloria, two lobster omelets, fresh fruits, an array of cheeses and a bottle of Dom Perignon, please." Jon winks at me. I give him a kick from beneath the covers. "Great, an hour would be perfect. Thank you, Gloria."

"What was that for?" I ask.

"What are you talking about?"

"Why did you wink at me when you ordered the Dom?"

Jon begins to laugh uncontrollably. "Well. . ."

"You sound like a damn hyena!"

"I can't help it. It was hilarious to find you and Veronica so wasted on the jet."

"I am sure it was, but for me, it was more embarrassing than anything else."

"Why were you embarrassed?"

"I didn't want you to see me that way."

"Oh baby, that's okay. I want you to be yourself. I want you to enjoy yourself. That is why I had the jet loaded up so that you and Veronica could enjoy yourselves."

"I was pissy drunk," I pout.

"And?"

"I don't want you to think that throwing up all over the damn place is the norm for me. I don't want you to think that you can't take me anywhere."

"Jade, wherever I take you. . .if you want to drink up all of the Tequila in Mexico, you can. It doesn't matter to me. I will be the one who will carry you to safety."

"Aww, Jon, that is so sweet."

"I mean it, Jade."

"I know you do." I pat him on the cheek and kiss his forehead. "Let's hop in the shower and get ready for breakfast. What's on the agenda today?"

"Whatever you want to do is what we will do."

"After breakfast, I would like to spend the rest of the day in bed, how about that?"

"Sounds like a good time will be had by all," he smiles, scooting under the covers and finding his place between my legs.

I kick the covers off the bed and wrap my legs around his neck. "Ooooh!" I grab the back of Jon's head, pushing his face deeper into me. "Hmm, baby, use your finger." He inserts his finger deep into my crevice, locating my G-spot. "Oooooooooh!" His lips caress my sensitive swollen clitoris. An indescribable surge builds inside me, causing my body to gyrate and my legs to stiffen, tightening around his neck.

"Baby, you're going to hurt me," he whispers on my clit. "Loosen your grip, babe."

"I'm sorry, baby, but that was one hell of an orgasm," I pant. "I have never felt that before."

"I'm glad I hit the right spot."

"You certainly did," I smile, stroking the top of his head. "Hmmm, I feel so good, Jon."

"Now, that's what I want to hear," he says, inserting his finger into my rectum.

"Oh hell no!" I jump.

"What's wrong, baby?"

"Could you please remove your finger from my ass?"

"You are very tight there."

"Well why wouldn't I be?"

"Jade."

"What?" I snap, not really feeling the finger in the butt thing.

"Be quiet and relax."

"Okay," I whimper. Giving in to him, I relax the tension in my body. I feel like I have to have a bowel movement and this is not cute. I can't help but to giggle, thinking about how ugly it would be if I were to fart on his finger.

Jon attempts to speak while his mouth covers my garden. "What's so funny?" he mumbles.

"Nothing. Don't stop!" I grind my hips to the bobbing of his head. "Baby, ooh, baby. The hood, get up under the hood," I stutter, getting that surge again. The desire to explode builds inside me. Again, I wrap my legs tight around his neck, probably cutting off the air passage to his brain. "Oooooooooooooooooh, shit, motherfucker!"

Jon raises his head and stares at me with a big cheesy smile. "That was a big one, huh?" he smiles.

I laugh at Jon's glistening face. "Did I do that?"

Ron

"Hi, baby. Sorry I'm late." I reach in to give Marion a kiss as I walk through his front door. To my surprise, he rejects me.

"Ron, we need to talk."

"What's wrong?" I reach to embrace him. He turns away from me. "What's up?"

"I spoke with your wife."

I chuckle because I don't believe my ears. "You spoke with who?"

"China. I spoke with China."

"What the fuck are you doing talking to China?"

"Lower your voice, Ron. There is no need for you to yell."

"I don't believe this shit. How did you come in contact with my wife?"

"You were sloppy."

"What the fuck are you talking about?"

"Ron, if you don't lower your voice and speak to me in a civil manner, you will have to leave."

"Okay, I'm sorry."

"Ron, you called me from your house. . ."

"Well, yeah, but China doesn't know your phone number. It's not like I have it written down or anything. I have it memorized."

"About ten minutes after you called, China called here. . ."

"But how did she know I called you? I didn't think anyone was around when I made the call," I say, pacing the floor. Then, it dawns on me. "Damn, she did walk in on me while we were on the phone." I walk over to the window and peer out at the headlights on the congested street below.

"Well, I guess she is not as stupid as you have made her out to be. I'm sure she is familiar with the redial feature."

"Shit!" I make a fist and slam it against my thigh. "What did you tell her?"

"I answered her questions."

I face Marion. It is bothering me that he is so nonchalant about all of this. "What questions?"

"Well, actually, it's quite funny. She thought I was a woman."

"What the hell is so amusing about that? Why didn't you tell her that Marion wasn't here or something like that?"

"Because I don't lie about my sexuality. I take it very seriously, which is something you need to consider doing."

"Damn! You didn't tell her that we were. . .you know?"

"I didn't want to tell her, but she insisted."

"Oh my God! What have you done to me?"

"I didn't do anything to you, Ron. I've told you repeatedly that lies and deceit bring nothing but pain and. . ."

I lunge at Marion and grab him by his collar. "You bastard! You have just ruined my fucking marriage. I ought to. . ."

"Ought to what, Ron? Beat me up? Kill me? What?" Marion breaks my grasp with his arms and stares into my eyes. "You know, Ron, for three years, I've put up with your bullshit. I've never asked you to choose between me and China. I've never kept you away from your children. I've never made any demands on you whatsoever. What I have done to you? I haven't done anything to you. You've done it all to yourself. The only thing that I am guilty of is loving you and not having that love reciprocated."

"But. . ."

"But what? But you didn't think she would find out? But your wife is not as stupid as you made her out to be? But you don't know what you are going to do? But, fucking, what?" Marion's eyes turn bloodshot. Tears roll down his face. "Ron, I think you should go."

"Are you ending us?"

"You need to go home and straighten things out with your wife."

"But, I don't want to lose you."

"Ron, you need to make a decision."

"You want me to choose between you and my family?"

"No. I want you to be honest with yourself. Either you are going to straddle the fence or you are going to accept the fact that you are a homosexual. Shit or get off the pot!"

"I am not gay!" I shout.

"No?"

"Fuck no! You're gay, but I ain't."

"Ron, I don't know of any straight men that love performing anal sex with another man as much as you do." Anger steadily rising, I turn to Marion, grab him by the neck and slam him against the wall. "Do you treat your wife like this?" he asks with a shaky voice.

Marion's words sting deep. I peer into his eyes, wanting to bash his head in for fucking up my life. I loosen my hold on Marion's neck. "I'm sorry. . .I, I. . ." Marion inches away from me, not taking his eyes off mine. "Marion, I. . .I don't know what to do. Please don't do this to us."

"Go home, Ron. Take a long look at yourself."

"But I don't want to lose you."

Marion walks toward the front door and picks up my cap from the green marble top end table. "You won't lose me if you make the right decision. But, I can't do this anymore, Ron. I will never forget the pain in China's voice. I caused that pain, Ron. We both did." Marion opens the door and extends me my cap. "Take care, Ron."

I walk by Marion and take my cap. My hand brushes against his. I stop in the doorway, with my back to the man who loves me just as much as I love him. "I do love you, Marion." There, I finally say what he has waited three years to hear. Only now, it's too late. I take a step into the hallway, and before I could utter a single word, Marion closes the door on me. Is this for good?

China

I packed as much as I could inside my '99 Ford Explorer.

I still can't believe the man that I married is into sexing men. When you think you know someone. . .how could he do this to me? He could give me AIDS or something. I can't believe that bastard would come home, climb in the bed and have sex with me. The nasty ass. How do I tell my children that their father is a faggot, or do I tell them at all? "Damn you, Ron!" I slam my fist against the steering wheel. I take a quick look over my shoulder to make sure I didn't wake up Ashley and André. Because of that bastard, I have my children on the Florida Turnpike heading toward Atlanta at one o'clock in the damn morning. "Ron, you will pay for this. Trust me." Mama used to say, "God don't like ugly." She spoke the truth. I just hope that Ron is able to accept and deal with the consequences that God puts before him.

I reach for the bag of audio tapes and search around for Pearl Cleage's *What Looks Like Crazy on an Ordinary Day,* slide it into the cassette player and lose myself in the world of literature for a few hours.

Jade

Lord have mercy, I don't know whether I'm coming or going. Jon has had me in a whirlwind of passion and fun for the entire weekend. Today is my last day in Montego Bay and the only sights that I've seen are Jon's bedroom, the kitchen and the beach. I haven't seen Paul or Veronica either. I wonder what they've been doing. Probably the same thing that Jon and I have been doing. Hell, if Paul is anything like his brother, Veronica's eyes have doubled back in her head at least twenty times. I am going to have to seek her out today, find out what's been going on with my new home chick. That sistah is off the hook. I hate that I haven't been able to see much of the island, but Jon says that I can come back anytime I get ready, and I plan to do just that. Now, if this isn't a girl's dream come true, I don't know what is.

Gloria softly knocks and cracks open the door, peeking her head inside the room. "'Cuse me, Ma'am," Gloria says in her strong Jamaican accent.

Gloria is a beautiful mahogany complexion with high structured cheekbones and a vanity mole delicately situated above the right side of her top lip. With eyes of coal, flawless skin and hair flowing down her back, it would be difficult to guess her age. I definitely wouldn't place her at being sixty years old. I hope and pray that I look half that good at sixty.

"Yes, Gloria. Please, call me Jade."

"Yes, Ma'am. . .care for lunch, Ma'am?"

"Umm, well, I would like to go out for lunch if that's okay."

"If that's what you want, Ma'am. What about dinner?"

I smile and hug myself. "I think I would like to go out for dinner too." Gloria nods with a smile and returns to her chores.

Since Jon has gone to town to handle business, I decide to be nosey and check out the areas of the house that I didn't get a chance to see on Jon's personal tour of *Meadowland*. I start my adventure in the basement in search of a bottle of Dom since my throat is a little dry. There has to be well over one thousand bottles of wine hanging on all four walls and from the ceiling, in every color, shape and size, with not a speck of dust on one bottle. Not one of these bottles resembles what I'm looking for. Hell, I don't need it no way. I'm already high off Jon.

I make my way upstairs toward the attic. Looking around, I see lots of trunks, boxes and old furniture. There are cobwebs all over the place and it smells like musty balls and cologne. It's obvious that Jon keeps his wine cellar cleaner than his attic. This place is scaring the shit out of me. It's safe to say that I will not venture up here again. I head back to my bedroom to call Jon, to see if I can meet him in town for lunch. While walking toward the room, my attention diverts to the only room on the floor that has a closed door. My curiosity gets the best of me. Plus, I'm nosey as hell. I open the door. This room didn't look any different from the other rooms, except for Gloria riding Paul like a mechanical bull, her arms flinging wildly in the air. Paul sees me and tosses Gloria to the side. "Jade!" Paul grabs the sheet, hops off the bed and wraps the sheet around his waist. "Jade, let me talk to you." I dart to my bedroom across the hall. "Wait, I can explain," he yells following behind me. "Jade, I need to talk to you!" Paul tries to open the door, but I beat him to it by locking it.

"There is nothing to talk about. I'm taking a nap."

"Please, we need to talk. . .about what you just witnessed."

"I didn't witness anything."

"Jade, please!"

"Listen Paul, who you screw is your business."

"Please, Veronica can't find out about this."

"If she finds out, it won't be from me. Now please, leave me alone."

"Thank you, Jade."

"Yeah, don't mention it." I sit on the edge of the bed, wringing my hands together, and then I fall out with laughter. "Paul is humping the sixty-year-old maid!" I exclaim, laughing so hard that I laugh myself to sleep.

Two hours later, Jon wakes me with a kiss on the forehead. "Hey there, sleepyhead."

"Hmm, hey you."

"Did you have a nice rest?"

"Yes. What time is it?"

"Almost two o'clock."

"Oh, I've been napping for a while."

"Gloria said that you've been locked in here for a few hours."

With the mentioning of Gloria's name, the scene of her riding Paul, like a rodeo buck, brought me to laughter again.

"What's so funny?" Jon asks.

"Nothing."

"Okay. . .you sure? I like a good joke too."

"If I told you, you probably wouldn't believe me."

"Try me."

"Well, I was taking a tour of the house and came across the only door on this floor that was closed. So, I opened it. . ."

"And?" Jon had a smile on his face, waiting for the punch line.

"And I saw Paul and Gloria knocking boots." The smile on Jon's face quickly disappears. "Ut oh. . ." Jon looks flushed.

"You saw what?"

"Well, maybe I saw wrong. . ."

"Goddamn him!"

"I'm sorry. I shouldn't have told you."

"It's not your fault. You aren't the one who copulates with every maid we hire. Damnit, I've told him time after time not to do that."

"He asked me not to tell Veronica."

"No, don't do that. That woman will tear this house upside down and Gloria's ass would be on fire for sure."

I watch Jon pace the floor. "Jon, it really isn't any of our business. So, let's not worry about it."

"No, but it is my business," he says, looking at me with a hint of embarrassment. "Gloria is not the first maid. We've had six maids within the past eight years and three of them turned up pregnant, by guess who?"

"Oh shit, for real?"

"I don't know why he keeps fucking the maids."

By now, I am laughing hysterically. "This shit is too funny."

"Yeah, well, their husbands didn't think so."

"Husbands?"

"Uh huh."

"Does Veronica know about his off springs?"

"Nope, and if she found out that Paul had impregnated three maids, all during the time she was here, she would do serious harm to him."

"Well, you need to have a talk with your brother. That shit is ridiculous."

"Been there, done that, and as you have witnessed, he's not a very good listener."

"Well ban his ass from coming here."

"Can't do that. This house is in his name too."

"What goes around comes around and when it comes back around, it's going to tear a big chunk outta his horny ass."

"He brought it on himself. Enough of Paul, how about dinner?"

"Yeah! Can we go into town?"

"Sure, I know a great spot. Let me call and make reservations."

"Good! Hey, how did you get in here? I had the door locked."

"Yes, and I do have a key. I own the place, remember?"

I chuckle. "Oh yeah."

Getting myself ready to head in to town with Jon for dinner, I decide to check my messages at home. My cell has been off all weekend.

"Hi Jade, it's me." My heart sinks when I hear Joy's voice. *"Look, I just wanted to apologize for the way I behaved in your office. It was uncalled for and it showed that I didn't trust you. I do trust you, Jade. I love you and I want you back. Can you ever find it in your heart to forgive me? Can we pick up where we left off? I miss you, Jade. You are the only one for me. I love you."* Beep.

I guess I do miss her and I could forgive her, but I can't go back to that. It has nothing to do with Jon either. I just can't be with anyone who causes me mental or physical harm because of his or her own insecurities.

During my relationship with Joy, her insecurities made it damn near impossible for me to be out in public with her. If she wasn't getting upset with me because someone was looking at me, she was getting pissed because I wore my skirts too short. To her, giving me oral pleasure was a way to make up and receive forgiveness. I can't go back to her. I won't go back to her. I'm not even going to return the call. But, knowing Joy, my not calling her back will piss her off. She will take that as a form of my disrespecting her and she will show up at my front door. "Humph, fuck her," I mumble to myself.

"What was that, baby?"

"Nothing," I smile. "Are you ready?"

"Yep, let's go."

Ron

I pull into the driveway, turn off the car and stare at the headlights shining on the badly chipped garage door. I pull a Newport from my shirt pocket, search my pant pockets for the lighter and light my cigarette. I take a long, deep drag, close my eyes and feel the nicotine wrap around my lungs. I recline my seat and exhale. I can't get China out of my mind.

"Fuck!" I yell, slamming my hand against the steering wheel.

Tears stream down my face. I peer at the house that I still have fifteen years worth of mortgage payments left. More than likely, she will want the house. I look over the manicured lawn that Ashley, when she was four years old, would jump and play in with the water sprinkler every time I watered the grass. I can still see China's image in the doorway, waving good-bye as I drove off to be with Marion. . .she didn't have a clue.

What have I done? The more I contemplate how Marion could've played it off and kept his mouth shut, the angrier I get. I toss the cigarette butt out of the window, smack the gear into reverse, tear out of the driveway and head to confront the bastard who ruined my life. At the stop sign, I listen to my conscience. *"Marion didn't ruin your life, you did."* I turn the car around and drive back home. Typically, I would enter the house through the garage door, but this time, I enter through the front. Standing in the foyer, the silence gives me a chill. The house is calm. I look around at everything in a house that says China—the living room and dining room furniture, the paint on the walls, even the wallpaper. I would give anything to hear Ashley calling André a pussy. What I would give to have everything back to the way it used to be—before Marion.

I walk into China's favorite room, the kitchen, and see the note attached to the refrigerator. A sudden feeling of emptiness and a wave of nausea rack my body. Hesitantly, I approach the refrigerator and remove the note from the magnet that is holding it in place.

Ron —

Our marriage is over. I can't fulfill the role of a man to satisfy you. I don't have a dick. Why would you go twenty years living a lie to me, yourself, our children? I put my life on hold and lived it the way that you wanted me to.

Ron, for three years, you've put my life in danger. Have you been tested for AIDS or any other STD? Why, Ron? I don't understand. Was I not enough for you? How long, before Marion, had you been interested in men? Was it something that I did to make you seek comfort from a man? When? Where? How?

I can't begin to figure out what I am going to tell the kids, or if I am going to tell them at all. Are you man enough to tell your children that you've chosen a different lifestyle over them?

I've taken the kids to Atlanta for a few weeks. When we return, I want your ass out of the house! Love doesn't live here anymore and neither do you.

China

P.S. Get tested. I know I will.

Jade

Returning from dinner, Jon and I stumble upon Veronica crying in the living room. "Ronnie, what's wrong?" Jon asks. She doesn't respond.

"Veronica, why are you crying, girlfriend?" Veronica looks up at me. Her eyes are cold and filled with scorn. "What happened, sweetie?"

She looks at Jon. "You knew, didn't you?"

"Knew what? Ronnie, what are you talking about?"

"You knew that Paul was fucking around on me!" Jon doesn't utter a word. Yes, he knew that Paul was screwing around and impregnating the maids and any pussy in his path. Jon stands there as she spews her anger toward Paul at him. "You bastard, you knew what he was doing and you did nothing about it. Why didn't you tell me? I've been loyal to you for ten years and in return, I get lies and pregnant maids!"

"How did you find out?" I ask.

She turns her venom toward me. "You know too? What the fuck? I must look like Boo Boo the Fool."

"Ronnie, believe me, I talked to Paul but it went through one ear and out the other."

"I can't believe this," she cries. "I can't believe this."

I take a seat beside her. "Veronica, how did you find out?"

"You know the bedroom across from your room?" I nod my head yes and glance at Jon. "Well, I was going to your room to see if you wanted to take in the beach since we hadn't spent much time together this weekend." She rolls her eyes at Jon. "Someone has had you quite occupied." She isn't holding any punches, not even with her boss. "Well, before I could knock on your door, I hear all this damn moaning and groaning. At first, I thought that maybe it was you and Jon, so I began to walk away, until I heard that bitch yell out my man's name." I look up at Jon. "I opened the door and," she turns to Jon, "your loyal maid, Gloria, with her old ass, was fucking Paul!"

"Ronnie, I am so sorry that you had to find out that way," Jon whispers.

"Uh huh, and you want to know what else I found out? Jon, you are going to be an uncle, for the, what third time?"

Jon is speechless. "Veronica. . ."

"No! Don't say shit to me. If you couldn't tell me before, then don't fucking tell me now!"

"Where is Paul?" I ask.

"Somewhere with his tail between his legs, the fucking dog."

I embrace her. "Ronnie, I am so sorry that you had to find out the way that you did, however, this isn't Jon's fault. You shouldn't take it out on him."

Veronica breaks my embrace, leans back and glares at me with a look of confusion. "He knew about it, didn't he?"

"Yes, he did but. . ."

"Then that makes him an accessory. Jade, you're my girl and all, but your man knew and he should've said something."

"I don't agree with that, Veronica. What goes on between you and Paul is between you and Paul. Jon has no control over a grown man. You're wrong for spewing your hatred at Jon. You need to go and beat Paul's ass and while you're at it, Gloria could stand a good ass whipping too."

"Wait. Let's back up for a minute." Jon takes a seat on the sofa across from us. "Ronnie, did you say that Gloria is pregnant?"

"Yes, that's what I said."

"She told you that she was pregnant?"

"Yes, and from what she tells me, this is not the first child of hers that your whorish ass brother as fathered."

Jon shakes his head in disbelief, knowing that everything that Veronica is saying is true. "Jon, I'm sorry. Jade is right. It's not your fault."

"No, it's not, but I could've done. . ."

"What's going on in here?" Paul asks, standing in the doorway of the living room, forcing a smile on his face. All eyes dart toward him. What a damn idiot. "Ronnie?"

"Paul, you have nothing to say to me."

"Baby, I think. . ."

"I'm not your damn baby! Do I look like anything that Gloria has popped out of her twat?"

"Ronnie, you and I need to talk."

"Say what you have got to say and leave me the hell alone."

"In private, please."

"Fuck you! You've done enough in private!"

"Fine. I love you Ronnie and I don't want to lose you."

Veronica stands to her feet and slowly approaches Paul.

"Ronnie, take it easy, girl," I whisper.

Veronica's five-foot-three-inch frame leans up to Paul's five-foot-nine masculinity and sniffs around his lips. "I can smell her. You love me. How dare you utter those words to me with her pussy on your breath," she snarls.

"I have an addiction. I need help, Ronnie."

"I don't want you anymore, Paul."

"But Ronnie. . ."

"I don't want you in my life anymore. You are no good for me, Paul." Veronica brushes against Paul and walks out of the living room.

"Um, I'll go with her and make sure she's okay." I leap from my seat and trot behind Veronica. "Hey, Ronnie, wait up." Veronica makes her way through the kitchen and out of the servants' door, jogging towards the beach. "Veronica," I yell. "Veronica, wait up." She comes to a halt, allowing me to catch up to her. "Girl, I can't run like I used to. You okay?" I pant, trying to catch my breath. I am so out of shape. Veronica stares out beyond the body of water that lies before us. "Hey, Ronnie, you okay?"

She faces me. "What do you think?" She turns her attention back to the white-ruffled waves crashing against the shore. "I love him so much." The salt air brushes Veronica's hair in her eyes.

"I know you do."

"I gave him all of me. Why would he do that? My God, the maid? That woman is old enough to be his mother," she cries.

I wrap my arm around her waist and pull her in to me. "You cry all you want. Everything will work out."

"What am I going to do without him?"

"You will do fine without him. You are a strong, beautiful sistah, who doesn't need a man to validate her. Do you hear me?" She cries in my neck. "Oh Ronnie, I don't have any answers to your questions," I console, stroking her hair. "I have asked those same questions. All I know is that God only gives us what he knows we can handle." I pull back, slightly breaking our embrace. "You are going to be just fine." I use my thumb to wipe away her tears. "Stop crying. You will be just fine. Paul will realize the goodness in you when you aren't around for him to take for granted."

Veronica gazes into my eyes. "Thank you, Jade."

"You're welcome," I smile. Veronica leans in and kisses me on the lips, catching me off guard. "Uh. . ."

"I'm sorry. I don't know where that came from."

"It's okay. I don't mind." She softly kisses me again. It doesn't feel sexual. It feels sisterly. "Jade?"

"Yeah?"

"Thank you for being the friend that I need."

"Girl, don't mention it." We take off our shoes, sit in the sand and run our toes through the cool, moist grains.

"I wish Paul could be more like Jon."

"I'm sure Jon has his flaws. They will surface eventually. They always do."

Jon

"How many times, Paul?" I pace the living room floor. "How many times are you going to fuck up?"

"Man, look. . ."

"No!" I yell. "You will listen to what I have to say." I walk over to the bar and pour myself a shot of Grey Goose. "Paul, you need help. I don't get it. You have a wonderful, faithful woman in Ronnie, you have more money than you can count, you are living the life and yet, you can't keep your dick in your pants. Not to mention, you are very careless with your dick, man. You don't use condoms when you are fucking these women. You are having these women bear your children. I don't get it. You are playing a dangerous game, bro."

"Jon, you don't understand."

"Okay." I take a seat on the sofa. "You have my full attention. Make me understand."

"It's like an addiction. I can't pass up sex."

"So, why can't you sex Ronnie night and day? Why the other women?"

"I don't know. It's a different flavor maybe, different moves. . .it's a different high."

"Yeah, that makes a whole lot of sense."

"Jon, I love the hell out of Ronnie. She is my world. . ."

"Then why the other women?"

"I told you, man, it's an addiction!" he yells. "Those other women mean nothing to me. They are just another piece of ass."

"Man, you are playing with fire."

"I can't help it. I need help!"

"Man, Gloria is pregnant?"

Paul takes a deep sigh and lowers his head. "Yeah, man."

"Damnit, Paul, she's old enough to be our mother!"

"She sure don't fuck like nobody's mother," he chuckles.

I peer at him with disgust. "You're on your own, Paul. I can't. . .I won't cover for you anymore."

"What? You just gone leave me hangin', Jon?"

"You're my brother and I love you, but this is something that you will have to work out on your own. I won't come to your rescue anymore."

"You're not perfect either, big brother," he says sarcastically.

"I've never claimed to be perfect. However, when I *know* that I have a good woman, I respect her and treat her the way she should be treated. I don't use some lame ass excuse to play around on her."

"I told you, I have an addiction!"

"Well, let's get you admitted somewhere because we don't want your *addiction* to effect Meadows & Meadows." I empty my glass and slam it on the end table. "I hope I am making myself clear."

"Yeah, loud and clear."

I turn to leave the living room when a thought crosses my mind. I face Paul. I glare into his eyes, trying to find the answer to my question. It's written all over his face. "If you are fucking around with anyone at the office," I take a deep sigh, "I suggest you end it."

"Naw, I don't fuck around at the office."

"Keep it that way."

Ron

I hold China's note between my fingers. As I stare into space, a tear streams down my cheek. Is this what Michael Baisden means by men cry in the dark? I've lost everything — my wife, my children, my life. I walk up the stairs to an empty bedroom. China's scent lingers, wafting through all of the memories of the good and bad times. I toss the note to the bed, fold my arms across my chest and look around at what used to be a room full of laughter and love. Sitting on the bed and resting my elbows on my thighs, I bury my face in the palm of my hands. "What have I done?" I reach for the phone and dial Free's number. "Is China there?" I ask through the sobs.

"Hello to you too, Ron."

"Hello, Maya."

"What can I do for you?"

"I need to speak with China."

"What for?"

"Huh?"

"Haven't you done enough?"

"Look Maya, this is none of your…"

"Don't even go there with me, niggah. This is my business. That's my sister you are fucking over." I couldn't say a word. She was right. I fucked over China like there was no tomorrow and she stuck around and took it. "Uh huh, can't say shit, can you?"

"Maya, is China there?"

"No, she's not here." Maya slams the phone down in my ear. I hit redial and fix my mind to chew Maya a new asshole for hanging up on me. "Look, I told you…"

"Maya, hang up the phone." Free's voice is calm. "I'll take it from here." Maya takes a deep sigh and reluctantly hangs up the phone. "Hello Ron, how are you?"

"Not so good, Free. Is China there?"

"No, she hasn't arrived yet."

"Well, I guess you've heard."

"Yes, I've heard."

"I'm sorry, I…"

"I am not the one you should be apologizing to."

I can't hold back. "I don't know what to do." I cry like a little bitch.

"Give China her space. She needs to think and sort things out. You hurt her, Ron. You hurt her bad. You see, a woman can deal with you having an affair with another woman, but another man isn't that easy to accept."

"But…"

"No, let me finish. It's bad enough that we have to deal with our men beating on us, chasing behind white women, porn videos and strip bars. But, when our men chase after men, we begin to ask ourselves what it is that we are doing wrong. No, that's not a very easy issue to deal with, Ron."

"I understand, Free. But, I don't know what I'd do without China."

"Well, dear brother-in-law, it looks as if you are going to have to figure that one out for yourself."

"When she gets there, could you have her call me?"

"No. I will tell her that you called. If she calls you, it will be her decision."

"I see."

"You take care, Ron."

"I guess you all hate me, huh?"

"Hate is a strong word. I don't like you though. You've caused my sister a lot of pain and I could never like you or forgive you for that, Ron. Our parents did not raise China to be a punching bag."

"Goodbye, Free."

"Take care, Ron."

I pull off my clothes, crawl under the covers, turn off the lamp and cry myself to sleep.

A few hours later, the doorbell rings. "Who the hell can that be?" Rubbing the crust from the corners of my eyes, I crawl out of bed. "Yeah, just a minute." I jog down the spiral staircase and slide my stocking feet across the foyer, to the front door.

"Hi baby, are you all right?"

I look over his head and around the outside. "What are you doing here? How did you know where I live?"

"I was worried about you."

I can't take my eyes off him. My bottom lip is stuck to the floor. "Well, um…"

"Aren't you going to ask me in? I know China isn't here."

"Uh, yeah, come on in." I step to the side for Marion to enter the foyer. "You shouldn't have come here."

"I figured you needed me."

"I was asleep."

"Ron, I can't stand you going through this alone."

"Marion, listen. I've got some things I need to work through and…" Marion slips his tongue down my throat and his hand inside my boxers, stroking my softness.

"Ron, it's going to be all right. Don't worry." Marion gets down on his knees and takes me inside his mouth. I moan with pleasure. I look down at Marion, knowing this is not appropriate at this time, but I rub his shiny baldhead anyway. With a mouthful of me, Marion gazes up into my eyes. I grab the back of his head and push myself deeper, nourishing him with me. "Hmm, that was good baby. You have any more for me?" I close the door, take Marion by the hand and lead him up the spiral staircase to my bedroom. I don't want to be alone tonight.

Jade

Posted for all to see:

HI JADE, I STOPPED BY TO SAY HELLO AND TO SEE WHY YOU HAVEN'T RETURNED MY CALLS. FROM THE LOOKS OF YOUR MAILBOX, YOU MUST BE OUT OF TOWN. PLEASE CALL ME WHEN YOU RETURN. WE NEED TO TALK. I STILL LOVE YOU, JOY.

After a wonderful weekend with Jon, the last thing I want is to come home to a big ass note from Joy plastered to my front door, for all of my neighbors to read at their leisure. No, I won't return any of her calls because I don't feel like the drama that is involved with dealing with her. "Damn, get a clue. If you call someone a million times and they don't return your call, it's because they don't want to talk to you!" I exclaim, slamming the door behind me. I drop my bags to the floor and head for the bathroom to take a long awaited pee. While relieving myself, I decide to run myself a relaxing bath. I reach over to the tub, turn the knobs and slip half way off the toilet seat, peeing on the floor. "Shit!" Before I could grab a few sheets of toilet paper to clean up the mess, the telephone rings. "Shit! Who the hell is that?" With the door ajar, I strain to listen for the caller to leave a message.

"*Jade, it's Maya. Girl, pick up the damn phone. Are you there? Okay, when you get this message, call me at Free's. We all are here. Free is having a cookout this weekend and we want you here! Call us!"* Beep.

I grab a glass of wine from the kitchen and yank the cordless phone from the wall to return Maya's call. "Hey, Sis, it's me."

"Hi Jade, how are you?"

"I am just peachy, how 'bout yourself?"

"Oh, I can't complain."

"Okay, so what's this message I get from Maya saying you're having a shindig this weekend?"

"Girl, Samuel wants me to meet all of his family and friends and…"

"Uh, Free, who is Samuel?"

"Didn't I tell you about Samuel?"

"No, you didn't tell me about Samuel," I mimic.

"Oh, well, that's my new boyfriend."

"Your new boyfriend?"

"What's your problem, Jade?"

"What do you mean?"

"Why does it shock you that I have a boyfriend? Maybe you should. . ."

"Aww hell, Free. Don't go there with me, damn. Besides, I am not with Joy anymore."

"Well that's good news. I am glad you came to your senses. I didn't like her no way."

"Why, because she was a woman and she was fucking your sister?"

"Jade, that is not necessary, and no, that is not why. I didn't like her because she was too possessive with you. She treated you as if you were her property. That time she came here with you for a visit, she was stuck right up under your tail. You couldn't pass gas without her being there to smell it. She didn't want to let you out of her sight. . ."

"I don't have to deal with that anymore. So, what's Maya doing there?"

"I'm not really sure. But, knowing Maya, she has probably gotten herself into some stuff and, as usual, she ran this way to avoid the consequences."

"Yeah, probably so. Okay, so what's China's excuse?"

"Well, to make a long story short, Ron had an affair. . ."

"What?"

"Uh huh, and. . ."

"Damn, I knew his ass was rotten to the core. If he ain't beatin' her ass, he's fucking around with some other woman?"

"Nope."

"Huh?"

"A man." There is complete silence. "Jade?" I can't respond. I feel like someone just hit me in my chest, knocking the wind from me. "Jade, you still there?" Free chuckles. "I can hear ya breathing."

"Poor China, she must be mortified."

"Yes, wouldn't you be?"

"Damn, Ron is fucking a man?"

"Uh huh, and why you so surprised? It ain't any different than you..."

"Shut the hell up, Free! We are talkin' 'bout China, not me."

"Uh huh. So, what happened between you and Joy?"

"Nothing."

"Why did y'all break up?"

"You were right, Free. Joy is too possessive and too controlling. I had had enough. She came into my office and tripped out on me. I had to beat her ass and send her on her way. I haven't spoken to her since." I take a deep sigh. "I am through with women."

"Hallelujah!"

"Well, you ain't heard nothing yet."

"Oh Lord, what? It can't be worse than Ron's extracurricular activity."

"I'll tell you this weekend."

"So you are coming?"

"Yep. I will have to take a late flight though."

"No problem. Call me back with your flight information."

"Okay. Well, I will talk to you later then."

"Okey dokey."

"Oh, by the way."

"What?"

"I got me a man." I hang up the phone before Free can respond. She is probably picking herself up off the floor.

When I arrive at the office the next morning, everyone is whispering. I just knew this shit was going to happen. All of my business is out for all to critique. Shit.

"Good Morning, Jade."

"Morning, Sherrell. How was your weekend?"

"Not as good as yours." Sherrell smiles as if she has just caught me in the act.

"Excuse me?"

"Nothing."

"Sherrell, my personal business is just that." I drop my briefcase to the floor, flop down in my chair and prop my feet up on my desk. Sherrell storms out of my office with a serious attitude, as if I give a damn. Only seconds after having exited, Sherrell buzzes in.

"Mr. Meadows is holding for you."

"Thank you." I show a little power by making sure Sherrell stays in her place. "Sherrell, close my office door, please."

It's obvious from her hesitation that my request threw her. "Uh, sure."

"Hello, sweetheart!" Sherrell rolls her eyes at me and closes the door. I guess she isn't too happy about having to get up from her desk just to close my door. Like I give a rat's ass.

"Hello, sweetness, how are you?"

"I am wonderful now that I hear your voice."

"It's good hearing your voice too. I missed you in my bed last night."

"I dreamt of you."

"Are you free for lunch?"

"Yep, dinner and breakfast too."

"Fine, I'll have Robert pick you up at twelve-thirty."

"I'll be waiting. Oh, and Jon?"

"Yes, baby."

"Thank you for a wonderful weekend."

"No problem. We can do it again this weekend if you'd like."

"I would love to, but," disappointment sets in my voice. I love my sisters, however, I'd rather be back in Montego Bay, having Jon clean the sand from his favorite nesting place. "I can't. I am going to Atlanta this weekend."

"On business?"

"Hardly. My sister, Free, lives in Atlanta and my sisters, China and Maya, are there. I guess you can call it an impromptu family reunion. It's been quite a while since we've all been together."

"When do you fly out?"

"Friday evening and thanks for reminding me, I need to make my flight reservations."

"Don't be silly. You'll fly there on *JonAir*."

"Huh? I couldn't ask you to do that."

"You didn't ask. I offered."

"Well, I am…speechless."

"Good, then I know that I am doing everything right."

"Well, um, would you like to join me? I am sure Free wouldn't mind."

"No, I couldn't intrude on your reunion with your sisters. I am sure you will be doing girly stuff all weekend."

"Hmm, do you have any plans for this weekend?"

"No. Probably hit the gym."

"Now you do. You are flying on *JonAir* with me and I won't take no for an answer. See you for lunch." I disconnect the call before he can object.

China

Maya is an annoying fly. She won't shoo.

"Maya, I don't want to talk about it."

"But China, talking about it is good therapy."

"And when in the hell did you receive your Masters in Psychology?"

"Funny. Listen, I just want to know where your head is."

"Attached to my damn shoulders. Now mind ya damn business!"

"China, calm down. We just want to help you," Free says, searching through the refrigerator for the mayonnaise. "We are your sisters and we love you. You know we've got your back."

"You keep asking me why my husband is fucking another man. Do I look like a crystal ball to you? How the hell do I know?"

"Well, that's some freaky shit, is all I'm saying. . ."

"Yeah? And you've done some freaky shit your damn self, Maya. You aren't perfect. I don't know why you're sitting here acting like your shit doesn't stink. What the hell are you doing here anyway?"

"Can't Maya come for a visit if she wants to?" Free slams the refrigerator door. "I'm out of mayo. . .wonder if I can use mustard."

"Sure, she can come for a visit. I just asked why all of a sudden." Maya turns away from me and stares at the wall. "Maya, 'sup, baby girl? What happened in Cali?"

"Nothing *happened* in Cali, China." Maya pushes herself arms length away from the table and glares at me, as if she's ready to give me the beat down of my life. "Why yo husband ass fucking another man?"

"All right now, Maya. I done told y'all I don't like that kinda language in my house!"

"It ain't a bad word, Free." Maya scrunches up her nose and pokes out her lips at the fruit flies flying around the rotten fruit bowl sitting in the middle of the table. "When you gone throw this rotten ass fruit away? What are you saving it for?"

"It's not rotten, it's ripe and who says it ain't a bad word? Can I use mustard to make potato salad?"

"Girl, fuck is an acronym and I ain't never heard of anyone making potato salad with just mustard," I chime in.

"I'll pass on the potato salad," Maya chuckles.

"A what?" Free looks at us in disbelief. "Okay, I've gotta hear this."

"Yep, China's right, for once."

"Go to hell, Maya!"

Maya rolls her eyes at me. "You will beat my ass there first!"

"Shut up, for God's sake!" Free yells.

Maya takes a deep sigh and plops her leg across the edge of the table. "It's an acronym and it means fornicating under the Consent of the King…F.U.C.K."

"Where did you hear that from? That's some of the dumbest mess I've ever heard." Free removes the pot of boiling potatoes from the stove and pours the hot water into the sink.

"Maya, that is not what it means," I say in disgust.

"China, you don't know everything. F.U.C.K. means..."

"I don't claim to know everything, but I do know that your meaning of F.U.C.K. is an urban legend. It means For Unlawful Carnal Knowledge."

"What? China, you just made that shit up," Maya teases. "You hate to be wrong!"

"Maya, your ignorance is showing," I snap.

"Both of you sound mighty ignorant to me," Free snaps.

"I believe it was in ancient England that if you wanted to have sex, you had to get permission from the King. Then a sign that reads FUCK is nailed to your door. Everyone in the damn village would know what you were doing."

Free and I fall out with laughter. "Maya, now that sounds like an urban legend to me," Free argues. "I don't care what it means, I don't like that word and I don't want to hear it in my house," Free chastises. "Now, I need mayo if I am going to make this potato salad. Let me see if I can catch Sam before he leaves."

"Aww, yes, the infamous Sam. I can't wait to meet him."

"Girl, he is fine too," Maya says, swatting the gnats away from the rotted fruit. "Drives a pretty red Jaguar and..."

"You've seen him, Maya? Oh wait, I forgot. You've practically moved in here."

"Hush up, China." Free dials Sam's home phone. "No answer."

"Call him on his celly," Maya says.

I glare at Maya. "How do you know he has a celly?"

"Huh?"

"Doesn't everyone have a cell phone these days?" Free says, scanning her wall of phone numbers. "I don't think I have his cell. . ."

"Yes, you do. It's in your bedroom, on your night stand," Maya says, picking up the bowl of rotted fruit and walking toward the trashcan.

"What are you doing going through my business, and where are you going with my fruit?"

"Free, this shit is rotten and I am throwing it in the damn trash. Hell, I will go to the store and get the mayo and pick you up some *fresh* fruit, okay?"

"Okay, thanks. Since you are going, let me give you a list."

"Aww shit, Free. I ain't trying to do no damn grocery shopping…"

"As long as you've been here, you need to do what she asks you to do and keep ya mouth shut."

"You know what, China? I am getting sick and tired of you. I ain't ya damn husband, so don't be taking that shit out on me!" Maya slams the empty bowl on to the kitchen table. "Free, what you need from the store?" she asks, her eyes are burning a hole through me. "China, I am sorry that your husband left you and went to a man, but…"

"That's enough!" Free scolds, placing her hands on her hips. "I have had enough! Maya, you have no right to stand there and talk to China like that."

"Well, she started it."

"I don't care who started it. We are sisters and we should not be talking to each other like we are thugs in the street. Yes, we all have issues, even Jade. None of us has the right to stand in judgment of anyone, not even me."

"Uh huh, tell her, Sis." I pull out a cigarette from the pack of Marlboro Lights that are sitting on the table. "Whose are these?"

Free reaches across the table and snatches the cigarette from my fingertips. "Since when did you start smoking, China?"

"I am grown, Free. I can do what the hell I want to do." I turn my attention to Maya. "Maya, before you head out, why don't you tell your big sisters what the hell happened in Cali that made you fly here so damn fast. Don't you have auditions to go to?"

"Fuck you, China. You get on my damn…"

"Well, well, well. I see things haven't changed in the Howard family."

"Jade! Girl, we didn't hear you come in!" I embrace my sister. "Girl, what are you doing here? I didn't know you were coming too."

"Free didn't tell you that I was coming?"

"Well, I thought it would be a nice surprise." Free pushes me to the side and embraces Jade around her waist. "It's good to see you, Jade."

Maya stares past Jade. "Maya! Hey, baby Sis!" Maya doesn't move. She slightly parts her lips. Jade walks toward Maya and whispers in her ear, "Will you please stop salivating over my man and give me a hug, bitch." Maya and Jade embrace. Maya's eyes are still on Jade's man. She's my sister, but I don't trust her as far as I can fart.

"Who did you bring with you, Jade?" Free asks, facing Jon. "You will have to excuse our manners. Some of us left them back in New York City. I'm Free, Jade's oldest sister."

"It's a pleasure to meet you, Free. I've heard a lot about you."

"Oh yes, sorry. Jon, these are my sisters, Free, China and Maya," she introduces, pointing at each one of us.

Free looks at Jade and smiles. Then, she takes a seat at the kitchen table and starts to jot down her list. "Maya, we need mayo and. . .can you think of anything else that we need?"

"I sure could use a drink," I chuckle.

"We've got that covered," says Jade.

"We can always count on you two liquor heads. . ."

"Kiss my ass, Free!" Jade snaps.

"Ouch!" Free falls out with laughter and embraces Jade. "Lord, I haven't heard that in such a long time. It's music to my ears. I am so glad we are all here together."

Jade gives Free a sisterly kiss on the cheek. "Free, is Sam here? I can't wait to meet him."

"Not yet. He should be on his way." Free tosses the grocery list at Maya, then reaches in her apron pocket and pulls out a twenty-dollar-bill. "I want my change."

"Uh huh, I need the keys to the car."

"Please. Allow Robert to drive you wherever you need to go," Jon offers.

"Who is Robert?" I ask.

"I don't ride nowhere with no strangers," Maya pouts. "He doesn't have gold teeth, does he? I have had my share of looking at men with a mouth full of gold teeth."

Jon chuckles, grabs Jade around her waist and kisses her on the neck. "Robert is my driver and no, he doesn't have gold teeth."

"Driver? Aww shit, you got some money?" Maya asks Jon, with wide eyes, looking like a deer caught in headlights.

"Mind your business and get to the store," Free snaps, smacking Maya on the behind.

"Okay, damn. I'll be back in a bit." Maya takes the twenty from Free, turns on her heels and grabs Jon by the arm. "Okay, let's go meet this Robert and head to the store."

Jon flashes Jade a smile and heads out with Maya. "She is such a damn flirt," I chuckle. "Okay, Free. Give us the. . ."

Free cuts her eyes at me. "Jade, your friend is very handsome. Where did you meet him?" Free cuts me off because she knows exactly where I am about to go.

"You didn't have to cut me off, heffa." I roll my eyes. "What do you need me to do?"

"Here." Free places a bag filled with ears of corn. "Shuck these for me."

"Ooh, Free. Girl, if you boil the corn with the shuck still on, it will be so sweet."

"Jade, is that some New York stuff, 'cause I have never seen anyone down here boil the corn without shucking it first."

"Free, get out the cotton fields. Lots of people boil the corn still in the shuck," I laugh.

"Well I don't, so get to shucking." Free faces Jade. "Okay, spill it. What happened to your girlfriend and where did you find that handsome fella?"

"Yes, do tell," I chime in. "And, after you tell your story," I look at Free. "I wanna know what happened in Cali."

"Huh? Cali? What happened in Cali?" asks Jade.

"Damnit, China, why don't you cut that mess out? Stop being so judgmental of Maya. You know she is weak. . ."

"What happened in Cali?" Jade persists.

"Well, I really don't know. I called Maya to see how she was doing and the next thing I know, I was booking her flight to Atlanta. She's been here for quite some time. . ."

"She's been here going on three weeks," I butt in.

"Three weeks? When is she going back?" Jade inquires.

"I don't think she is. When that girl landed, she had more bags than the other passengers. I think she is here to stay," Free chuckles.

Jade retrieves a cookie from the black and white speckled, cow-shaped ceramic cookie jar sitting on the counter top, against the floral printed tiles. "Wow, I wonder what happened."

"Tell her, Free."

"Tell her what?"

"Tell her about Jonah."

"Who is Jonah?" Jade inquiries.

I look Jade straight in her eyes. "Jonah is Maya's pimp."

"Maya's pimp!" Jade turns to Free. "What the fuck?"

"Yes, Maya's pimp. Your baby sister has been selling her ass to keep food on her table," I sarcastically say.

"Damn, but I thought she was doing well in California. It seemed like she had an audition every single day," Jade frowns. "My baby sister is a prostitute?"

"Yeah well, a lot of those auditions she couldn't make for the ass whippings and the late night tricks she had to turn."

"All right, China, why don't you give Maya a break?" Free angrily interjects.

"Because as much as I love my sister, I don't trust her as far as I can smell her."

"Damn, is it that deep, China?" Jade asks.

"Yes, and you better watch your man. She damn near pissed her drawers when he walked in here."

"China, you are talking silly," Free snaps angrily, turning to the oven and checking on the pineapple upside down cake.

"Free, you need to watch her 'round your man too," I snap back.

Free takes a seat at the table and begins to play with the napkin that she's been holding in her hand for the last hour. "Well, I don't think that Maya would back stab us like that."

"Uh huh, All right, don't say I didn't warn you."

"So, what's up with you, China?" Jade asks, changing the subject.

Free turns her attention to Jade. "Jade, I asked you a question a half hour ago. Do you mind answering it for me?"

"Sure, Free. What was your question?"

"What happened to Joy and where did you meet Jon?"

Jade takes a long deep sigh and rests her chin in the palms of her hands. "Well, it's a long story. . ."

"Ut oh, will I need a drink for this?" I ask.

"This is not the corner liquor store, China," Free chuckles.

"Not to worry, y'all. I am well stocked. Be right back." Jade leaves the kitchen. When she returns, she has three unfamiliar looking bottles in her arms. "Okay, here we are! See, told y'all I was well stocked!"

"Yes, we see. What is that?" Free asks.

"Shut up, Free. Ya sounding ignorant," I snap.

"How am I sounding ignorant? Because I don't know the name of whatever is in that bottle?" Free jumps up from her seat, leaves the kitchen and returns with three crystal wine glasses from her china closet. "Don't break up my glasses."

"It's Dom Perignon, and do you have a cork screw?" Jade asks, rifling through the utensil drawer.

"Naw. It doesn't have a twist off cap?"

Jade and I fall out with laughter. "Lord, Free, get your ass out the country!"

"It's okay, we can use a knife." Jade proceeds to pop the cork with a knife, which results in a few small pieces of the cork floating in the bottle. "Oh shit!"

"Girl, that's okay. It's still gone be good. Hurry up and pour me some," I say, excited as hell because the closest I've ever been to Dom Perignon is Mad Dog 20/20 and I doubt if you can even compare the two.

Free shakes her head in disgust. "China, you are such the lush."

"Go to hell, Free." I take my first sip of Dom Perignon and savor it. "Ooh, tingly. I can feel it in my nose." I take another sip. "Okay, Jade, fill us in."

"Well, to make a long story short, Joy and I got into a fight in my office. . ."

"At your job?" I ask.

"Yep and. . ."

"You whipped her tail, didn't you?" Free asks. "Embarrassing you on your job like that, humph."

"Yep and. . ."

"Girl, I knew them lesbians were like cats. Did she try to scratch your eyes out?" I ask.

"Yes and. . ."

The Dom Perignon made a beeline to my head. "Where that bitch at now? I say we go fuck her up!" I slam my glass on the table. "Where she at, Jade?"

"China, will you please be careful with my glasses?"

"Will y'all please let me get the story out before you form a lynch mob?"

"Okay, go ahead and finish. You tell it too slow," Free says, enjoying her drink as well. Free is not much of a drinker, so she'll be drunk in two minutes. "I've gotta finish cooking my food. The folks will be here tomorrow at noon."

"Anyway, as I was saying, Joy came to my office and we got into a fight. She tried to take advantage of me. . ."

"What you mean?" Free asks.

"What?"

"You said she tried to take advantage of you."

"Yes, and?"

"How did she do that?"

"She tried to rape me, Free."

I am working on my second glass of Dom Perignon. "How can a woman rape another woman? She ain't got a dick!" My words are slurring and my tongue feels swollen. I hold up my glass. "What is in this stuff, Jade?"

"China, slow down, will you? It's not water, it's alcohol," Free reprimands.

"Free, shut up. I know what the hell it is."

"China, you don't need a dick to take advantage of someone. The girl had her hands down my pants and was squeezing the hell out of my clit, to the point where it was very painful."

"Tsk, tsk, tsk. Damn shame. What you do next?" Free asks.

"I felt an ink pen beneath my butt. I reached for it and rammed that bitch in her face and then I had her ass thrown out!"

"Humph, women are something."

"Free, men aren't any different," I say. "I can count the number of black eyes that niggah gave me on both hands and one foot." I pour my third glass. Jade and Free give me silent stares. "What y'all lookin' at?"

"China, what's going on?" Jade asks.

"Nothing really. My husband decided he wanted to be with a man instead of me." Jade gasps, covering her mouth with the palm of her hand. "Yep, I had the same reaction, Sis."

"I don't get it. What makes a man want another man?" Free questions.

"I guess for the same reasons women turn to each other," I slur, shrugging my shoulders.

"Jade, why is that?"

"Free, I can't speak for all women, but I was fed up with men. I was tired of being used, abused and hurt by them. I met Joy and, well, she was more sensitive to my needs and my feelings. I fell in love with her as a person, not with the fact that she is a woman."

"Okay, so tell me this, Jade. How does pussy taste?" I quiz. Jade, with her nasty ass, spreads her legs apart and offers me to taste her. "You just nasty!"

"No," Jade laughs. "I just want to satisfy your curiosity."

Free joins in on the laughter, but I don't see shit funny. "Both of y'all just go to hell and fry!" I pick up the bottle of Dom Perignon—it's empty. "Jade, open up the other bottle."

"Whoa, China. You need to slow ya roll, Sis," Jade warns. "Don't drink yourself into a stupor because of a man. It ain't worth it."

"Why can't I just be drinking to enjoy myself with my sisters? Why it gotta be over a damn man?"

"Okay, let me get back to my cooking. Where is Maya with the mayo?"

"Uh huh and where is Jade's new man?" I glance at Jade. "Don't trust that tramp with ya man."

"Well, if she can take him, he wasn't mine to begin with."

"Whatever. . ."

"That's a good attitude to have, Jade. I don't fuss over any man. . ."

"Free, shut your lying ass up! You probably have fits every time you see Sam coming," she giggles.

"I don't have time for this foolishness," Free snaps.

"Oh, you don't have time when it's your business, huh?"

"I just have a lot of work to do for tomorrow."

"Leave Free alone. She finally has a man and I am happy for her," Jade smiles.

"Yeah, I'm happy for her too. If she would stop shittin' on herself, she may be able to keep him!"

Jade falls out with laughter. "China, what?"

"Yeah girl, she ain't told you?"

"Tell me what?"

"Hush up, China. I swear your mouth runs like an uncapped hydrant!"

"What is she talking about, Free?"

"Nothing. She is just talkin' to hear herself talk."

"No I ain't either. Jade, Free went on her first date with Sam and knew damn well she couldn't eat a whole lot of seafood. . ."

"Oh shit, you didn't, Free."

"Yes she did too. Shitted all over herself and that man's leather seats!" I slap the table with laughter. "And that ain't the half of it. Girl, her stomach was so messed up that Sam had to pull over for her to take a shit in one of those Port-O-Pottys. It was dark as shit and she couldn't find the toilet paper, so she wiped her ass with her underwear, flushed them down the toilet and *then* she called Earl, using her bra to wipe her mouth and that ended up down the toilet too! Some first date, huh?"

"That's not funny, China. I swear you make me sick! Where is that damn Maya with my mayonnaise?"

"Free, don't even worry about it. A similar situation happened with me and Jon."

"Oh damn, this shit runs in the family," I laugh.

"Well, let me tell y'all something. I have found the man of my dreams."

"Jade, I never knew you dreamt about men," I chuckle.

"China, kiss my ass, damnit!"

"Leave Jade alone, China. I told you that whatever it was that she was going through was just temporary. She done come back to her senses, so let's drop it."

"Uh huh, whatever. When he breaks her heart, she will end up back in Joy, Tracy or Wendy's arms," I snap, finishing off the third bottle of Dom. "Jade, you got any more of this stuff?"

"No, China. You have had enough. You are going to start embarrassing yourself and us too," Free scolds.

"Free, you are the oldest, but you aren't our mother. So, you need to go somewhere with that shit."

"Aww, go to hell, China!" Free slams the kitchen cabinet and storms out of the kitchen. "Where in the hell is that damn Maya with my fucking mayonnaise?" she yells.

Jade and I look at each other in disbelief. We can't believe that Free just said the 'F' word. "I guess I must've really pissed her off, huh?"

Jade nods her head. "Yes, I believe you did. I will be happy when we all can get together without all of the drama."

"Humph, all we have in our lives is drama."

"Speak for yourself. I am very happy and drama-free."

"Yeah well, my life has been nothing but drama and I guess it always will be."

Jade gently places her hand on top of mine. "Girl, you are going to be just fine."

"I sure hope so."

"You have to be for my two babies. Where are they anyway?"

"Most likely, somewhere getting into some mess."

"Well, let's help Free out here."

Jade and I searched Free's kitchen for a pot to use for boiling the corn. We decided to make things up to Free by finishing the cooking. Jade made her famous cornbread, pasta salad with pepperoni and baked beans. I chopped up the eggs, celery and onions to make the potato salad and seasoned the chicken and ribs to marinate overnight. We rinsed the dishes and placed them in the dishwasher, swept the floor and wiped down the counter tops. I took the Pineapple Upside Down Cake out of the oven and placed it on the cake rack to cool. For the first time in a long time, I actually felt needed by someone other than Ashley and André.

Where is Maya with the mayonnaise?

Maya

One block away from Free's house and I can't seem to maintain my control. They will just have to wait for the mayonnaise until I finish taking care of business. Hell, it's been weeks and I need some attention. Jon did say that Robert was at my disposal, and my pussy is twitching. Besides, I do not feel like going back just yet and dealing with all of China's fifty million questions.

"Excuse me, Robert."

"Yes, Ms. Howard."

"Could you please pull the car over?"

"Is everything all right?"

"Yes, everything is just fine. I am not ready to go back just yet."

"Will do, Ms. Howard." Robert looks in the rearview mirror and smiles. After pulling the car over, he turns off the engine and turns to face the back of the car where I was sitting. "Are you sure everything is all right?"

"Yes, I'm sure. Just need a break from my sisters." Robert nods his understanding. "So, are you married, Robert?"

"No, I'm very much single."

"And why is that?"

"Well, my job keeps me very busy. I do a lot of traveling with Mr. Meadows."

"What does Mr. Meadows do?"

"He is only one of the wealthiest black men in all of New York City. He and his brother run their own architectural firm."

"Oh, how nice. Hey, it's somewhat lonely back here. Would you mind sitting back here with me so we could talk?"

"Well, uhh. . .I'm really not supposed to do that."

"Who is going to know? I won't tell, will you?"

"Well, no, but. . ."

"Aww, come on back here."

Robert slides out of the driver's side, closes the door and hesitantly makes his way to the rear of the rented black Lincoln Continental. Before Robert opens the door, I take off my underwear and prop one leg up on the seat. I start to play with myself, causing the sweet smell of my pussy to drift throughout the car. It's a good thing I douched today. It's been a long while since I have seduced a man of my choosing. Robert stands in the door and peeps inside, afraid to enter. "What are you waiting for? Come on in." Robert looks like a virgin seeing pussy for the first time.

"I'm sorry, I can't do this. I could get into a lot of trouble."

"Listen, Jon said that you were at my disposal. Are you saying that he is a liar?"

"Oh, no. Not at all. I just don't feel that this is appropriate."

"Well, you know what? I don't give a fuck what you feel. Your boss is fucking my sister and if you don't get your ass in this car and close that damn door, I will tell him that you do not follow instructions." Robert hesitantly gets into the back of the car. "Take off your jacket and get comfy." Robert, with his eyes facing the front of the car, removes his jacket. "Robert, look at me." Reluctantly, Robert focuses his eyes with mine. "Are you a faggot?"

"I beg your pardon?"

"Are you a faggot? Are you scared of pussy?"

"No. I just can't do this."

"Okay, the pussy is here for you to take, so what's your problem? Do I have to tell you what to do?"

"I am sorry, but this is totally inappropriate."

"Okay, fine. You want to play hard to get." I lean over and unzip his pants. I pull out his softness, take him inside my mouth and think to myself, "This is going to be a task. I've never seen a penis the size of a stack of four quarters."

"Oh my God!" Robert exclaims. He gives in and grabs the back of my head, gyrating his hips and pushing himself further into my mouth. He doesn't moan, groan, nothing. He just stares off into space.

I remove him from my mouth and look into his face. "Pull your pants down." I instruct. He pulls them down around his knees. I straddle him and take him inside me. I can't feel a thing and he isn't moving at all. What a lame fuck. I definitely miscalled this one. I pull myself off him and plop down beside him. "What's the problem? You impotent or something?" He stares past me. "Look, you done got me all hot and bothered. You gone eat the pussy or do something, niggah. What you think this is?"

"I think it's time that we get back to the house."

"You will get back to the house when I tell you to get back to the house. Now, get on your knees, niggah, and eat some pussy."

"No."

"No? Did you tell me no? Well, we will just have to see what Jon thinks about you telling me no."

"I really don't care. I am not a slave and you are not my mistress. Mr. Meadows is my boss, not my master. Tell what you want."

"Yeah, just as I thought, you a fucking faggot."

"No, I am not, Ms. Howard." Robert pulls up his pants. "I just don't prefer whores." Robert opens the door, closes it and makes his way to the front of the car. He starts the engine and speeds off down the street to Free's house.

Once he pulls up front, I get out of the car and slam the door. I storm into the house and up the stairs toward the guestroom where I've made my new home. After taking the time to compose myself, I decide to leave the comforts of my room and join my sisters downstairs before they come looking for me. However, during that hour or so that I was alone in my room, I came to realize one thing. I am not the type of person who likes to be alone. I have feel needed by someone in order for me to feel good about myself. I have to find happiness within myself, somehow, someway.

Upon exiting my room and advancing toward the stairs, I come to an abrupt halt. My body jolts at the sight of my niece between my nephew's legs. "What the. . .? André, Ashley!" Before I realize it, I snatch Ashley by her hair and toss her out of the room and into the hallway. "China! Get up here right now!"

"Please, Aunt Maya. Please don't tell Mama. I won't do it again," Ashley cries.

"She made me do it, Aunt Maya," André pleads.

"What the hell is going on up here?" China asks, running up the stairs.

"China, you need to have a talk with your kids."

"What is going on?"

"Mama, she made me do it. I didn't wanna do it. She said she saw Aunt Maya do it with the man in the car up the street, and she wanted to play the game too!"

"André, what game? What the hell are you talking about?" When China gets no response from André, she turns to Ashley. "What is he talking about?"

"Mama, Aunt Maya was doing it. . ."

"Aunt Maya was doing what? Somebody tell me what is going on here!" China faces me. "Maya, what is going on?"

"China, I walked in on Ashley with her head between André's legs."

China turns red as a beet. Her eyes are as big as bowling balls and her nostrils are flaring up like a bull ready to charge after the Matador. "You lying ass bitch," she spews.

"What?"

"What do you have against my kids? You're the only slut in the family!"

"Okay, let's calm down. There must be a misunderstanding or something," Jade says from the bottom of the staircase.

"No. There's no misunderstanding. I told y'all I didn't trust this bitch. Sister my fucking ass! How dare you accuse my child of some sick ass shit?"

"But China, why would I make such an accusation if it weren't true?"

"Because you are a lying ass, selfish bitch. That's why! You are the whore in this family, Maya!"

Without warning, China takes a swing in my direction, landing her fist to the side of my head. "China!" Jade yells. China wraps her fingers around my throat and begins to bash my head against the wall. "China, stop it!" Jade tries to release China's grip from my throat.

"Get off of me. I am going to kill this bitch!"

I can't breathe and my lips are turning blue. China is trying to cut off my oxygen and bury me next to Mama and Daddy. Jade and Free aren't having any luck getting this psychotic nutcase off me, so Jon steps in. Why in the world did he do that? I guess flashbacks of Ron beating her ass floods her mind because she flicks off on Jon, ignoring me, thank God, and starts whipping on his ass like he stole something. Coming to her man's rescue, Jade jumps on China's ass. Free yells for them to stop and Sam is looking at us all like we've just lost the good sense God gave us.

"Stop!" Sam yells in a deep baritone authoritative voice. "Stop, right this minute!"

"Sam," Free cries, "these people are crazy!"

"Free, what is going on? Why are y'all fighting like animals?"

China pulls herself up from the floor. "That whore," she snarls, pointing at me, "accused my child of performing oral sex on her brother! What kind of sick, twisted shit is that to come from my sister?"

"It's true, Mama," Ashley whispers. "It's true."

"What?" China's beautiful almond complexion drains, favoring Casper the friendly ghost.

"I saw Aunt Maya doing it with the man who's driving that big black car that Aunt Jade and her friend rode in," Ashley admits with her head hung low, practically touching the floor.

"What? I don't believe. . ."

"I'm sorry, Mama. I didn't think I was doing anything wrong. I just wanted to do what Aunt Maya was doing."

Somberly, China begins to cry and falls to her knees. She lowers her face into the palms of her hands. "Oh my God, Ashley, you are twelve years old," she weeps. "You should know better. Didn't you know what Aunt Maya was doing? Do you realize that you have just molested your ten-year-old brother? Oh, dear God!" China looks into Ashley's innocent eyes, searching for answers. All of a sudden, rage overcomes her. "You knew what you were doing, didn't you? You knew what you were doing!" China lunges at Ashley, pounding her into the wall.

"Mama, please! I didn't know! Mama!"

"China, for God's sake, stop it!" Free grabs hold of China, trying to pry her hands from around Ashley's neck. "What are you doing?"

"Get off of me!" China screams, taking a step back from Ashley. "For years you have given me nothing but back talk and trouble! You are just like your damn daddy! You knew what you were doing! You sucked your ten-year-old brother's dick, you nasty little whore! You are just like your damn daddy and your Aunt Maya." China turns her back on Ashley. "Get that little tramp out of my sight." China walks into her bedroom to wallow in her tears, blaming it all on herself. "What have I done to deserve all of this, dear God?"

Glaring at her mother's back, Ashley cries out, "Mama!" China doesn't respond. Jade embraces Ashley, Free embraces Jade and I embrace everyone except China. "Everything is going to be all right, Ash. Your mother will come around. She just needs some time. She's been through a lot," Free explains.

"It's all my fault," Ashley cries.

"No. It's not your fault, baby." I stroke her hair. "Auntie Maya should have been a little more discrete."

"Yes, you should have," Jade snaps. "The driver, Maya? I don't believe this. I am so ashamed of this family." Jade turns her back on me and storms down the stairs. "This family is going to hell in a hand basket!" Jade storms out of the door and down the street, with Jon, holding his left cheek from China's powerful blows, in tow.

Free

Sam suggests that we take a ride to get away from the chaos that is taking place in my own home, chaos that I have absolutely no control over.

"Sam, I just don't understand." I recline the seat and enjoy the breeze coming through the moon roof of Sam's Jaguar. I've always loved Jaguars.

"You aren't supposed to understand, babe."

"What do you mean?"

"Life is full of complications and not everything will make sense, nor are you suppose to figure everything out."

"That makes no sense to me. I mean, this is ridiculous. I swear, those three sisters of mine will make me lose my religion for sure. I just don't know what to do."

"Let them live their own lives."

"That's what I've been doing and look at how they've turned out. Jade turned to women. China is with a man who mentally and physically abuses her, not to mention he was caught in an affair with a man. . ."

"A man?"

"Yes. I didn't tell you because I just didn't want all of that mess to interfere with what we are trying to build."

"Nothing will interfere with us because we won't let it. Hell, I won't let it."

"I sense that something isn't right with Maya. How could she be away from her life in California for three weeks? She's not being totally upfront with me at all."

"Listen baby, you've got to let them work out their own problems. They are all grown women."

"Ashley performing oral sex on her brother? What kinda mess is that? I swear, I just don't believe she picked that up from Maya. Something else has been going on in that house. Something just doesn't smell right to me."

"Free, let them be. Let them take care of their own mess."

"Sam, before my mama died, I promised her that, as the oldest, I would watch over my sisters, that I would always be in my sisters' corners, no matter what. I am going to keep my word to Mama. Besides, I'm the only sane one, so I have the obligation to keep things in order."

"Free, you can't be mother to three adult women. You have to let them live their lives and you live yours."

"Yeah, I know that you're right. But, you saw for yourself, they are so mixed up." Sam pulls off the road and into King National Park. "Baby, what are we doing here? The sign reads, "closed after dark."

"Shh. It's okay. I just want you to chill before we head back."

"Yeah, we will be chilling in a jail cell if we hang around here."

"Woman, don't you ever take chances?"

"No, what for?"

"For the excitement. . ."

"Please, I have enough excitement in my life, or did you forget about what just took place in my house?"

"Aw come on, Free, be daring for once."

"I'm daring. . ."

"Good, prove it." Sam reaches for the remote control attached to his key chain and pops the trunk. "Come on."

"What are you doing? Where are we going? It's dark as heck out there, Sam."

"Come on, baby."

Reluctantly, I climb out of the passenger seat and into the darkness. "Sam, if you get my behind arrested, I will. . ."

"You will what?"

"I will let that mean ass China loose on you," I chuckle.

"Ha! Hush now and come." Sam takes me by the hand and leads me to the rear of the car. He pulls out an army-green wool blanket from the trunk of the car and spreads it out on the grass. "Have a seat, baby."

"Why Samuel Meeks, what do you have planned?"

"Just a quiet moment between me and my woman. Is that all right with you?"

"Looks like it's going to have to be, huh?" I take a seat on the blanket and gaze up at Sam. "Aren't you going to join me?"

"Yes. Are you chilly?"

"Just a little."

Sam retrieves another blanket from the trunk, takes a seat beside me and with his arms around my waist, wraps us in the blanket. "How does this feel?"

"Nice." I smile and feel myself blushing between my legs. "Sam, is it safe out. . ."

Sam presses his index and forefinger against my lips. "Woman, do you ever shut up?" He kisses me on my cheek. "I love being with you, Free."

"I love being with you too."

Sam kisses me on my neck. "I love the way you smell, Free."

"Likewise." I feel a moisture bubble between my legs. "Ooh, look at the stars. They are out in droves tonight."

Sam kisses my ear. "I love your name. . .Free, Free, Free. . ."

"Sam, you are a fool." Sam presses his lips against mine. His kiss is warm and soothing. His hand wanders under my skirt and over my thighs, to the opening of my crotch. "Sam. . ."

"Shh," he whispers, lying me backward onto the blanket. "Ooh baby, you are really wet. You are coming through your drawers." I grab his hand. "It's okay, baby. Just relax." He kisses me again. "I want you to forget about all that bullshit that's going on at your place." He strokes my lips with his tongue. "I want you to close your eyes and let me love you. Let me take you to a place you've never been."

"Okay," I whisper. "Do you have a condom, Sam?"

"No baby, I don't have any. I'm clean. Are you?"

"Well, yes. . ."

"Then we are fine."

"No, we aren't fine. I am not having sex with you unless we use a condom."

"Baby, you are spoiling the moment."

"Sam, I mean it."

"Okay, okay. I won't penetrate, okay?"

"Sam, I am serious. . ."

"I won't stick my dick in you, all right, Free? Can we please just enjoy being in each other's company?"

"Fine, Sam, but there's no need for you to get nasty."

Sam pulls himself off me and plops down beside me like a spoiled brat. "Baby, I'm not getting nasty and if I appear nasty,

I am sorry, okay? I just want you to trust me and know that I would not put you or myself in jeopardy."

"Okay, I'm sorry, Sam." I tug at his collar. "Come on down here and show me what 'cha working with. . .meoooooow."

"Aww sookie, sookie now." Sam rolls on top of me and gently strokes my breasts. "These are so beautiful."

Sam never fails to compliment me on everything from the top of my head down to the crust between my toes. I guess I should be thankful. I have a man who makes me feel like the woman I truly am. "Sam, what are you doing?"

"Shh."

"No, Sam! I said no penetration."

"Oh shit, baby!"

"Sam, you are too big. Please, take it easy!"

"I will, baby, I will," he pants. The gate is open and he's off. "Baby, open your legs and wrap them around my waist, baby. It will go in easier." I oblige. "Oooooh damn, you got some good ass pussy!" I'm looking at him like he has lost his mind. "Yeaaaaaaaaaaaaaaah! Whose pussy is it? Whose pussy it?"

"Huh?"

"Is this my pussy?"

"No, it's my pussy."

"I don't want another motherfucker in my pussy!"

"Sam, you need to slow down!"

Sam grabs my leg and bends my knee back to touch my ear. "Oh shit!" I yell. "That hurts!" Sam slows his roll and slightly eases out, leaving the tip of his penis inside. He adjusts himself, slightly raises his hips and strokes the roof of my vagina. "Ooh, what are you doing?" He smiles down at me. "Sam, what is that? What are you. . ."

"I found that motherfucker, huh?"

"What, motherfucker? What are you talking about?"

"Baby, you fucking up my concentration. Please, be quite."

"But. . ."

"Naw baby, all I wanna hear you say is that this pussy belongs to me."

"Uh well…ooh shit…damn that feels good!" I raise my hips. I feel like I have to pee. "Sam, stop!"

"No."

"I've gotta pee!"

"Oh, that motherfucker ready to pop," he announces, stroking me with hard thrusts. "Yeah, baby. Give me that other leg, baby." He grabs my other leg and bends it back to my ear. My behind rises. His strokes are deeper. "Yeah, yeah, yeah. . .uh huh, my motherfuckin' pussy! Whose pussy is it?" He is stroking me so hard I can hardly breathe. I can't even answer his question. "I. . .said. . .," he yells with a hard thrust. "Whose pussy. . .," he growls with another hard thrust. "Is. . .it?" He groans through clenched teeth. "Aw shit. Yeah, yeah. . .bitch, work that pussy for me." With one last power thrust, Sam collapses his weight on me.

"Are you done?" I ask.

"Whoooohoo, you got some good shit, baby," he pants.

I give him an open-hand slap to his face. "Make that the last time you call me a bitch, Samuel!"

"Damn, baby. . .I didn't call you a bitch."

"Yes, you did!"

"Well, it must've been in the heat of the moment. I guess I got carried away."

"The next time you call me a bitch that will be the last time you see me." I push him off me. "I'm ready to go." I stand to my feet and adjust my clothing. "You call this intimate?"

"Yes, I do."

"Humph, I feel like I've just been raped." I get in the car and slam the door. "Take me home!" I yell.

Sam packs up the trunk and slides into the car. "Free, you feel like I raped you?"

"Yes, I do." I have serious attitude and am not feeling him right now. "Yes, you raped me!"

Sam places both hands on the steering wheel and stares out of the window. "Raped you," he whispers. "Baby, I love you. . ." His voice trails off into tears. "I don't. . ."

Now I feel like shit. "Sam, you didn't rape me. . ."

"How could you come out of your mouth with something like that?"

I place my hand over his. "Baby, you were too rough with me. I haven't been with a man in years and, well, I don't like it rough. I like it tender and loving." I palm his face and turn his glare toward me. "Samuel Meeks, you are the man for me. The times that we've made love have been wonderful. This is a side of you that I've never seen before and I don't like it."

"I am so sorry. I guess I wanted you that bad. . ."

"Sam, I love you too." I kiss him on the lips. "Let's go home, baby. It's okay."

Sam and I ride in silence. Half of me don't like that forceful sex stuff, but the other half of me loves having Sam take me the way that he did. Maybe if it hadn't been out in public. Maybe had it be in privacy, I would've been more receptive. I don't know, I guess my sisters are right, I am a prude.

"Sam?"

"Yes, baby."

"May I. . ."

"What?"

"Umm, well. . .err, umm. . ."

"What's wrong, Free?"

"I don't know how to say this."

"Just say it."

I take a deep sigh. "Unzip your pants."

"For what?"

"Just do it before I lose my nerve."

Sam quickly unzips his pants. "Now what?"

"You leave that to me." I lean over, pull out his penis and begin stroking his shaft. By the time we got home, Sam had released himself twice. Am I supposed to swallow that stuff?

Jade and Jon are cuddling on the living room sofa, drinking that Dom Petey stuff. I've never been a drinker and I guess I never will. Looks like Jade caught herself a big fish and he seems to be a nice person. He's very attentive to her needs and I like that, just like Daddy was toward Mama.

Daddy was so attentive toward Mama. She never had to worry about pumping her own gas, changing the oil in her car or doing anything other than cleaning the house and taking care of us. She never worked a day in her life. Although taking care of four girls was a job in itself. I can remember when Mama used to line us up, according to hair texture, and comb our hair every morning. Jade was always last because her hair was like a brillo pad and always took the longest. Sometimes, I would be so sleepy that she would comb my hair with my head in her lap. Since Mama never worked, she ran the household while Daddy worked two jobs to keep food on the table and clothes on our backs. I remember the time Daddy was been laid off his jobs and one night, we were so hungry that Mama took us to a cornfield and had us pick corn for our dinner. We were stealing, but never caught, and we did this on a regular. We would steal potatoes from the neighbor's potato fields and have potato pie, fried potatoes, stewed potatoes, any way Mama could cook a potato we had it. I wish Mama were here to straighten out her girls.

"Hey, Sis, y'all have a nice drive?" Jade asks, wiping the sleep from her eyes. Jon is barely awake.

"Yes. The night air was exactly what I needed." I try to refrain from blushing. If Jade knew that I had just finished screwing Sam in the middle of a big field, she would never let me live it down. "Where is everyone, sleep?"

Jade shook her head. "Naw, Maya went to some club and China and the kids went to a movie."

I take a deep sigh. "Jade, I just don't know. . ."

"Jon, how about a drink?" Sam suggests.

"Sure. I've got plenty of Dom Peri. . ."

"Naw, my man, that stuff don't put no hair on yo' chest." Sam waves his hand for Jon to follow him. "Let me school yo' ass on how and what to drink." Jon and Sam leave the living room in laughter. "Besides, man, I don't drink juice I can't pronounce!"

Jade smiles as Jon leaves the room. "Girl, you look like you've got love in your eyes."

"Who me?" Jade grabs the pillow and cuddles it closely to her chest, inhaling the faint traces of Jon's scent. "You think so?"

"Yes, I think so. . ."

"Jade, you look like a pig wallowing in slop, with that big ass grin on your face," China says, coming through the front door with the kids on her heels. "Go upstairs and go to bed," she instructs Ashley and André.

"Yeah well, I do like him very much."

"Why? Is it the bulge in his pockets or the bulge in his crotch?" China fills the room with laughter. "Girl, he is fine though. But tell us, Jade. Can he fuck?"

"China!" I exclaim.

"What?"

"Mind your business, that's what. What kind of question is that to ask someone?"

"A question that I want an answer to," China laughs. "Jade, is the man good in bed or what? Your ass went from pussy to dick all within the same breath. Help a sistah out in understanding. . ."

"China, you are just too much into other folks' business. You need to mind your own business and maybe your twelve-year-old daughter, who should definitely know better, wouldn't be giving head to her ten-year-old brother. . ." I gasp at my own words. I extend my hand toward China. "I'm sorry, China. I was totally out of line."

"No, no, it's all right." China heads for the stairs. "That's quite all right, Free. Me, André and the little whore will be out of your fucking house in fifteen minutes." China runs up the stairs with tear-filled eyes.

I am stunned at the words that I have spoken. "Dear God." I take a seat beside Jade on the sofa and grab the pillow that was lying beside me. "What have I just done?"

"You spoke the truth." Jade scoots herself closer to me, resting her arm across the back of my neck, with her hand draped over my shoulder. "Free, you didn't say anything that wasn't on all of our minds, as well as China's."

"No, Jade. I was out of line. China already has so much to deal with and now, I open my mouth and give her more to deal with."

"Whatever China is dealing with, you have nothing to do with it and there is absolutely nothing that anyone can do to make it worse."

"I'm really happy for you, Jade. I am glad that you found someone to love."

"Thanks, Free. I knew you, more than anyone else, would be excited about me being with Jon."

"Yeah well, I was getting worried about you for a minute."

"Uh huh, I know, and besides, you weren't going to let me rest until I stopped dating women."

"Jade, can I ask you a question?"

"Sure you can, sweetie."

"What's it like eating…um…you know?"

"Well, it's like eating chicken…"

"Eating chicken? You mean it taste like chicken?"

"Haha! No, it tastes like pussy, and if a sistah doesn't ash her ass, it could taste like fish!" Jade embraces me as she laughs in my ear. "I love you, Free and so does China and Maya."

"I love you too."

"Good. Now, let's go upstairs and straighten out China, shall we?"

"After you," I smile.

As we make our way up the stairs, China meets us at the top landing. "Free, I just want to tell you that…"

I grab China, embrace her and refuse to let her go. "China, I am so sorry. I was out of line and I hope that you can find it in your heart to forgive me."

China's heart softens. "It's okay, Free. You were right." China cries in my arms. "I don't know what to do. Everything in my life is turning upside down. My husband is fucking a man and my daughter has committed incest with her brother!" China's knees begin to buckle. "Free, what did I do to deserve this?"

Ashley slowly and quietly closes the door. She turns her back and leans against the door, with the palms of her hands cupping her backside. She stares into space with disbelief and mumbles, "My daddy's a faggot?" She slides down to the floor, stretches her legs out in front of her and silently beats the back of her head against the door. "My daddy is a faggot," she whispers. She begins to beat her fists against the floor. "My daddy is a faggot." The banging becomes louder. "My daddy is a fucking faggot!" She ceases her head banging as impure thoughts of her father infuriate her. She leaps to her feet, grabs the brass door knob and flings the door open, allowing the doorknob to become a temporary fixture with the freshly painted periwinkle-colored wall. "Good, the pity party ended," she spews. She dashes out of her room, across the narrow hallway, and with her right foot, kicks open the bedroom door to André's room. Standing in the doorway, she gawks at André with disgust. Slowly, she walks toward him and leans in close to his face. André scrunches up his nose. He can smell the popcorn and nacho cheese sauce on her breath from their outing to the movies. "Your daddy is a faggy and you will be one too," she spews, taking her hatred out on him. She quickly turns and heads for the tiny hallway. She darts down the stairs and into the living room where her mother and two aunts are talking. "My father is a faggot and it's all your fault!"

Sitting before her daughter and unable to speak, China's mouth is wide open and becoming dry from deeply inhaling the dry heat. Free has the heat is pumping. She takes a dry swallow and looks into the eyes that once belonged to her innocent twelve-year-old daughter, but now to a stranger. "Ash, I am so sorry. How did you. . ."

"I heard you and your sisters talking about Daddy. You said that Daddy was fucking another man!" Ashley yells to the top of her lungs, causing Jon and Sam to make a hasty exit from the kitchen into the living room. "Isn't that what you said?"

"Yes, that is what I said. I shouldn't have. . ."

"It's all your fault that Daddy is fucking men!"

"Ashley, watch your mouth! I will not have that kind of talk in my house!" I stand to my feet, ready to smack this grown ass child into next week.

Ashley doesn't take her eyes off her mother. "It's all your fault that I don't have Daddy anymore. You wouldn't open your legs and now he is fucking a man in the ass!"

In a split second, Jade lunges at Ashley, landing an open-hand smack to her face. Ashley stumbles backward and regains her balance by grabbing hold of the banister. "Who in the hell do you think you are? Don't you know I will beat the black off your ass? You have lost your fucking mind up in here!" Jade hollers. Ashley feels a second open-hand slap land across her left cheek. "Get out of my sight. I will deal with you later." Ashley doesn't shed one tear. She rolls her eyes at Jade, snaps her neck and turns her back. She slowly walks toward the stairs and glances back at Jade. "Um, Ashley, let me make something very clear to you. If you so much as roll your eyes one more time, you will be picking them up off the floor! I am not a child and you don't play with me, because I will beat your ass!" Ashley darts up the stairs to her room and slams the door. I cringe. "What's wrong with you, Free?" Jade asks.

"That little bitch is going to tear up my damn house!" The room fills with laughter. "That shit ain't funny. I just replaced those damn doors and painted this whole damn house and now she is tearing up my shit!"

Jade is laughing so hard, she has to sit down. "Free, do you hear yourself?"

"What?"

"Free, Lord have mercy. Thank you! This is exactly what I need," China laughs.

"What are y'all talking about? As much as you heathens cuss, none of you have any room to talk."

"Girl, do you hear the words that are coming out of your mouth? You are cussing like a damn sailor!" Jade exclaims.

"I ain't saying anything that you heathens haven't said since you've been here. Shit this, fuck that, go to hell, kiss my ass and whatever else rolls off your tongues," I snap.

"It's all right, baby," Sam laughs. "You go 'head and cuss all you want to. I like my woman feisty."

"I think a few bottles of Dom Perignon are in order!" Jon exclaims.

"Yes!" Jade and China sing in unison.

"Oh hell naw. You got stock in that shit or something?" Sam asks, laughing.

"All of y'all are a bunch of fucking lushes!" I laugh. I have to admit, all of this cussing makes me feel liberated. I don't know why, it just does.

"Oh no, Free. Please, no more cussing. It doesn't sound right coming from you." Jade's laughter is uncontrollable, with tears streaming down her cheeks and dripping onto my new carpet.

"Kiss my ass, Jade. Who want some fucking sweet potato fucking pie?" I laugh, sashaying into the kitchen with my sisters, my man and my hope-to-be brother-in-law on my heels, like a litter of puppies.

Maya

Leaning on the bar at the X'tacy Night Club in downtown Atlanta, I feel a swipe across my behind. I turn to face my offender, a six-foot-four-inch lanky bastard. "Excuse me, do you have a problem?" I yell over the loud house music.

He takes a step backward and smiles, looking me up and down, rubbing his tongue over his pearly whites and one gold tooth sitting in the front of his mouth that appears to be tarnished. "Nope, no problem. Saw a nice, round ass and wanted to know what it felt like."

"Suppose I let you feel my foot enlarged in your musty nuts?"

"Bitch, have a Coke and a smile and be glad somebody wanna touch your skank ass."

"I got your bitch, motherfucker. Don't put your damn hands on me."

"Yeah, whatever, you stank hoe."

I watch that bamma walk away from me, making sure he is out of my presence before I turn my back on his ass.

"Do you need some help?" the bartender asks.

"No, I'm fine. I don't appreciate being disrespected."

"What 'cha drinkin'?"

I bat my eyes. "One hell of an Orgasm, please."

"Sure. Coming up," he chuckles.

While preparing the drink, the bartender doesn't take his eyes off me. Leaning on the bar, I raise myself up on the tips of my toes to get a better look. He stands about six feet tall, two hundred and fifty solid muscle mass and big ass feet. I am a sucker for a flavor savor, baldhead and a beautiful smile. Just looking at him is making me wet. "Here ya go, beautiful."

"Thanks. How much?"

"It's on me."

"Really? Thank you so much. That is so sweet of you."

"Don't mention it."

"You must allow me to return the favor," I say, tossing him a flirtatious wink and a smile.

"It's just a drink. You don't have to pay me back."

"Oh, but I want to," I smile, licking my lips.

"Oh, I see," he says, leaning on the bar. "What do you have in mind?"

I part my lips with my tongue and moisten my bottom lip. "My name is Maya, and you are?"

"Hello, Maya. Nice to meet you. I'm Daryl," he winks. "So, Maya, you don't look like a regular."

"Good observation. I'm here from California, visiting my sister."

"You know a beautiful woman, like yourself, shouldn't be coming to a club alone."

"I can take care of myself."

"You never know who you are going to bump into," he says, using a white, soiled towel to wipe down the bar. "Everyone you meet doesn't always have the best intentions."

"Well, like I said, I can take care of myself. Thank you very much."

"Yeah, so I see. So, Maya, are you single, married, divorced or widowed?"

"I'm available."

"So, you're married, huh?"

"Do you see a ring on my finger?"

"No, but most married women that I've come across are always *available*."

"Well, I am happily single. What about you?"

"I fly solo."

"What time do you get off?"

"In a few hours, when the club closes. But, I do have a break coming up shortly."

"How long is your break?"

"Thirty minutes."

"And when will that be?"

Daryl looks at his Mickey Mouse watch. "In exactly ten minutes."

"I'll tell you what. I will run to the restroom and meet you back here in ten minutes. Is that cool?"

"Sure. I'll look forward to it."

I down the rest of my Orgasm. "See you in a bit."

I make my way through the crowd to find the restroom. What is with the gold teeth? I wish these brothas would stop grinning up in my face, showing me every gold tooth and cavity they possess. So far, Daryl is the only man that I've come across that doesn't have a mouth full of fake gold. He seems very decent too. He just may be worth my time.

A line, as long as the China Wall, is waiting to take a piss. After standing in line for five minutes, I excuse myself past the line and into the restroom. "Um, 'cuse me. But, where you goin'?" asks the Fly Girl reject.

"I am going into the ladies room," I snap, not looking in her direction.

"Well, the line starts back dere."

I turn to face her. She looks like Chris Rock in drag. "Look, I don't have to pee. I just want to powder my nose."

"Oh, a'ight den. You can go 'head." Damn, she has a mouth full of gold too.

"Well, gee, thank you very much." Amongst the snickering and the 'she think she cute' whispers, I make my way into the restroom.

"It smells like piss in here," I mumble under my breath. It's a damn shame that the men's room is probably cleaner than the ladies room—toilet paper soaking in piss on the floor, water all over the countertop, overflowing trashcans, people taking dumps and not flushing the toilet, or bloody Tampax or sanitary napkins clogging up the toilet? Just trifling. Don't make any damn sense for women to be so nasty. I can't hold my breath any longer, so I take one last glimpse in the mirror and get the hell outta dodge. Besides, I don't want that smelly shit to get in my clothes.

A few minutes later, I am leaning against the bar. "Hey, Daryl. You ready?"

"Yes, and you are still beautiful."

"You know exactly what to say, don't you?"

"I only speak the truth. Let's go somewhere quiet so we can talk."

Daryl takes me by the hand and leads me to a room in the rear of the club that houses a bed, sofa and a dressing table. "Wow, do all clubs have beds in the back?" I ask.

"I don't know, but this is the only quiet place in the Club. If it makes you feel uncomfortable, we could step outside."

"No, this is fine. What's with the bed?"

"This is the changing room for the female and male dancers, and it's also a place where we can come and rest our eyes for a half hour."

I don't notice the bottle of wine that Daryl has hidden behind his back, until he pulls out the corkscrew to pop the cork. "Yummy," I say as he pours the wine. Daryl hands me a glass and takes a seat on the sofa. I take a seat on the bed positioned across from the sofa. After ten minutes of chit chat, I feel a tingle between my legs. I haven't had any decent dick since my last trick, and I am really craving the touch of a man. The wine has taken control of my good senses. I kick off my shoes and kneel on the bed. Forming a bridge with my body, I stretch from the bed to the sofa and into Daryl's lap. "Let me see what you have," I whisper. Daryl obliges me and unzips his pants, allowing his one-eyed tiger to peep through the opening. With my weight on the palms of my hands, I lean in close and brush the one-eyed tiger with my lips, letting my tongue stroke the opening of the eye. The flinching of Daryl's body tells me that I have found his weakness. I part my lips and begin to please him.

"Damn, baby, you suck a mean dick." His pulsating veins warn me of his potential release. Since I don't know him from Adam, I remove him from my mouth. My arms weaken, so I make myself comfortable by straddling him. "Your mouth felt good," he moans, stroking my hair.

"I'm glad you liked it."

"You gone let me stick it?"

"You gone lick it?"

"I don't eat pussy I don't know anything about."

"Oh, but you will stick pussy you don't know nothing about? Talk about contradiction."

"Look, I just don't eat pussy, a'ight?"

"That's cool, but if you can't lick it, you can't stick it."

"So, do you always suck the dicks of men you don't know?"

"Well, I did check out ya dick and you ain't got no sores."

His face distorts. "You can't be teasing a brotha like that. I want me some pussy!"

He stands to his feet and I quickly wrap my legs around his waist. "Damn, you almost dropped me. What's up?" He tosses me on the bed, drops his pants and falls on top of me. "What are you doing? Get off of me!" Daryl reaches between my legs and rips my underwear from me. "You are hurting me!"

"Shut up!"

"Fucker, you better get the fuck up off of me!"

Daryl shoves my torn underwear inside my mouth. "Shut up, whore. This is what you want." I slap him across the face, trying to fight him off me. With one hand, he grabs both my wrists and pins me down to the bed. My mind is going one hundred miles per minute and flashbacks of Jonah's attempts at raping me flood my mind. With his other hand, Daryl grabs me by my neck. "If you don't keep still, I will cut your fucking throat," he snarls. "I fuck a whore the way a whore likes to be fucked. I have no sympathy for you." My body goes limp from exhaustion and my cry for him to stop continues. Daryl inserts himself inside me, pounding me roughly. "Aw shit, just as I thought. You are a black hole. I knew you were a whore," he grunts. I can't do anything but cry. It feels like he is ripping my insides to shreds. Daryl raises himself off me. "Don't move," he snarls. Afraid for my life, I do as instructed. Daryl raises my legs up around his waist and roughly spreads my butt cheeks apart. I close my eyes and cry harder, shaking my head from left to right, begging him to stop. Daryl ignores my plea and with force, inserts himself into my dry rectum. I use my tongue to push the torn underwear from my mouth and yell to the top of my lungs for help. The music in the club is too loud, so no one can hear my cry. My yelling is only turning Daryl on more, making him stroke my rectum harder, drawing blood. After five minutes of torture, Daryl ejaculates inside me. He releases my legs and falls back onto the sofa. "Damn, that was some good shit," he smiles. "You know girl, you look good and you got some good pussy too. Thanks!" I lie there, staring at the ceiling and afraid to move. "Whew!" Standing to his feet, Daryl adjusts his clothing. "I really needed that. It's been a while, ya' know?" I don't respond for focusing on the pain between my legs and praying that the throbbing in my rectum would cease. Daryl reaches into his back pocket and pulls out his wallet. Opening it, he retrieves a card and tosses it at me, where it lands on my chest. With his hand on the doorknob, "It's been a pleasure to serve you, Maya. Take care of yourself," he smiles.

Once the door closes behind him, I rise up on the bed, adjust my clothes and gather my bearings. The card falls face up onto the floor. I lean over to read it. The lettering is too small, so I pick the card up off the floor and hold it in my hand. My hand starts to tremble and I feel light about the head. The card reads,

"Roses are red,
Violets are blue,
Someone infected me,
Now I've infected you."

Ron

"Happy birthday to me. Happy birthday to me. Happy birthday to the fooooooooooooooool. Happy birthday to me."

I extinguish the half-smoked cigarette and drag my way down the spiral staircase, that China insisted on having built six years ago, to answer the obnoxious pounding on the front door. "Yeah, I'm coming!" I bark.

Marion looks me up and down and, using his fingers as a clothespin, pinches his nose close. "Oh my word, you look and smell like a mess!"

"Marion, not now."

"Ron, I've been calling and calling. Why aren't you answering the phone?"

"What do you want, Marion?"

"Well, I came to see my man and to wish him a happy birthday. I haven't heard from you and I wanted to make sure you were still alive."

"Do I look dead to you?"

"Aren't you going to ask me in?"

"No."

"Look, China has moved on and it's time for you to do the same. Get over it and let's start living our lives, together."

I refrain from ramming my fist into his face. "Fuck off!" I slam the door in his face.

I head back to the bedroom and resume my slouching position in the chair, staring at the four walls. I haven't slept in days because I refuse to sleep in a bed where my wife is not and where I disrespected her. I can't believe I defiled my marital bed. What in the hell is wrong with me? Have I really gone over the edge?

I reach for the Absolute vodka that is sitting on the end table beside the chair, fill my snifter to the rim, take it to the back of my throat and close my eyes. I feel the alcohol burn my insides, praying it will burn away the desires I have to be with Marion. Sitting beside the bottle of Absolute is the Smith & Wesson .38 caliber that China forbade me to bring into the house. Little did she know, it's been under the bed in a shoebox for five years. "Oh God, what have I done?" I cry.

I make one last attempt to communicate with China. She has to face me, us, the issue, eventually. "Hello, Free, it's Ron," I slur.

"Hello, Ron. Is everything all right? You don't sound too good."

"No, everything is not all right. I need my family, Free. I need my wife," I sob hysterically like a baby.

"Ron, well…"

"Is she there? Please, Free, I need to speak with China."

"Well, I will see if she wants to speak with you. I don't think she's ready to confront the issue yet, Ron. Why don't you give her some time? She will come around," Free consoles.

China snatches the phone from Free. "Ron, I am not ready to talk to you. Please leave me alone. Go ass fuck your boyfriend and leave me alone!"

"But, baby. . ." China throws the handset against the wall. I hold the phone to my ear, hoping this is all a bad dream.

"If you would like to make a call, please hang up and dial the number again," came from a recorded telephone message from Coastal Bell.

I stare at the phone, grasping it tightly. "I'm sorry, China." I hang up the phone and slouch back into the chair. I take another glass of Absolute to the back of my throat and stare at the gun, contemplating my reasons for living. I have none. I don't have China, and I don't have Ashley and André. I rest my hand over the gun. "There's no point in living if I can't have my family." I aim the trembling metal at my temple. My heart beats faster as beads of perspiration dance upon my forehead. I close my eyes and inhale. I am calm and at peace. . .until the phone rings. In hopes that China is on the other end wanting to reconcile and take me back, I snatch the phone and whisper, "China?"

"Daddy, is that you?" My heart softens from Ashley's delicate voice and instantly, life is worth living. I return the gun to the table.

"Yes, baby girl. How are you? I miss you so much."

"I'm fine, Daddy." Ashley sucks her teeth and takes a deep breath. "Daddy, is it true?"

"Is what true, baby?"

"Is it true what Mama said?"

"Well, what did your mother say?"

"Daddy, is it true what Mama called you?"

At this point, I don't need a bullet. The words coming from my daughter are killing me slowly, knocking the breath out of me, causing my heart to skip beats. If I answer her question honestly, what will my baby girl think of me? Will she still love me? Will she still respect me? What will André think?

"Daddy, Daddy, is it true?"

"Is what true, Ashley?"

Ashley cries into the phone. "Mama told Aunt Jade and Aunt Free that you like men."

"Baby, I. . .I. . ."

"Daddy, are you queer?"

Ashley's words pierce my heart like a rusty dagger. I pour myself another full glass of Absolute and repeat the process of taking it to the back of my throat. "Yes, baby girl, it's true." I hear a click and then a dial tone. I pick up the gun and aim it steady at my temple. "The Lord is my shepherd; I shall not want. He maketh me to lie down in green pastures. He leadeth me beside the still waters. He restoreth my soul. He leadeth me in the paths of righteousness for his name's sake. Yea, though I walk through the valley of the shadow of death, I will fear no evil, for thou art with me. Thy rod and thy staff they comfort me. Thou preparest a table before me in the presence of my enemies. Thou anointest my head with oil; my cup runneth over. Surely goodness and mercy shall follow me all the days of my life and I will dwell in the house of the Lord forever." I blankly stare at the wall and cock the gun. I close my eyes and slowly pull back the trigger. "Amen."

Free

It's three in the morning and the shrieking ring of the telephone awakens me. I snatch the phone from the cradle.

"Who is this calling my house at three in the morning?"

"Free Howard, please."

"This is Free."

"I know it's late and I do apologize for calling. My name is Cynthia Winters and I am calling from the Shady Village Assisted Living Community. Ms. Cherry has you down as next of kin."

"I don't know a Ms. Cherry," I snap. "I think you have the wrong number."

"Are you sure? Ms. Ethel Cherry."

"Ms. Ethel? Yes, I know her." I pull myself upright.

"Ms. Howard, I am so sorry to have to tell you…Ms. Cherry passed away in her sleep."

"Oh no!" My heart is in my throat. I take a deep swallow. "Well, how? Why?"

"She went peacefully."

"Was she sick? I just saw her a few days ago."

"No, I guess it was just her time."

I remove Sam's arm from around my waist, pull back the covers and press my feet against the cold, newly buffed and glazed hardwood floor. "I appreciate you calling me, but why didn't you call her son? He would be her next of kin, right?"

"Mr. Cherry passed away six months ago."

"Oh, Jesus!"

"After her son died, Ms. Cherry changed her contact information, as well as her last will and testament, and claimed you as her next of kin."

"I don't know what to say. . ."

"I understand. The Managing Nurse will contact you some time later today."

"Thank you."

I sit the phone on the nightstand and lean sideways, resting my shoulder and head against the headboard, and stare into darkness. A lump rises in my chest, making its way to my throat. I gasp for air. I feel like I've been here before. It feels like losing Mama all over again. I can't help but to cry.

"Everything okay?" Sam asks.

"I'll tell you later. Go back to sleep." I pull my legs under the covers and slide down under the warm sheets to cry in silence, but I hear sounds coming from downstairs. I get out of bed, reach for my robe that is lying across the paisley print chair and toss it around my shoulders. Barefoot, I walk into the hallway. Careful not to wake Sam again, I pull the door close and creep down the stairs. "Maya? Is that you? Why are you sitting in the dark?"

"I didn't want to wake you up. Who was that calling this time of night?"

"Oh, you remember Ms. Ethel, who'd come into the shop every single day?"

"Yes, I remember."

"She passed away and that was the assisted living community calling. They say she had me down as her next of kin."

"Her next of kin?"

"Yes. It seems her son died six months ago. I didn't know that and she never told me."

"I'm sorry to hear that, Free. I know how fond you were of her."

I take a closer look at my baby sister, in a fetal position in the corner of the sofa with her shoes still on. For goodness gracious, I just had that sofa cleaned. "Maya, what's wrong? Are you crying?"

"Free, I really fucked up tonight."

"Besides teaching your niece how to suck dick, what else have you done?"

"Free! That was not my fault!"

"Keep your voice down, Maya," I whisper with a stern tone. "You shouldn't have been messing with Jon's limo driver in the first place. What is wrong with you, girl?"

"Just never mind, Free. I can't talk to you anymore," she snaps.

I take a seat beside her. "Maya, you have always been able to talk to me."

"Not anymore. You are so damn judgmental of me."

"No, I'm not."

"Yes, you are! You sit your ass in judgment of all of us. Free, what makes you think you are better than we are, huh? You have your flaws too."

"Well, I'll be damned, you ungrateful tramp. Where do you get the audacity to speak to me this way in my house, after everything I've done for your selfish behind? I have never sat in judgment of you or anyone else. How dare you come at me like that, Maya!" I stand to my feet. "Well, let me break it down for you, darling. I have respect for myself and I have morals, which is more than I can say for you! You look a hot mess. Where did you go tonight? You were probably out having sex with some man you just met!" I head for the stairs. "Maya, if anyone sits in judgment of you, it's because you allow yourself to be judged by exhibiting such ungodly behavior. I don't need this. Goodnight!"

"What is going on down here? I can hear you two all the way upstairs. Maya, what's your problem?" China snaps. "Do you ever keep your damn nose clean?"

"Indeed! You two are just too loud," came from Jade, following behind China. "What are you two arguing about now, Free?"

I choke with tears. "All I ever try to do is be here for my sisters. I've never closed my door to you all."

Jade props her hands on her hips "Free, you are always here for us. Who the hell is questioning that shit?"

"Evidently, Maya doesn't think so," I sob.

"Oh, who gives a shit what Maya thinks?" China barks. "If it wasn't for you, she wouldn't have been able to flee California. . ."

"Flee? What the hell are you trying to say, China?"

"I don't know. You tell me, Maya. You've been here for over three weeks. When are you taking your ass back to California? I thought you had a slew of auditions and shit!" China sits on the arm of the sofa. "We are all ears, Maya. What's the deal?"

"Fuck you and your uppity ass, China! You need to worry about why you drove your husband to the asshole of a damn man."

"Enough! I have had enough!" I yell. "This is crazy. We are sisters and we shouldn't be talking to each other like this. Mama would have a fit if she knew…"

"Well Mama ain't here, Free, and I wish you'd stop trying to take her place," Maya snaps.

"I'm not trying to take Mama's place," I cry.

"Stop beating around the bush, Maya. What happened in California?"

"Nothing happened in California."

"Okay, so when are you going back?" Jade asks Maya, while consoling me with her arms wrapped around my shoulders.

"I don't know if I will be going back. I am trying to start fresh, here in Atlanta."

"Oh? So, why aren't you out looking for work?" China inquires.

"You know, China, you get on my fuckin' nerves. You wanna know why I left California? Fine, I will tell you so that you can shut the fuck up and get off my fucking back!" Maya stands to her feet. "I killed a motherfucker before he could kill me!"

"Jonah?" I ask.

"Yes."

Jade and China are about to step on their bottom lips and their eyes look like they are about to pop out of their heads.

"Well, good for you, Maya! You should've done it a long time ago," I say.

"Free, what are you saying? You are condoning her killing somebody?" Jade scolds.

"Jade, that Jonah character was a pimp and I am sure no one is missing him."

"But, she committed a crime," China chimes in.

"And so did your daughter. Are you going to report her to the police?" I ask, but I wish I hadn't.

China is flabbergasted. "Excuse me, Free?"

"Yes, Ashley committed a crime by sucking her brother's dick!" I snap. "It's a damn shame that you have so much hatred towards Maya. What did she ever do to you, China?"

China stands toe-to-toe with me. "She didn't know what she was doing," she snarls. "Maya knows. . ."

"Bullshit!" I snarl back, cutting her off. "What twelve-year-old do you know who doesn't know about oral sex or any other kind of sex for that matter?"

"Ashley didn't know any better!" Jade chimes in.

I face Jade. "No wonder that child is mixed up. Look at who she has for aunts."

"It's not my fault. It's Maya's fault for tricking with the limo driver in broad daylight!" Jade retorts.

"No, it's all of our faults. She is a child who looks up to her aunts, and her mother, and we need to lead by positive examples."

"Are you saying that we are bad influences, Free?" Maya asks.

"Maya, if the shoe fits. That girl has issues. For years, she stood by and watched as her father mentally and physically abused her mother. She has an aunt who is a prostitute and had to witness how freely she gives of herself. Her Aunt Jade don't know if she's gay or straight. . ."

"Wait a minute, Free, don't go there with me!" Jade defends herself. "I ain't got shit to do with this scenario."

"You're wrong, Jade. We are sisters and we all have something to do with what goes on with each other. . ."

"I was raped tonight," Maya mumbles. She reaches into her jacket pocket and pulls out a card. "I was raped and I am going to die."

I snatch the card from her hand and read it aloud. "Roses are red, violets are blue, someone infected me, now I've infected you." The burning of the words on my fingertips causes me to drop the card to the floor. "Maya, what is this all about?"

"I met this guy who works at the club I went to tonight. He forced himself on me. Afterwards, he threw that card at me."

"What does that mean, he's infected you?" China asks, with her hand on her hip. "You mean that AIDS thing?"

Maya nods her head yes. "But, his dick didn't have any sores on it."

"So, what does that have to do with the price of tea in China? Now you are an expert on sexually transmitted diseases? Besides, he probably just wanted to scare you." Jade says. "And he succeeded."

"Well, it's a sick ass joke for someone to make up cards and pass them out to everyone he screws." I sit down beside Maya and wrap my arms around her. "It will be okay, Maya. First thing Monday morning, you will be tested and all we can do is pray for the best."

"Yeah, and after that, we are going to the police and file charges against his ass for attempted murder!" China barks. "Don't worry, Sis. You aren't in this alone."

"I honestly don't know what I would do without my sisters," Maya cries.

"You would probably be less screwed up!" Jade chuckles.

"Free, I am so sorry for the mean things I said to you. I didn't mean them," Maya cries, clinging on to me for dear life.

"It's okay, baby girl. I know it didn't come from your heart."

"What mean things?"

"Let it go, China," I plea.

"I know she didn't come half-cocked toward you after..."

"China, shut the hell up," Jade snaps. "She's apologized and Free has accepted. Why do you like to keep shit going?"

China rolls her eyes at Jade. "Ain't nobody talking to you."

"I'm hungry. Who wants some sweet potato pie?" I ask.

"Yummy, sounds good. But, hey, didn't we eat that pie up already, with the guys?" Jade asks.

I look over my shoulder. "Hmm, well, I will just have to bake another one. Come on!" Jade, China and Maya follow me into the kitchen.

"Free, it's four in the morning," Maya says while pulling out the canned milk, butter, sugar, vanilla extract and cinnamon. Jade turns on the oven and China puts the sweet potatoes on to boil. "It's kind of late to be baking a pie, don't you think?"

"It's never too late for Mama's sweet potato pie."

"Who was that ringing the phone so late at night? Was it Ron again?" China growls.

"Nope. It was Shady Village Assisted Living. . ."

"Isn't that where Ms. Ethel lives?" China asks.

"Yes. They were calling to tell me that she passed away."

Jade embraces me. "Oh Free, I am so sorry."

"Thank you, Sis." I break her embrace and try to hold back the tears. "She didn't have any next of kin, so they called me. I guess I will have to make the funeral arrangements."

"I thought she had a son," Jade says, retrieving the carton of milk from the refrigerator and pours herself a glass.

"He died six months ago," Maya interjects.

"Wow, Free, are you sure you want to take on that responsibility?" China asks. "What about other family members she may have?"

"China, Ms. Ethel left instructions for me to be called as her next of kin. Now, that tells me that she didn't want anyone else to handle her arrangements or her business. So, if that is what she wishes for me to do, then that is what I will do."

Jade raises her glass of milk to make a toast. "Free to the rescue!" Jade says.

"Yeah, just like Silver!" China laughs.

"You mean Tonto, right? Silver was the horse," Maya says as we fill the kitchen with sisterly laughter.

"Nope, Tonto was the Indian. China, you mean the Lone Ranger, you jack ass," Jade laughs.

"Just kiss the darkest part of my black ass, Jade!"

"China, one day you will invite the wrong person to your nasty ass," Jade laughs.

I take a deep sigh and smile at my sisters. They all have issues, but they are mine. "I love you girls so much," I say with a bright smile. "No matter what happens to pull us apart, we always find our way back together."

"Here, here," Jade toasts, with a half-empty glass of milk.

"I second that!" Maya exclaims.

"We all need psychiatric care," China says with a smirk. She walks over to the stove and pierces a fork into the sweet potatoes. "Hard as a rock."

"It takes time, China," I say.

"Put them in the microwave," Maya suggests.

"Mama's recipe doesn't call for zapped sweet potatoes, "I snap.

"Well, I'm going to bed," China says, dragging her feet across the kitchen floor.

"Yeah, it's been a long day and even longer night," I agree.

"Yeah, let's go to bed and bake this pie later," Maya says, returning the spices to the cupboard.

I turn off the flame under the pot of sweet potatoes, drain the water into the sink, toss the entire pot into the refrigerator and head off to bed.

"Maybe Billy Dee and I can pick up where we left off," I chuckle. "Only in my dreams."

I slowly climb back into bed, trying not to wake Sam. I close my eyes, take a deep sigh and try to clear my mind of all the events that will not allow me to sleep. I have so much to do tomorrow.

"Free?"

"Oh Sam, sorry I woke you."

"You didn't wake me. I can't sleep."

"Was it the ringing phone?"

"No."

"What's wrong, honey?" I ask, turning over to face him. "Are you not feeling well?"

Sam smiles, his hands slowly moving downward and skimming my body all the way down to my thighs. He leans in close and whispers, "I love you, baby," his lips brushing against mine as he speaks. His kiss is gentle yet hungry, leaving me burning with fire.

"Wait!" I exclaim, tossing Sam to the side.

"What's up?"

"I forgot to do something. Be right back." I hop out of bed and shoot into the bathroom, praying that I haven't used all of my Today's Sponges.

"Okay," I say, opening the bathroom door. "Where were we?"

Climbing into bed, Sam uses his arm to scoop me under him. "You were gone too long," he says, covering my mouth with his. Heat and desire for him exude from my pores. "You feel so good, baby."

Now aroused by his touch, I pull him on top of me. Together we find the tempo that binds our bodies together. Sam moans aloud with erotic pleasure.

"Shh!" I whisper, covering his mouth. "They are going to hear you," I smile, tasting the sweet nectar of his kiss.

Sam buries his head in the crevice of my neck. "Ooh," he says. "I don't care if they hear me," he moans.

As our bodies move in unison, I wrap my legs around his waist and pull him deeper inside. The involuntary tremors of arousal begin. His smell intoxicates me, taking me to greater heights. "Oh yes!" he exclaims, the tremor of his body heating me inside and out.

Once the snoring begins, I tiptoe into the bathroom and close the door. I sit on the commode and take a deep breath. I've never had so much sex in all my life. Sam is going to exhaust me. But, at least it was more passionate this time. I pull myself up from the commode, raise one leg on the commode and insert my finger to pull at the string. "Oh shoot!" I exclaim. "What am I going to do now?" I attempt to tug at the string again. I still can't feel it. I crack open the bathroom door and call for Sam. He doesn't budge. I call him again, louder.

"What?" he says, springing up in the bed and looking around the room. "What's going on? What's wrong?"

"Sam, I can't get it out."

Rubbing his eyes, trying to adjust them, "What are you talking about?" he asks.

"The sponge. I can't get it out."

"How did you get it in there?"

I take a sigh of irritation. "I can't find the string that is used to pull it out."

"Lie down on the bed. Let me see if I can find it."

"Are you crazy? That won't be happening."

"What's the big deal? Just lie down and I will pull it out for you."

"Nope, sorry. Could you get China for me?"

Begrudgingly, Sam crawls out of bed, slides into his slippers and heads for the door.

"Where is your robe?" I ask. "You can't go out there naked, Sam!"

"Oh, sorry, wasn't thinking. Still trying to wake up." Sam slips into his pajama bottoms and pulls on a tee shirt.

Knocking on China's bedroom door, he whispers, "China, Free needs to see you."

The door flies open. "What's wrong?"

"She'll tell you." China follows on Sam's heels. "She's in there," he says, pointing to the closed bathroom door.

China places her ear against the door. "Free? You okay, honey?"

"No, I'm not," I whine.

"What's wrong?"

"I can't get this sponge out."

China looks at Sam and falls out with laughter. "Pull the string, Free."

"Don't you think I've tried to do that?" I snap. "I can't feel the string!"

"Let me get Jade and Maya. They might know how to help you. I haven't used any form of birth control in years."

"No, wait! I don't want everyone to know, China."

Maya knocks on the bedroom door. "Y'all having a party and didn't invite me?"

"Aww shit!" I snap. "Look, all I want to do is get this sponge out!"

"What sponge?" Maya asks. "What is she talking about, China?"

"That fool done gone and got a sponge stuck up in her twat and now she can't get it out."

"Pull the string," Maya suggests.

"If I could pull the flippin' string, you wouldn't be here!"

"Whoa, hold up, Free. You are the one with a sponge stuck up in your coochie," Maya teases.

"You two get on my nerves! Just tell me what I can do."

"Okay, lie down in the tub, raise your hips and try to get it out that way," Maya suggests.

"Okay." I begin drawing the bath and sit on the commode. "I can't believe this is happening to me."

"Don't worry about it, Sis. You aren't the only one that this has happened to," China consoles, while giggling under her breath.

"Go to hell, China!" I spat.

"What? All I'm saying is that it's no biggie."

"Okay, I'm in the tub, my hips are raised and nothing."

"Free, is there water in the tub?" Maya asks.

"Yes, and I still can't get it out."

"And you won't," Maya laughs. "Girl, don't you know that a sponge will soak up water and that bitch will grow inside you?" She laughs uncontrollably.

I pull myself out of the tub, slip into my peach terrycloth robe and fling open the door. "You two are worthless, I swear!"

"Baby, why don't you lie down on the bed. . ."

"I said no!" I yell. "You are not going to dig up inside me. Maya, go downstairs and get me a fork."

"Free, what in the hell are you going to do with a fork?" China asks.

"I am going to use it to pull this thing out," I growl. "Stop asking dumb ass questions and just do as I ask!"

"Free, you cannot use a damn fork. Girl, you will tear yourself up!"

"Well, what in the hell am I suppose to do?" I cry. "I can't keep this thing inside me. I could get an infection."

"We'll have to go to the Emergency Room," China laughs.

"Oh, I can't do that."

"And why can't you?"

"That is too embarrassing," I sob.

"Free, you're being stupid. Now get dressed and let's go!"

"This house is full of drama. What is going on now?" Jade asks, peeking her head into the bedroom. "Free, what's the matter?"

"She can't get the sponge out," China says.

Jade looks at us like we are all crazy. "What sponge? Get it out where?"

"The sponge, Jade," Maya says. "She and Sam where fucking and now she can't get the sponge out."

"Shut the hell up, Maya. Why did you have to go there?" China scorns. "Your mouth is too goddamn big!"

"Okay, okay," Sam yells. "Can we just get Free taken care of, please?"

"Sweetie, come into the bathroom. I will help you. I've been there, done that," Jade smiles. "It's going to be okay."

Jade escorts me into the bathroom. "Free, do you have any tweezers?"

"Yes, they are in the medicine cabinet."

Jade looks over her shoulder. "We do not need any help, thanks," she says to Maya and China and closes the door behind her. "They can be so juvenile, it's ridiculous," she says while reaching into the medicine cabinet. "Okay, here they are," she says, holding them between her fingers. "Free lie down on the floor, raise your legs up in the air and let's keep our fingers crossed."

"I don't know, Jade."

"Okay, either I do it or you go to the Emergency Room. It's your choice."

"But. . .I mean, you are. . ."

A questionable look crosses Jade's face. "I am what, Free?"

"Nothing. I'm being silly."

"No, let's get this out in the open."

"Well, you are a lesbian and I don't want a lesbian playing around in my stuff," I say, lowering my head at the ignorance that just fell off my lips.

Jade relaxes her posture, her arms fall down to her side. "Free, I am your sister. I am hurt that you would think that I would take advantage of you."

"No, it's not that. . ."

"I am not a lesbian. I chose to be with Joy because, at the time, she loved me the way that I wanted to be loved. Yes, it was hard at first. . .being with a woman. But, I got over it."

"I'm sorry, Jade."

"No apologies needed. One can't help for being ignorant."

Free gasps. "I deserved that."

"Yes, you did. Now, do you want me to get the sponge out or what?"

I assumed the position on the floor. Free maneuvered that pair of tweezers like a pro and within seconds, the sponge was dangling from the grasp of the tweezers.

"See, that wasn't so bad," she smiles.

"Nope. Thank you so much," I smile, embracing her.

Her smile fades. "Free, along with using the sponge, do you use a condom too?"

"Absolutely!"

"Good."

"What about you? I know about your high sex drive. Do you use a condom?"

"All the time."

Jade

I have a serious headache from all of the drama that has transpired under the roof of this house. This is exactly why I don't do family reunions. My sisters are three of the most dramatic women you will ever meet in your life. If I had any inkling that I was going to have to deal with all of this shit, I would've kept my ass in New York. Poor Jon, I know he thinks we all belong in a mental institution. I can just imagine what he must think about Maya's hot tail, trying to screw his driver that she doesn't know from a pile of horseshit.

I had no idea Maya was so free with her body. To screw a man she meets in a club, in the back of the club at that, is just repulsive. I pray that she has not contracted a STD or a life-threatening disease like HIV. I don't wish any harm to come to my baby sister, but contracting a STD may be what she needs to calm her hot ass down, because I doubt if anything else would have an impact. A prostitute? I had no idea that life was that bad for her in California. The morals that Mama and Daddy instilled in her went right out one of those car windows when she hitchhiked three thousand miles to California. Yes, despite what she may think, we all know that she hitchhiked. How else would she get there with only one hundred dollars in her pocket?

Jon begins to twist and turn, awaking from his slumber. I stroke the top of his head. "Morning, sleepy head." Jon slowly opens his eyes, squinting as if there is a bright beam of light shining in his face. "A headache, huh?" Jon nods his head. "You want some coffee?"

"No, babe. I don't want you to go to any trouble. Besides, caffeine is not my best friend," he smiles. "I will be acting as batty as your family," he chuckles, until he realizes what has just escaped from his morning breath, crust-infested mouth. "Oh, I'm sorry, Jade. I was out of line."

I reach down and kiss his forehead. "No need to apologize when you're speaking the truth."

"But, sometimes, the truth can be very hurtful. That is the last thing I would want to do."

"Jon, please. I was just lying here thinking the exact same thing. Yes, my family is batty as all hell. I have a damn drama headache. Everywhere I've turned this past twenty-four hours, there has been nothing but drama."

"Not the weekend you envisioned, huh?"

"Not really. I thought we would've outgrown this shit by now."

"You mean this is the norm?"

"Uh huh. It's always something."

"I really like Sam. He's cool people."

"I like him too. He seems to be very attentive toward Free, and I like that. Free hasn't had a man in her life for a very long time. I believe she blocked so many blessings because of self-esteem issues."

"Free doesn't appear to lack self-esteem to me."

"But, she does. Well, she did. I don't know if you've noticed, but Free is the darkest of the sisters."

"And?"

"And she always felt that men weren't interested in her because of her deep chocolate complexion."

"Why do you think that is?"

"I'm not really sure, but I believe it has to do with this boy calling her Puffy as a child."

"Puffy?"

"Uh huh, as in a puff of smoke. He would always make that poof sound."

"How awful."

"Yep, kids can be so cruel."

"And she's carried that throughout her adult years, huh?"

"I believe so."

"I think Free's complexion is beautiful. And, not to mention, she has flawless skin."

"Humph, you don't miss a beat do you?"

"I just pay attention to my surroundings, that's all." Jon pulls the covers back and crawls out of the bed. "Excuse me, love. I need to use the bathroom." As he advances toward the bathroom, I pull the covers back, grab my robe and toothbrush and follow him. He stops in his tracks. "Jade, where are you going?"

"To the bathroom."

"So am I."

"And your point is what, Jon?" I chuckle.

"You want to come in there with me?"

"Sure, why not?"

"That is just a little bit too personal, don't you think?"

"Jon, I only want to brush my teeth."

"Fine. Wait until I finish and then you can go in and brush your teeth."

"Jon, what's the big deal about me being in the bathroom while you're taking a piss?"

"Jade, there are times when I'd like to be to myself, and urinating is one of them."

"Fine!" I push my way past Jon and into the bathroom. "You can *urinate* when I am done brushing my teeth!" I slam the door in his face.

Just to be mean-spirited and since this is the only bathroom in Free's house besides the one in her bedroom, I take my sweet time. Not only did I brush my teeth, but while Jon was standing on the outside, probably holding his dick, I decide to take a nice, long shower. Ten minutes later, Jon bangs on the door. "Jade, you are so wrong!"

"You are welcome to come in and *urinate* if you'd like to. I'm not stopping you." I chuckle to myself. He is such the prude, and if he's going to be with me, he is going to have to lighten up.

I guess he couldn't hold it any longer because, within seconds, Jon was in front of the porcelain, aiming and sighing with relief. When his stream slows, I turn off the shower and slide the shower curtain open. "Now, that wasn't so bad, was it?"

"What was the big deal?" he asks, with his hand on his hips, obviously irritated.

"That's what I want to know, Jon. You don't want to pee in front of me, but you will keep your face buried in my bush for hours," I snap in a low, irritated tone, not wanting to disturb the occupants of Free's Inn.

"You're being childish, Jade."

"I'm being childish?" I snatch the towel from the towel rack and wrap it around me. "If that is how you feel, fine." I step out of the shower and storm off to the bedroom.

Jon follows behind me like a lost puppy. "Jade, I didn't mean it like that."

I turn to face him. "Then what did you mean?"

"I'm just not used to all of this." Jon sits on the bed, patting the empty space beside him. I take a seat beside him. "Jade, the only family that I have is my mother and Paul. I can't remember the last time we've had a disagreement. All in one day, your sister tries to rape my driver, your niece decides to imitate your sister and your brother-in-law is a fudge packer."

"Well. . ."

"I'm sorry, Jade. But, this is all new to me. It's going to take some time for me to get used to being a part of a family with so much pain and heartaches."

"A part of?"

"Yes, I plan to stick around."

"You do?" I smile.

"Yes. I really care for you, Jade. I want to see where 'us' will lead."

"So do I, Jon." He leans in to kiss me. I pull back. "Umm, baby. . ."

"Morning breath?"

"Uh huh." Jon hurries off to the bathroom, brushes his teeth and, within minutes, is back in my arms. "Better," I smile, stroking his cheek while our tongues dance around.

"I have an idea. Why don't I take us all out for a night on the town?"

"That sounds desperately needed!" I exclaim.

"Okay, I'll talk with Sam to see what six adults can get into."

"Wait. What about the kids? They will need a babysitter."

"Robert can watch them."

"Who is going to drive the car?"

"I do know how to drive, you know."

"Ooh, I can't wait to tell the girls!" I screech. "What am I going to wear?"

Jon reaches into his billfold. "Do you prefer cash or credit?"

"What are you talking about?"

"To go shopping. Do you prefer to use cash or credit?"

"Well, umm. . ."

"Okay, all I have is three thousand on me. Will that be enough?"

"Well. . ."

"If this isn't enough, you can use my credit card. I don't have a limit with the card."

"Jon, you are. . ."

"Why are you crying?"

"I've never been treated so good."

"You deserve it," he smiles, using his thumb to wipe away the tears. "Here is the cash and the credit card. I want you and your sisters to have a day of shopping. Buy whatever your heart desires. The sky's the limit."

"This is just unreal."

"Go wake up your sisters and tell them to get ready. You should start out with breakfast somewhere nice."

"Well, what are you going to do while we're gone?"

"Don't worry about us guys. We will be fine. You should take Ashley with you. I have a feeling she needs a lot of attention right now."

"I think you're right."

China

Lying in bed, listening to Jade's loud talking, I can't seem to stop thinking about Ron. It's strange. Since I've been here, I really haven't thought of him at all. But, for some reason, I woke up with Ron on my mind and an eerie feeling accompanied with a knot in my stomach.

There's a soft knock at the door. "China, you up?"

"Uh huh, thanks to your loud ass. Come on in."

"Aww, boo boo. I didn't mean to wake you. I'm sorry."

"You really didn't wake me."

"You okay?"

"Not really. I've got Ron on my mind."

"China, I just don't know what to say."

"Neither do I."

"What are you going to do?"

I take a deep sigh. "I don't know, girl. Everything is just going so fast. I feel like I am on a serious, non-stop roller coaster ride."

"I can't say that I know how you feel…"

"What I'm feeling, I don't wish on my worst enemy."

"Are you going to file for divorce?"

"Most likely. I mean, there is absolutely no way that I can continue my marriage with Ron. . ."

"Because he had an affair with a man?"

"It's not just that. Ron lied to me, period. He deceived me, Jade, and I don't think I could ever forgive him for that. I will never be able to trust him again."

"Knock, knock."

"Damn, can't there ever be just two of us in one room at a time?"

"Shut up, China. Don't start so early in the morning," Maya barks, opening the door. "What y'all doing?"

"Nothing girl, just talking," Jade says, waving for Maya to come in.

"Well, Free will be in here in thirty seconds," I chuckle.

Maya pulls the covers back and crawls into bed. "China, I am so sorry."

"It's not your fault, Maya." I pull my baby sister close to me. "Ashley knows better."

"She's just a child," Jade says, coming to Ashley's defense.

"Yes, a child who is a few months away from being a teenager. She knows better."

"China, her mouth is awful. I couldn't believe the foul language she was spitting at you."

"Yeah, that was kind of raw," Maya says, with her thumb in her mouth.

"Maya, you still sucking on that crusty ass thumb?"

"Whatever, Jade."

"Leave her alone. You know she's the baby," I tease.

"Humph, yesterday, you were ready to kill her ass." Jade pushes Maya in the middle of the bed and climbs in. "Y'all know what?"

"What?" Maya and I respond in unison.

"We've got some issues in this damn family."

"You ain't never lied," China laughs.

"But look, I've got some good news," Jade says.

"You're pregnant?" China chuckles.

"Ha! Please. No. . ."

"Well, you don't date women anymore, so that's definitely good news."

"Whatever, China. We are going on a shopping spree, thanks to Jon."

"Why?" I ask.

"He feels sorry for us," Maya chuckles.

Jade pops Maya upside the head. "He is just generous. He wants to take us all out tonight, so he is treating us to a shopping spree. Now, get your funky asses in the shower and let's start with breakfast!"

"Okay, I'll go in there first. China you can go next," Maya instructs.

"Hold up, what about the cookout? Y'all know Sam's people are coming over today," I remind them.

"Hell, we can cancel it," Maya says with her selfish ass.

"Maya, how do you sound?" China snaps.

"Like a sistah who wants to get her shop on." Maya snaps her fingers in the air.

"Just selfish. . ."

"Okay y'all, it's too early," Jade interjects.

"Yeah well, let's check with Free to see if the cookout is still on," Maya sings.

"I'll wake up Free and see what she says. Oh, and China, Jon thinks we should take Ashley with us."

I take a deep sigh. "You think we should? I would hate to have to knock her out in public because of her mouth."

"Yes, I think we should. I think it's what she needs," Maya says.

"And what do you know about what she needs, Maya? If you knew what she needed, you wouldn't have allowed her to see. . ."

"Look, I didn't know she was watching me. Hell, we were about six blocks up the street. What was your child doing roaming the streets?"

"China! Not today. Let's just go out, spend Jon's money and be sisterly to each other for a change," Jade snaps and rolls her eyes. "I swear!"

"I'm not going!" Maya storms out of the bedroom.

"I swear, China. You are just. . ."

"Just what, Jade?"

"You are just bitter! You are taking out your frustrations with Ron and your marriage on us and I'm sick of it!" Jade storms out of the room too. "Free, get up! We are going shopping, damnit!" Jade yells as she slams her bedroom door.

Bitter? Who is she calling bitter? I am not bitter. Angry, yes. Bitter, no. They just don't understand. I am a failure. I've failed at being a wife. I've failed at being a mother. I don't know what hurts the most, my husband having an affair or my daughter being a slut. Well, I can't worry about Ron. He is an adult. He has to accept responsibility for his actions. But Ashley needs psychiatric help. During all of this, I never stopped to think about André. How is he handling all of what is going on around him? I should not have to tell him that his father is a homosexual. Ron should be the one to tell him. Besides, I wouldn't know where to start.

"China!" Free yells from her bedroom. "Telephone!"

"Coming!" I didn't hear the phone ring. Somewhere else in my thoughts, I guess. "Be right there, Free!" I throw my robe around my shoulders and slip into my leopard print, faux fur-lined slippers. I knock on Free's door. "May I use the phone in here?"

"Sure, come on in," she says.

I enter Free's bedroom with my hand covering my eyes. "Girl, please, we are in bed and clothed. There ain't nothing to see," Free chuckles, while Sam is calling the hogs. "I guess you will be able to hold a conversation with Sam's snoring."

I take the phone from Free and glance over at Sam. "Ooh chile, how can you stand that?"

"It hasn't been easy."

"Hello, this is China."

"China, this is Marion."

"How. . ."

"China, I'm. . ."

"Sorry? You should be sorry. How dare you call me! Don't you think you've done enough?"

"China, please, I need you to listen to me."

"I don't need to listen to shit you have to say."

My loud voice arouses Sam from his peaceful slumber. He looks up at Free. "What's going on?" he stretches.

"Shh, I'll tell you in a minute. Soon as I find out," Free replies.

"China, you need to come home," Marion says.

"I don't need to do shit but. . ."

"China, Ron is dead!"

I think my heart stopped. I feel myself weaken. I fall back onto Free's bed, landing on her leg. "China, are you there?" Marion begins to cry. "China, are you there?"

"What happened?" I mumble.

"Last night, I stopped by your home because I was worried about Ron's state of mind. He came to the door, told me to fuck off and slammed the door in my face. I got in my car and was about to leave, but changed my mind. He had been drinking. He didn't look or smell too good. Just as I was about to ring the doorbell, I heard a gun shot."

"Oh!" I gasp. "Where did he get a gun from? I never allowed one in the house."

"I don't know. After I heard the gun shot, I pulled out my cell and I called 911. The police had to knock down the door. By the time the paramedics got to Ron, it was too late. I feel like this is my entire fault. I knew he was married, but I let my feelings stand in the way of my good judgment," he cries.

"Where is he now?"

"The County Coroner has him. The police wanted to call you, but I asked if I could call you instead. I don't know why, but I thought it would be better coming from me."

"I appreciate the call. Thank you."

"China, I know this is going to sound crazy, but if you need anything, anything at all, please don't hesitate to call me. I've left my phone number attached to your refrigerator."

"Thanks." I hung up the phone. "Oh Lord," I whisper in my palms.

"China, get off of my leg and tell me what's wrong," Free snaps.

"Would you like for me to leave the room?" Sam asks.

"No. No, you don't have…Free, Ron's dead," I sob.

"What! Who was that on the phone? What kind of sick games…"

"That was Marion, Ron's lover. It's no game. Ron committed. . .committed. . ."

Free places her hand on my knee. "Oh, Sis, I am so sorry."

Sam sits up in the bed and rubs the crust from the corners of his eyes. "China, is there anything I can do?"

"No, there's nothing anyone can do. What's done is done. Thank you anyway."

"Well, I'll do what you need me to do, Sis. You know that."

"I guess I'll have to start making arrangements. I need to head back home. Free, will you do the floral arrangements for me?"

"Of course."

"Okay. Oh my, I have to find a way to tell Ashley and André."

"How do you tell a child that their parent committed suicide?" Free asks.

"I don't know."

"I would suggest you seek counseling for you and the kids, China," Sam says, putting in his two cents. I nod my head in agreement.

Jade knocks on the door. "Free, have you heard the good news?" Jade plops down on the bed beside China. "Morning, Sam!" She stares at China. "What's wrong with you?"

"Jade, I don't think we will be going shopping today."

Jade throws Free a bewildered look. "Why not?"

I broke down. I can't suppress it any longer. "Oh Jade!" I cry hysterically. "Ron's dead. The man that I've loved all of my life is gone. The father of my children." I fell into Jade's arms. "What am I going to do?"

Jade cradles me in her arms and kisses the top of my head. "Not to worry, Sis. We aren't going to let you travel this road alone. We are always in your corner, you know that."

"I don't want to spoil your shopping trip."

"Don't talk nonsense, China," Free snaps. "We've got work to do." Just like when Mama died, Free goes into her take-charge mode. "First thing we are going to do is book us a flight to Florida, just me and you. Second, we. . ."

"Free, what about the shop?" Jade asks.

"Maya is here, until whenever. She can run the shop for a week or so."

"You're going to trust Maya with your money?" I ask. We all stare at Free, waiting on her response.

"She will do fine," Free smiles. "Someone has got to start trusting her."

"Baby, I will call my folks and tell them the cookout has been cancelled," Sam says.

"But Sam, I've prepared so much food and you were looking forward to me meeting your family and friends."

"Nope, this takes priority. You'll have more opportunities to meet them."

"Well, okay, I appreciate that, honey."

"As a matter of fact, I think it would do you all some good to go shopping," Sam smiles. "I'll take the guys out." He faces me. "China, I'll take André too."

"Sam, oh, we can't do that. China has so much to do. . ."

"Baby, I don't mean to be insensitive, but Ron isn't going anywhere. The planning can wait one more day."

"China, let's make some calls and find out what we can do from here, okay?" Jade smiles. "I am sure Jon doesn't mind detouring to Florida on our return trip."

"Jade, I can't ask him to do that."

"You aren't asking. I am."

I look at my sisters with a mixture of sadness and joy. I feel sadness for Ron and our life we had together, and joy because I have the best sisters in the world. "I love you wenches so much, you know that?"

"You only love us because we are the only ones who tolerate your mean and nasty behind," Free chuckles. "Now, let's go get some breakfast. I'm hungry."

"Free, your ass is always hungry!" Jade teases.

"Y'all go ahead without me and the kids. I want to take them to breakfast and break the news to them. I'll catch up with y'all at the mall."

"China, you sure you don't want company?" Jade asks.

"No, we'll be fine, thanks." Heading back to my room, I hear André moving about in his room. I tap on the door. "Dré, you up?"

"Yep. Morning, Mama."

I open the door and peek my head in. "Morning, baby. You want some breakfast?"

"Uh huh, I'm starvin' like Marvin."

"Good. I'm going to wake up your sister and the three of us will go to IHOP. How does that sound?" André nods his head and smiles.

China

I can't stand IHOP! Those damn pancakes are so good and they don't do shit but aid in the spreading of my ass, and Lord knows, I don't need that. A sistah has more back than she cares to acknowledge. My favorite is the Country Fried Steak and Scrambled Eggs, with just a hint of cheese, a bowl of grits, a stack of pancakes and a double order of sausage links. Humph, and I constantly wonder why I keep advancing a dress size.

"Mama, what you gone order?" André asks.

"The same stuff she always orders, you pussy!" Ashley taunts.

"You know something, Ashley. You better stop calling me a pussy or. . ."

"Or what? What are you going to do to me? Not a damn thing!"

I reach across the table and pop Ashley in her mouth. "What did I tell you about your mouth?" I snap. Ashley gasps in astonishment. I've never laid hands on her in public before. I guess my popping her in her mouth shocked her. She's lucky I didn't do what Mama used to do to us, pull her pants down and beat her ass. "Can we please come out in public without having to experience a lot of bullshit?"

"You didn't have to hit me, Ma," Ashley cries.

"You deserved it," André laughs. "You are always calling me names. What did I ever do to you?"

"You were born, that's what."

"I didn't ask to be your brother, so you need to stop trippin' before I tell on you."

"You ain't gone do nothing but sit there and shut up, you pussy."

"Enough!" I yell, halting the surrounding IHOPers from shoving wads of pancakes, dripping in Maple Syrup, in their mouths. "What is wrong with you two?"

"Mama, she always starts it!"

"I don't care who started what. Both of you listen to me and you listen to me good. When I am dead and gone, all you will have is each other. Do you understand me?"

"We will have Daddy," Ashley pouts.

"No, you won't."

"Yes, we will! If you die first, Daddy will take care of us."

I lower my head and stare at the dried up food stains on the table. "No, you won't have your daddy, Ash." I raise my head and look into my baby girl's eyes.

"He probably doesn't like you anymore," André snaps.

"Shut up! Daddy loves me!"

"You both shut up. I have something I need to tell you." My hand shakes as I take a sip of water, spilling drops down the front of my shirt. "You know that I love you both. I love you more than anything in this world, right?" They both nod and answer, "Yes," in unison. I don't notice the tears streaming down my face until I feel the drop on my hand. I reach for a napkin from the dispenser and gently wipe around the edges of my eyes.

"What's wrong, Mama?" André asks. "Why are you crying?"

"Your ugly mug would make anybody cry," Ashley laughs.

"Shut up, something's wrong with Ma."

Ashley stares in my face, looking for an answer to André's question. "I don't know how to tell you. . ."

"Mama, just tell us, please. You are scaring me," André whimpers, on the verge of crying himself.

"Your daddy died last night." I lower my head because I don't want to see the hurt in their eyes. What are they going to do without their father? How will I raise my son to be a man? That's a father's job, isn't it?

"Mama, that's not a funny joke. That's mean for you to say," Ashley pouts, as she wrinkles up her nose at me.

"Mama is not telling any jokes, baby. I would never say something like that if it weren't true."

"But I just talked to Daddy last night and he sounded fine to me," Ashley retorts.

"I didn't know that you spoke with your father last night. When? Why didn't you tell me? Did he call you?"

"No, she called him. And it's her fault that Daddy died, because she's so fucking mean!" André cries. "I can't stand you anymore, Ashley. Daddy is dead and it's because of you!"

Ashley stares at André as her eyes well and her face droops. "I didn't do anything," she cries.

"It's no one's fault," I say, taking both of their hands in mine and attempting to console them. "Your daddy was dealing with some demons."

"What kind of demons?" André asks.

"The queer demons," Ashley answers. "You're right, Dre. I did kill Daddy," she cries. She wipes her eyes and nose with the back of her hand. "Mama, I called Daddy last night and I asked him if he was a faggot. . ."

"You did what?"

"Yes, she did, Mama," André chimes in. He gets a thrill out of telling on his sister, no matter what the circumstance. "She came into my room last night and told me that Daddy was a faggy and I was going to grow up to be one too."

"Ashley that is a cruel thing to say. Why would you say something like that?"

"Because it's true, isn't it?"

"No, it's not true and you shouldn't go around talking about topics you know nothing about."

"I think we need counseling," André suggests.

"Excuse me?" I couldn't believe my ears. My ten-year-old son is suggesting that his family seek counseling. "Baby, what a mature thing to say. You want counseling?"

"Yes. I want someone to talk to."

"You mean a Psychiatrist? Those are for crazy people and you're not crazy. Ugly, yes, but you're not crazy," she chuckles.

I smile at Ashley, while noticing that André has his fist bald up, laying flat on the table. "Baby, are you alright?" I ask him.

André opens his fist and places his hand in his lap. "Yes, Mama, I'm fine." I smile at him and blow him a kiss. He catches my kiss and tucks it inside his jacket pocket. "I'll keep it there for good luck," he smiles.

When André was five years old, after dropping him off at preschool, I would always blow him a kiss and tell him to put it in his pocket for good luck. His teacher was appreciative and always looked forward to it because it stopped his wailing, making him feel secure. That boy had a set of lungs on him. He would tell his teacher that he carried his mother around in his pocket.

"What are we going to do now, Mama? Are we going to stay here with Aunt Free?" Ashley asks.

"I don't know, Ash. What would you like to do?"

"I want someone to talk to."

"You want counseling too?" I ask her.

"Yes, Ma'am."

"You need a facelift!" André exclaims.

"Shut up, you pussy!"

"See, Mama, she still calling me a pussy," he pouts. "Ashley, why do you call me that?"

She looks at him and then darts a look at me. She rolls her eyes up towards the ceiling and takes a deep sigh. "Because I love you, you little pussy."

André's mouth drops open from not believing his ears. He looks at me and forms a smirk on his face. One of those "I'ma get you back," smirks. He turns to Ashley. "I love you too, you dick!"

Maya

I am convinced that the Howard family is cursed. Within one week, China finds out that her husband likes men, she leaves him, thinks about filing for divorce and he eliminates that thought by committing suicide. I might have a STD, or worse, something that could kill me. And my niece is trying to follow my example. Jade and Free, however, are happy as a dog rolling around in his own mess.

China is right. I have to take responsibility for my actions. This is why I am here at the Women's Community Clinic, alone. My sisters wanted to come and give me support, but this is something that I have to do by myself, if I am ever going to stand on my own two feet. I can't believe all of the women that are sitting here waiting to be tested. I thought AIDS was something that only affects homosexuals.

This is the most morbid waiting room I've ever been in. The walls are gray, the carpet is gray, the chairs are gray and the people working behind the desk are wearing gray. Well, if I didn't feel gray before I came through the door, I sure as hell feel gray now.

Looking at my watch, wondering how much longer I will have to wait before the doctor sees me, I reach for the National Geographic to occupy myself before I go crazy. There isn't anything on television except for the news, and all it's reporting is the bad that is taking place in and around Georgia and around the global world.

"In other news…Jonah Roberts, a well known pimp and drug king, was murdered in Los Angeles, California. Police say that a neighbor called in complaining of a foul odor coming from Roberts' apartment. Police say that there are no suspects, however, neighbors told police about a young woman who was occupying the apartment with Roberts. A description of the young woman was given to police." A sketch of a woman looking like me flashes across the television screen. I slide down in my seat and look around at the faces staring at the television. *"Police have no leads and no suspects at this time."* I raise the National Geographic up to my face. "Oh no," I whisper to myself. "Shit! What am I going to do?"

A young woman sitting beside me, about twenty years old, wearing burgundy hair and several body piercings, overhears me and leans in to me. "Girlfriend, all I can say is good riddance to stank rubbish," she snarls. "He deserved what he got. Killing off his community with drugs and whores!"

Whore? Who is this trickster calling a whore? Hell, she's the one sitting in the Community Clinic, probably for some type of incurable shit. Humph, I was a damn good whore and look at where it got me, in the same Community Clinic. Drugs? I didn't know Jonah was into drugs. Wow, when you think you know someone, you really don't.

"Maya Howard," shouts the mid-forties woman, dressed in all gray and standing in the doorway leading to the back of the clinic.

"Yes, that's me."

"We're ready for you," she smiles, flashing a gold tooth. She leads me to a cold, white room with Exam Room 4 painted on the door. "I need you to undress from the waist down." She pulls out a paper skirt and tosses it onto the examining table. "Put this on." Without looking at my face, she turns her back to me, reaches under the counter and pulls out a neatly filled package. She opens the package, exposing a small tube of KY jelly, a long cotton swab and an instrument that looks like a mini toothbrush. "Are you allergic to plastic?" she asks.

"Uh, allergic to what?"

"Plastic. You would be surprised how many people are allergic to plastic."

"No. No, I don't think so."

"When you're done undressing, press this button right here." She points to a red button sticking out from the wall. "That will let the doctor know that you are ready."

"Okay. Thank you."

"Oh, you ain't allergic to latex are ya?"

"No."

"Good." She turns on her heels and leaves the room, closing the door behind her.

Standing in the middle of the cold room, holding the paper skirt, I kick off my shoes, unzip my pants and watch them fall to my ankles. Stepping out of them, I pick them up and lay them across the red plastic chair that leans to one side because it's off balance. I slip off my panties and stuff them inside my pants pocket. I hold up the flimsy paper skirt and slip in one leg at a time. I push the red button and hop up on the examining table to await my turn.

Ten minutes later, a woman dressed in all white scrubs enters the room. "Are you the doctor?" I ask. She looks like she's seventeen years old.

"Yes, that's me. I'm Dr. Phyllis Rose. How are we today?"

"Just fine, thank you."

"So, what's the problem?" she asks, flipping through the papers that I completed three hours earlier.

"Well, I would like to be tested for a STD?"

"I see. Okay, lie back, slide down a little bit and place your feet in the stirrups." Dr. Rose turns toward the counter and pulls out latex gloves from the box sitting next to the jars of cotton balls, Q-tips and packages of alcohol wipes. Facing me, she snaps the latex gloves on each hand. Taking a seat on the chrome swivel stool, she pulls a long-necked chrome lamp toward my knees, aiming the light directly between my legs and onto my vagina. "Let's see what we've got here." She uses her gloved fingers to spread apart my vaginal lips. "No lesions," she says. "No discharge." She leans in closer. "No foul odor." I lie there with my hands clasped flat across my stomach. She swivels on the stool to face the counter and retrieves the cotton swab. "Okay, Ms. Howard, just relax. I am going to take a culture. You may feel me scraping, but that's it." I nod my head as she inserts the swab that's the length of a drinking straw. Withdrawing the swab, she turns to the counter and swipes the swab across a small glass. "Okay, one more culture," she says, retrieving the mini toothbrush. "You will definitely feel some scraping, but nothing major." I nod, close my eyes and hold my breath. "Okay, all done."

"Wow, I didn't feel that one."

"See, nothing to it," she says, taking off the latex gloves. "Now, your urine analysis shows no signs of puss. However, staying on the side of caution, I would like to draw some blood, test it and hopefully, we will come up with nothing."

"Okay, that will be fine."

"Good. In the meantime, I am going to give you this." Dr. Rose hands me a pill bottle with seven pills. "These are antibiotics. Take one pill a day, for seven days. This will clear up any infection you may have."

"Okay. Um, shall I call back for my test results?"

"Yes. In about three to five days, call us and we should have your results back. Would you like for us to test for HIV as well?"

A chill comes over me. "HIV?"

"Yes. I recommend you be tested for HIV if you are sexually active, and especially if you aren't using condoms." From the look on Dr. Rose's face, I must have just turned white as a ghost. "Are you all right, Ms. Howard?"

"Yes. Yes, I am fine. I just. . .I never imagined that I would be tested for HIV."

"Well, I am sure you have nothing to worry about. Like I said, I prefer to stay on the side of caution."

The one thing Jonah always stressed was that I use a condom with all of my Johns. Seeing as though most of them were married, still, Jonah didn't want me to take any chances. Although, I never used a condom with him. All I can do is hope and pray that God will have mercy on me, once again.

Jade

Sitting in the back of the limo, cuddled in Jon's arms after a long, exhausting weekend with my sisters, I now understand why I kept my ass in New York after college. The drama with them is too intense. Free definitely has her hands filled with Maya, China and her rugrats all under her roof. She is going to go insane, that's for sure.

"What a weekend," Jon says, stretching his arms around my shoulders.

"It was a typical weekend with my sisters," I chuckle.

"There was never a dull moment, that's for sure," he says as the limo approaches my apartment on W. 134th Street. "I can tell that you all are very close."

"What is she doing here," I think to myself, as Joy crosses W. 134th Street, in front of the limo. Thank goodness, the windows are tinted. I really don't feel like dealing with her shit tonight. She must be coming to my place and I don't want Jon to have a face-to-face with Joy.

"Jade?"

"Huh?"

"What's on your mind? You seem distant."

"Oh yeah, we are very close," I say, trying to figure out what to do or say next. "Baby, I feel like having a drink. Can we go somewhere?"

"Sweetie, I really don't feel like dealing with a crowd. . ."

"We can go somewhere secluded. . ." I pout.

"Jade, I am whipped, babe. Here," he says, reaching into the mini refrigerator, "we have plenty of champagne. Let's just go up to your place and relax."

"All right," I sigh, accepting defeat. "Are you staying with me tonight?"

"Do you want me to?" he asks, his eyes undressing me.

"You are such a flirt," I chuckle, trying to bide my time.

"What?"

"What?" I mimic. "Yes, I want you with me tonight. . .every night I want you with me."

"You mean that, don't you, baby?" he asks, my focus now off him and out of the back window, as Joy vastly approaches. Her stride is confident and determined. She approaches the limo as Robert opens the rear door. She peeps inside. She sees me and without breaking her stride, she passes by. I step out of the limo and watch her cross the street and turn the corner, walking out of my life.

Once inside, I kick off my shoes, retrieve two champagne flutes and drop down on the sofa beside Jon, draping my legs across his. "It's good to be home," I sigh.

"Yes, it certainly is," he says, taking the bottle to head. I place the flutes on the table and follow suit. "Jade, thank you."

"You're welcome. What did I do?"

"You gave me something that I've never had."

I nestle under him. "And what's that, sweetie?"

"A family," he says, kissing me on the forehead.

"Ha! You can have them, at no cost," I chuckle.

"I've never experienced that type of love before. The arguing, calling each other names, the fighting. . ."

"Oh, you don't get out much," I laugh. "You call that love?"

"Yes, I do."

"Jon, get real. There is nothing loving about sisters trying to break each other's neck and calling each other names."

"Well, not the part about trying to kill each other, but there's something warm when family can call you a bitch, trick, and any other name in the book and you know it's not given from the heart."

"Yeah, I guess I know what you mean."

"I am so sorry about what's going on with China. Are you sure you don't want to fly down for the funeral?"

I shake my head. "Naw. Besides, from talking to China, there isn't going to be a funeral. Just a small memorial service followed by cremation."

"I could never understand why anyone would want to commit suicide."

"Me either. I believe China handled the matter wrong."

"How would you've handled it?"

"By not fleeing to Free's place, for one. I would've stayed at home, confronted the issue and given his ass an ultimatum."

"Really now? And what would that ultimatum have been?" he chuckles.

"There's only one that I know of when you are caught cheating...get your shit and get the fuck out!" We both laugh.

"Suppose he doesn't want to leave?"

"Then I'll just have to cut his dick off in his sleep," I smile, grabbing his crotch.

"Remind me not to cheat on you," he smiles. "Don't think I could get used to sitting down to take a leak," he winks.

Feeling at peace with myself, satisfaction with my life and horny as hell for my man, I take Jon by the hand and lead him to the bedroom. Once inside, Jon places the champagne bottle on the nightstand and gathers me into his arms. The sweet intoxicating musk of his body overwhelms me. Without a word, he turns me around. Pressing his palm in the arch of my back, his hand moves gently down the length of my back. He falls to his knees and nuzzles his face between my legs. With a swift motion, my chenille pants fall down around my ankles and Jon's tongue stimulates the throbbing between my legs. "Jade, you are hypnotic," he whispers. "I could love you forever."

Rolling over onto my back, I bring him inside me, my body heaving as he enters. "Yes, Jon," I moan. "Yes. . .mmm, yesss."

Our bodies pump in unison and our passionate lovemaking turns into fucking.

China

Ashley is chewing on her ponytail and André is pacing the floor. I can't say that I blame them much. The idea of going before a psychiatrist scares me too. But, they both wanted to do it. They have no idea of the intensity of divulging your innermost feelings to a stranger.

"Ashley, stop chewing on your hair. That's disgusting," André taunts.

Ashley doesn't respond, which is not normal for Miss Mouth Almighty.

"Leave her alone, André."

"I'm not messing with her. Just telling her to stop chewing on her nasty hair."

Ashley continues to stare at the floor.

"Honey, are you all right?" I ask.

She doesn't respond.

"Just like a retard not to answer."

"André, shut up and go sit down!"

"Aww, Mama, I ain't. . ."

"Mrs. Douglas?" the receptionist calls out. "We're ready for you now," she smiles.

"Thank you," I smile, taking Ashley by the hand. "Come on, baby."

She doesn't budge.

"Ashley, what is wrong with you? Come on!" I demand.

She doesn't budge. Instead, her eyes remain plastered to the floor.

"Look. . ." I begin.

"I don't want to go in there," she whimpers.

I bend down before her. "Why not?"

"I'm afraid."

"Oh Ashley, there's nothing to be afraid of, sweetheart."

"I don't like doctors," she says, now peering through me. "I don't like them, Mama."

"Baby, Mama is going to be in there with you. I won't let any harm come to you. Besides, this is not a regular doctor. There are no needles involved," I smile.

"Who's the pussy now?" André asks sarcastically. "Come on, Mama. Let's me and you go on in and leave the *pussy* out here," he says, tugging me by the arm. "I've got some things to get off my chest."

I slap André's hand. "Boy, stop tugging on me. Ashley, you don't have to go in, but I thought this was what you wanted?"

"I thought I did," she says. "But I don't know now."

"Okay, I'll tell you what. Let's go in. If you are still feeling uncomfortable after we start, we can leave. How's that?"

Ashley nods her head and smiles. She grabs my right hand while André continues to tug at my blouse. "Boy, will you stop that? Why are you tugging on me like that?"

"'Cause I love you, Mama!" he exclaims with a giggle. He is enjoying this entirely too much.

"Mrs. Douglas?"

"Yes, and this is my daughter, Ashley and my son, André."

"Hello, Ashley and André, my name is Dr. Allison Kirby. It's a pleasure to meet you both. Please," she says as she points to a group of chairs sitting in front of her desk, "have a seat."

Ashley drops down in the seat next to me and André, with his grown ass, plops down on the sofa. "André, wouldn't you be more comfortable sitting in this chair?" she asks, pointing to the chair next to Ashley.

"Nope, I'm comfortable. . ."

"Boy, do what you are told," I snap.

"No, it's quite all right," she smiles. "So, let's get started, shall we?"

"Yes and I have some things to say," André blurts out.

"All right, we can start with you, André. What's on your mind?" she inquires with her pen to paper, ready to jot down any and everything.

"Well, first of all, I am not a pussy."

Dr. Kirby glances in my direction and smile with embarrassment. "Okay," she says, leaning back in her chair. "I would agree with you, André."

"Well, I wish you would make Ashley agree too," he pouts.

"Does Ashley call you a pussy?"

"Yes, and I'm sick of it. I ain't done nothing to her," he says as I cringe at my money for a private school going down the drain.

She turns her attention to Ashley. "Ashley, why do you call your brother a pussy?"

"Because he is," she responds, sticking her tongue out at André. "He is such a baby. He's always whining to Mama about something. He's always getting me in trouble and I don't like him."

"Dr. Kirby, this isn't why we are here," I interrupt. "We are here because my husband committed suicide. I want my children to talk about how they feel about that and how it affects them."

"Okay, Mrs. Douglas. We can shift gears."

"Thank you."

"Well, I'm glad Daddy is dead," André says, picking at the leather sofa.

Ashley perks up. "How could you say something so mean? See, I told you he was a pussy!" she yells.

"André, why do you feel that way?" Dr. Kirby asks.

"Because."

She removes her glasses and rests them on the desk. "Because why?"

"Because he would beat Mama all the time."

She glances toward me. "Is that so?" she asks me.

I nod my head yes and look out of the window.

"André, how do. . ."

"If he didn't do it, I was going to do it."

"André, what did I tell you about that?" I snap.

Dr. Kirby raises her hand to silence me. "André, is there anything else you didn't like about your father?"

"He played with men," he says, lowering his head in embarrassment. "My father was gay."

"Is that a bad thing?" Dr. Kirby asks.

"Yes," he whispers. "It's not natural. I don't want to be like that," he begins to sob.

"Baby, you won't be like that," I say, turning towards my weeping son. "André, look at me," I say. "Sweetheart, homosexuality is a choice, a preference. . ."

"Well," Dr. Kirby interjects. "Although I haven't done much research on sexuality versus genetics, I do believe that one's sexual orientation does have something to do with genetics."

I look at Dr. Kirby with disgust. "What kind of doctor are you? Why would you tell a child something like that?"

"Mrs. Douglas, it is my position to be as upfront with my clients. . ."

"No, it is not your position to damage a child!"

"Daddy was a sick man," Ashley says, breaking her silence and facing her brother. "Right, André?" André nods his head in agreement.

"What are you saying, Ashley?" I ask.

"We've seen the porn tapes that you and Daddy used to watch," she says.

My body becomes erect. "I don't know what you're talking about, Ashley."

"Those same tapes," she says while looking at me, "are the same tapes that Daddy would have me and André acting out."

I gasp in disbelief and Dr. Kirby leans in toward Ashley. "Ashley, what do you mean by your father having you and your brother acting out?"

"I mean," she says, becoming irritated, "Daddy would turn on the tape, call me and André into the room and make us do what was on the tape."

"Oh my God! Ashley, you are lying!" I yell, unable to believe what I am hearing. "Did you hate your father so much to make up such a story?"

"It's true, Mama," André confides. "That's why Ashley doesn't like me, because Daddy would make me do those things to her."

"What things?" Dr. Kirby asks.

"Oh sweet Jesus, do you have to go there?" I ask.

"Yes, I do. Mrs. Douglas, it's very important that your son understands that whatever acts your husband had him and his sister do aren't their fault."

"Mostly, he made us suck each other. You know, I ate her pussy and she sucked my dick."

"That bastard!" I howl like a wounded dog. "How could he do this to his own children? That man was sick!"

"Yes, he was very sick," Dr. Kirby intervened. "Mrs. Douglas, if I could," she says, retrieving a card from her Rolodex. "I have a colleague who specializes in children and molestation cases. I would like to refer you to him. He holds a chat session with a group of children who have similar experiences as Ashley and André. It rather makes them feel like they aren't alone. They can talk about their experiences and hopefully, grow into strong, healthy adults."

"Yes," I say, taking the card. "I think that would be best."

After leaving Dr. Kirby and hearing Ashley and André's confessions, I regretted that Ron killed himself. I would've loved to pull the trigger my damn self.

Jade, Jon, & Joy

Her watch reads two-fifty a.m. as she slowly inserts her key into the door lock. Joy slowly enters Jade's apartment, taking slow steps. She gently closes the door, making sure not to make a peep. She looks around the apartment. Rage engulfs her when she inhales Jon's scent trailing from the bedroom to her nose. "That scathing bitch," she thinks to herself. "I can smell her stank pussy," she mumbles under her breath. The sound of Jon's snoring directs her attention down the hall toward the bedroom. Tears of pain stream down her face as she mumbles, "He can't have you," to herself. Her face becomes flush and her brows have left their neatly arched position, meeting in the middle.

With the bedroom door partially open, Joy gently presses her hand against the door, her eyes roll toward the bed. She reaches inside Jade's top dresser drawer, feeling under the lace panties and other unmentionables in search of the revolver that Jade purchased three years ago after the apartment on the third floor was broken into and the occupant was raped and brutally murdered.

Joy approaches Jon's naked sleeping figure and places the gun to his temple and her hand over his mouth. He awakens, fear dances in his eyes and his life flashes before him. "If you as much as flinch, I will kill her first and then you," she whispers between clenched teeth, careful not to arouse Jade. "Do you understand me?" Jon barely nods, afraid of having his brains becoming the new décor for Jade's bedroom. Joy looks over at Jade and back at Jon. "Her pussy is good, no?" He doesn't budge. "I want you to *slowly* get your ass up and sit in that chair," she says, directing him with her eyes to the chair on the other side of the room. "Don't be stupid," she warns. She begins to tie him up to the chair with the scarves that drape over the dresser mirror. Once he is tightly secure, she reaches under her skirt, removes a soiled sanitary napkin and dangles it in front of his face. She aims the gun at his face, barely touching the tip of his nose. "Open wide, sunshine," she smiles in a low faint, psychotic voice. Jon reluctantly opens his mouth and she forcefully rams the soiled napkin into his mouth. His head jerks and his body begins to heave. "Not a word," she snaps under her breath.

When completely satisfied that Jon will be going nowhere, Joy turns her attention toward Jade, who is peacefully sleeping with her breast partially covered. She approaches the bed and stares down at Jade, admiring her beauty. She uses the mouth of the gun to move the sheet slowly down around Jade's brown voluptuous thighs. She gazes at Jade's pubic area, a devious smile creeping upon her lips. Jon helplessly watches as Joy inserts the mouth of the gun into Jade's canal. "Wake up, muffin," she says, moving the nozzle around, scraping Jade's canal.

"Oh my God!" Jade screams, sitting up in the bed. "Jon!" she says, as her man sits tied to a chair, unable to come to her rescue.

"Your boyfriend is a cutie, Jade," she smirks.

"Jon, are you all right?" she cries. "Joy. . ."

"I told you if I couldn't have you, no one will have you!"

"Joy, why are you doing this? I thought you loved me."

"Oh cut the bullshit, Jade. You know I love you, but you continue to hurt me by doing dumb shit like fucking Pretty Boy Floyd over there." Joy's face distorts. "You are tainted, spoiled goods." A look of sadness comes over her. "Jade, I love you and I gave you my all." She jerks her head toward Jon. "What does he have that I don't have? A dick? I don't need a fuckin' dick to please her," she yells at Jon. "Isn't that right, Jade?" she asks, her glare piercing through him.

Joy turns toward Jade. "I've missed you, babe. I can't live without you and you can't live without me." She kneels down beside the bed with the gun aiming at Jade's chest. Joy, with her eyes in a yearning stare, inhales deeply. "I've always loved pleasing you, Jade. You like it too." She glances over her shoulder at Jon, her face expressionless. "You can't replace me," she snarls. "Jade, slide down and let me show this motherfucker how to work that pussy."

"Joy, you are fuckin' crazy. You need help!"

Joy uses the gun to pry open Jade's legs. Jade resists. "Oh no, don't close your legs now," Joy spews. "Please don't make me angry, Jade," she cautions, aiming the gun at Jon.

"Okay, okay. I'll do whatever you want, just don't hurt him, please!" Jade cries.

Jade slides to the edge of the bed. With the gun steadily aimed at Jon, Joy lowers her face into Jade's abyss. Jade, with her eyes affixed to Jon, flinches at the stroke of Joy's tongue and grabs hold of the cotton percale sheets, balling them into a fist. With the anticipation of climaxing, tears fill in Jade's eyes, stream down her cheeks and onto the sheets. Jon watches defenselessly, unable to wiggle free.

After Joy brings Jade to full climax, she slowly stands upright, rounding her shoulders and ridding her lips of Jade's leftovers. "Please leave, Joy," Jade cries. "You've gotten what you want."

Joy peers at the Dom Perignon bottle sitting on the nightstand. "I don't have you, Jade," she frowns. "Are you going to get rid of him?" she asks, pointing at Jon. "He doesn't love you. He's a man. He's a dog. He won't do shit but hurt you. He will cause you pain, Jade. Don't you know that?"

"Joy, listen. . .baby, okay, we can try to work things out," Jade says, looking toward Jon. "You're right. He's no good for me. Why don't you just give me the gun and let's go back to the way things were."

Joy's temper begins to flare. "What do I look like to you, Jade?"

"I don't know what you mean, baby?"

"Baby? Look, bitch! You have to get up awfully early in the morning to pull the wool over my eyes," she says, scorn oozing from deep within.

"No, I. . ."

"Cut the crap! You don't want me. If you wanted me, you would've answered my fuckin' calls. If you wanted me, you wouldn't be with him!"

"Joy, calm down, okay? I do love you. I was confused and I didn't know what I wanted. . ."

"Shut up! Just shut the fuck up before I poke out your boyfriend's eyes and skull fuck him!"

Joy picks up the champagne bottle and breaks it over the nightstand. She holds tightly to the broken glass in her hand.

Jade scoots up toward the headboard, her knees in a bent position.

"Joy, what are you going to do with that?" Jade asks, while Jon continues to wiggle in the chair, trying to break free. "Please, Joy, don't do this."

"How many times do I have to tell you? If *I* can't have you, no one will." Joy aims the gun close to Jade's forehead. "Open your legs."

Jade doesn't put up much of a fight because she knows that Joy is obviously mentally challenged and capable of doing just about anything, even killing her. Jon continues his attempt at breaking loose, which is virtually impossible considering Joy was a Girls Scout and tying knots were one of her many specialties.

No doubt, Joy is mentally unstable. From the age of three, her mother's boyfriend, Ian, repeatedly molested her. Joy's mother worked nights. On the nights when Ian's not drunk on the sofa, he would spend the evening in Joy's bedroom. "We are going to play a game," he would say. "This game is called 'Find the Lizard' and you can't tell anyone, not even your mommy. This is our game," he would constantly tell her.

The game, Find the Lizard, consisted of Ian unzipping his pants and allowing the tip of his head to peep through. Once Joy saw the tip, she would get a prize each time she touched it. Her prize? To be fondled by Ian. By age eleven, the rules of the game changed and Joy's reward increased to sodomy. Ian threatened to kill her and her mother if she breathed a word. By age thirteen, Joy had a bun in the oven. She had heard that a girl at her school, the same age, had been pregnant and aborted by using a vacuum hose to suck out the fetus. She was too afraid to go that route and too afraid to tell her mother that she was pregnant by Ian.

For the duration of her pregnancy, she wore large-sized clothing and carried her child in her hips. Her mother never even noticed, never paid any attention to her whatsoever. When she needed her mom the most, she couldn't because they never had a real mother-daughter relationship. Joy didn't know how to approach her mother with her pregnancy, so she didn't approach her at all.

Joy gave birth to her daughter in the bathroom of the junior high school she attended. She named her daughter Genevieve and left her in the toilet. Genevieve was placed in foster care and Joy has never felt a man's penetration since.

With hesitation, Jade spreads her legs. Joy reaches in with the broken bottle and aims directly for Jade's vaginal area. With her right foot, Jade kicks Joy in her temple, causing her to fall backward and hit her head on one of the four-corner bedposts. Joy lands on the floor like a piece of fallen timber. She's out cold. Jade leaps from the bed and over to Jon and removes the soiled napkin from his mouth. Jon regurgitates from having Joy's body fluids in his mouth for so long. He gags and coughs.

"Who in the hell is that, Jade?"

Jade looks down at the body lying before her. "That's Joy."

"I don't believe this! That bitch is nuts! I'm calling the police." Once untied, Jon rushes to the phone and dials 911 as Jade sits in the chair, staring down at Joy.

"Did I kill her? She isn't moving."

"No, you didn't kill her. You just knocked the wind out of her."

"Are you okay?" he asks, staring down at Jade with concern in his eyes.

"Of course I'm not all right. She tried to kill me, Jon!"

"What is Free's number? I think you need your family now."

"No! Don't call Free. It's over. Free has enough on her hands. I'll be fine."

As the police are taking Joy away in handcuffs, she stops before Jade and says, "I love you. Don't you ever forget that."

Free

Well, well, well. That was one hell of a weekend and my house is peaceful once again. But then again, as long as Maya is around, there will never be any peace.

Sam still feels that I am being too much of a mother to three grown women. He's right. It's time to let go. Well, not totally. I will just loosen the apron string, slightly. Once a mother, always a mother, I suppose.

I am so embarrassed that Sam's first encounter with my sisters was less than desirable. But, oh well, no point in putting on airs for folks. I am a package deal. You want me, you have to deal with the retards. I love my sisters dearly, but sometimes, I feel like calling the Jerry Springer Show because Oprah wouldn't touch us for nothing in the world. I can picture China on the panel. "My husband had an affair with a man and my daughter molested her ten-year-old brother." China has something on her hands, for sure.

Ms. Ethel's home going was done exactly to the specifications she left in her will—two gospel choirs and a church filled with roses from Free's Floral Design Boutique. Because her son died over six months ago, Ms. Ethel was his only heir. And since she changed her will to make me her beneficiary, I now own three houses and fifty thousand dollars cash. I still haven't a clue as to why she made me her beneficiary, but if it's what she wants, it's what she gets.

On China. . .

After telling Ashley and André that their father committed suicide, China sought counseling to help them deal with the pain, which is long overdue. Unfortunately, she found out that not only was Ron a homosexual, but he was also a pedophile. Humph, life is funny. You can be with a person for years and still not know them. She has put the kids in group counseling with other kids with similar issues.

China feels that going back to Orlando and living in the house, which is now a crime scene, would be too much for her and the kids. So, instead, she is selling the house and moving into one of the houses here in Atlanta that I inherited from Ms. Ethel. She has decided to take refresher courses at the community college and hope to find a job in her field.

Because Ron forced his children to do such disgusting acts, China felt that the best revenge on him would be to cremate his body. She drove around with his ashes in a cardboard box in the back of her truck, searching for the appropriate place to discard his remains. Her search led her to the toilet, where she flushed that no good sonofabitch where he belonged…in the gutter with the rest of the shit.

On Jade. . .

Jade is going to be all right. She is in love with Jon Meadows. At first, I thought it was the money and that Dom Petey stuff she was in love with, seeing as though she was high strung on that woman, Joy. But, after seeing her glow the entire weekend, I know differently. As for Joy, since Jade never returned any of her calls, I suppose she got the hint. Besides, Jade has made plans to move from her apartment and in with Jon. Can you believe that? Is that fast or what? I've already started drawing up the guest list.

On Maya. . .

Maya's test results came back negative for HIV. However, she did contract a very bad yeast infection and a urinary tract infection, both can be cured with medication. She's lucky. . .damn lucky. I don't think she realizes how lucky she really is. I believe Maya still thinks that life is a big game. Well, I have news for her. If she is going to stay under my roof, there will be rules and she will work on her trifling ways. Yes, she is a grown woman, but she will not be coming in and out of my house at all hours of the night. I run a flower shop, not a 7-11 and I am not open 24-7. She has to go back to school, get her degree and help me run the shop. She reluctantly agreed, of course.

I saw the newscast on Jonah Roberts. I think she saw it, too, because after she left the Community Clinic, she made a beeline to the Hair Cuttery. She is now sporting a burgundy crop haircut. Since she has a fair complexion, and despite what I think about black women with burgundy hair, I think it looks very nice on her. I believe she will do just fine.

On Sam. . .

Sam and I are going to be just fine. If he can deal with my sisters, I can put up with his snoring. I've yet to meet his parents, but I am sure they are just as wonderful as he is.

On sisters. . .

They are always in your corner.

The End

Visit Jessica Tilles
at
www.jessicatilles.com.

Send comments to:
JTilles@aol.com.